Witch Is Where Squirrels Go Nuts

Chapter 1

"You look awful," Jack said when I came downstairs for breakfast.

"I didn't sleep very well. I had a horrible nightmare."

"I'm going to have a fry-up. Do you want one?"

"Yes, please."

He took the bacon, sausages and eggs out of the fridge. "What was this nightmare of yours?"

"Mr Cheese was chasing me, and I couldn't get away from him because my legs had turned to jelly. Literally. They were wobbling around all over the place."

"*Mr Cheese*? That's probably down to all the cheese you've been eating recently."

"It wasn't because of that. When I was working on the NOCA case, I had to go to Chuckle House a couple of times. They have framed photographs on the wall of famous clowns over the years. I made the mistake of looking at them, and that's when I saw Mr Cheese."

"Why did he pick such a stupid name?"

"Because of his nose."

"Sorry, you've completely lost me now."

"Instead of having the usual red nose like most clowns, he had a lump of cheese in the middle of his face."

"That's just wrong."

"Tell me about it. I've not been able to get that image out of my mind."

Florence came running down the stairs. "Mummy, can I learn some new spells this week, please?"

"I'm not sure if we should allow that."

"But you said I only had to miss one week."

"I said you had to miss *at least* one week, but that it might be more if you hadn't learned your lesson."

"I have learned my lesson."

"What do you think, Daddy?" I said.

"Please!" Florence said. "It was an accident. I was just trying to get the scissors from Wendy's desk. I didn't mean for all that other stuff to fly across the room too."

"That's not the point though, is it, Florence?" I said. "You shouldn't have been using magic at all. If you wanted the scissors, what should you have done?"

"Walked to Wendy's desk and asked if I could borrow them."

"That's right. It was lucky that the headmistress thought it was an electrical surge."

"I won't do it again, Mummy, I promise."

"You'd better not."

"What spell can I learn this week?"

"I thought I'd teach you the 'faster' spell."

"What's that?"

"It will let you run really fast."

"Cool! I'll be able to win all the races at school."

"Florence! What have we just been talking about?"

"I was joking. When can I learn it?"

"We'll need plenty of space, so I thought we could go down to Tweaking Meadows. But we can only do it if there's no one else around."

"What day?"

"Let's see what the weather's like. Probably Thursday."

"Yay!" Florence did that cute little dance of hers. The one she always did when she was happy. "I'm going outside to play with Buddy."

As I took a seat at the kitchen table, I noticed that Jack had left his laptop open, so I had a quick nosey.

"Wash Golf Club? Are you serious about taking it up?"

"I'm not sure. Tommy Gray mentioned that he's a member."

"You should join."

"Can we afford it?"

"How much are the fees?"

"A lot."

I clicked on the link marked *fees*. "You aren't kidding. Do people really pay that much to hit a ball around a field?"

"I should have taken that bellboy job at your grandmother's hotel." He grinned.

"You should definitely join. It'll do you good to get regular exercise. We'll find the money somehow."

"I'll give it some thought."

My phone rang; it was Kathy.

"Jill, make a note to keep your diary free for a week on Friday."

"Why? What's happening?"

"My new shop opens. Nine o'clock sharp."

"I can't keep pace with you. Don't you have enough shops yet? Where's this one?"

"I have told you several times."

"Sorry, my mind is all over the place at the moment."

"It's in Washbridge, but on the south side."

"I still don't understand why you need two in the same town."

"Washbridge is a big place. My research showed that a second shop would be profitable."

"What are you doing for the opening?"

"Just bubbly and nibbles. Will you be able to make it?"

"I'll do my best."

"By the way, how's your search for another PI going?"

"I've identified a promising candidate. I'm going to interview him next Monday."

***

I was about to get into the car when I heard raised voices coming from somewhere just up the road. If I'd had any sense, I would have ignored them and gone to work. Instead, curiosity got the better of me, and I took a walk into the village to find out what was going on. As soon as I turned the corner, I saw the source of the commotion: Just outside Tweaking Tea Rooms, Miss Drinkwater and Grandma were having a blazing row. Even from that distance, I could see that the wart on Grandma's nose was glowing red, which was never a good sign. A small crowd of onlookers were rubbernecking while maintaining a safe distance.

"Grandma! Miss Drinkwater!" I shouted, as I hurried towards them, but neither of them heard me because they were too busy flinging abuse at one another.

I could tell by the look in Grandma's eyes that she was on the verge of using magic, so I forced my way in between the two of them and pushed them apart.

"Get out of my way, Jill," Grandma spat the words. "Let me deal with this woman."

"No, I won't. What on earth is going on here?"

"Your grandmother refuses to see sense," Miss Drinkwater said. "Can you try to talk some into her?"

"It's not a question of seeing sense," Grandma snapped.

"I will not be dictated to by you or anyone else in this village. Hotel First Time will be hosting afternoon teas from this Saturday, and there is nothing you or anyone else can do about it."

"We'll see about that. I've been running this tea room for almost twenty-five years, and I'm pretty sure who the villagers will back."

"It certainly won't be you." Grandma scoffed. "No one in this village likes you."

"Don't be ridiculous. I'm well respected and liked by everyone."

"In your dreams. Jill, tell her, will you? Tell her that everyone thinks she's an ogre."

There was no way I was going to get dragged into that argument, but I couldn't just walk away in case Grandma did something stupid. Without another word, I grabbed Grandma by the arm and, despite her protestations, dragged her back to the hotel.

"What do you think you're playing at, Jill? Why didn't you let me sort that woman out?"

"Because you'd totally lost it. If I'd left you to it, you would have used magic on her."

"So what? The woman's a rat, so it would have served her right if I'd turned her into one."

"And what good would that have done you? The rogue retrievers would have been all over you like a rash, and that would have been the end of your hotel."

"I'm not backing down over the afternoon tea."

"I don't expect you to. Just ignore Miss Drinkwater; don't rise to the bait."

"Okay, you've made your point."

"Do you promise not to go back down there?"

"Yes, I promise. I've got better things to be doing with my time, anyway." And with that, she stormed into the hotel.

I made my way back to the tea room where the crowd had dispersed. Miss Drinkwater was inside, sitting on a stool next to the counter; she met my entrance with an icy glare.

"What do *you* want," she snapped.

"I'm hoping to make you see reason."

"Unless you've persuaded your grandmother to abandon her plans to offer afternoon tea, you're wasting your breath."

"That's never going to happen, so you may as well get used to the idea. Instead of wasting your energy arguing with my grandmother, you should be thinking about how best to compete with her. You said yourself, you already have a head start because you've been in the village for such a long time. Use that to your advantage."

"I don't need you to tell me how to run my business, young woman."

"I'm just trying to help."

"Well don't. I'd like you to leave now."

"Okay, but whatever you do, don't go up to the hotel."

When I got back to the car, Jack was standing in the garden.

"I wondered where you'd gone. I looked out the window and the car was still here."

"I've just been breaking up a fight between Grandma and Miss Drinkwater."

"Oh dear. What was that all about?"

"Afternoon tea, what else? I'll fill you in on the gory

details tonight."

I was just about to drive away when I heard muffled sounds coming from the glove compartment. When it didn't open, I figured it must be stuck, so I pulled it open.

And immediately wished that I hadn't.

Henry was in there, but he wasn't alone. He and a female elf were locked in a passionate embrace, and neither of them had noticed me.

"Ahem!"

The two of them finally realised I was there.

"Jill? Do you mind?" Henry said.

"Do *I* mind?"

"Some privacy, please."

"I—err—" I was lost for words, so I pushed the glove compartment closed.

Unbelievable!

***

There wasn't a scarf on the door handle, so I walked straight in.

"Good morning, Mrs V."

"Good morning, Jill. Did you have a nice weekend?"

"Yes thanks, but I didn't sleep very well last night, I had a horrible dream about a clown called Mr Cheese."

"You never were very fond of clowns, were you? Why was he called Mr Cheese?"

"Because instead of a nose, he had a lump of cheese in the middle of his face."

"How horrible. No wonder you were upset."

"Aren't you recording a video today, Mrs V?"

"No, and you'll be pleased to hear that I won't need to

use the office to record them from now on."

"How come? Have you given up on them?"

"On the contrary, I'm planning to up my output. I showed Armi what I'd done so far, and he thought they were very good. In fact, he came up with the idea of using the spare bedroom as my studio. Over the weekend, we cleared the furniture out of there and we've set up my recording equipment."

"Good for you, but what will you do with yourself all day here in the office?"

"I'll go back to my knitting and crocheting."

"Right."

"And any work you may have for me, of course."

"Only if you have the time." She shot me a look. "Just joking."

I walked into my office to find Winky standing on the sofa, dressed as a pirate.

"Winky, why are you wearing that getup?"

"Isn't it obvious?"

"Not to me, no."

"It's the pirate fancy dress competition next week of course. Surely I've mentioned it to you before?"

"You haven't. Trust me, I would have remembered. It's a very striking outfit. Where did you get it from?"

"I had it specially made, which is why I'm a nailed-on certainty to win. Everyone else will be wearing the same off-the-peg rubbish from the costume hire shops."

"That sword is very realistic."

"That's because it is real." He began to wave it around his head.

"Be careful. You'll have someone's head off."

"I'm a master swordsman. You have nothing to worry —
"

The sword slipped from his grasp, flew across the room, and wedged itself into my desk.

"Idiot! You could have killed me."

"Sorry, it slipped."

"Look what you've done to my desk."

He jumped off the sofa, walked across the room, and tried to pull it out, but it wouldn't budge.

"It's stuck."

"Well, you'd better un-*stuck* it before my new client arrives. What kind of impression will he get if there's a sword sticking out of my desk?"

Winky put his back paws on the desk to give himself more leverage. He pulled and pulled, and when the sword did eventually yield, it sent him tumbling onto his backside.

"There you are." He pointed to the desk. "Good as new."

"Apart from that big gash, you mean?"

"You can barely see it."

"This desk is an antique. It'll have to be repaired, and you're going to pay for it."

"Okay, no big deal. I'll pay for it out of my prize money when I win best costume in the Jolly Roger awards. I expect us to win the best couple category."

"*Us*? *Couple*? Who's your other half?"

"My new girlfriend. Her name is Mimi."

"When do I get to meet the unlucky lady?"

"She'll be popping in on Friday. I'll introduce you to her then."

"Will she be dressed as a pirate too?"

"Of course."

A little later, Mrs V brought my drink through. "Sorry, Jill, I forgot to mention I took a phone call for you before you arrived."

"From a prospective client?" I asked more in hope than expectation.

"I'm afraid not. It was Betty Longbottom."

"What did *she* want?"

"She asked me to tell you that she'll be coming to carry out her inspection on Friday morning at ten o'clock."

"*Friday*? I hope you told her that wouldn't be convenient."

"She wasn't really asking. She gave me the impression that she expected you to accommodate her. She asked if you'd have all your books ready for her to inspect."

"She'll be lucky."

***

My first client of the week was a gentleman by the name of Raymond Double.

"Good morning, Mr Double. I'm Jill Maxwell."

"Good morning, young lady. And it's okay, I know what you're thinking."

"You do?"

"I saw it in your eyes as soon as I walked through the door. Don't worry, I'm used to it by now. It happens all the time."

"Right. What does?"

"You thought I was Rock Masters, didn't you?"

"I'm sorry, you've lost me. Who's Rock Masters?"

"You've never heard of Rock Masters?"

"I'm afraid not. Should I have?"

"Rock was a big movie star back in the eighties, but he's retired now. Might even be dead—no one seems to be sure."

"Right. I'm sorry, but I don't remember him."

"It was back in the seventies that I realised I bore a striking resemblance to him. Since then, my face has been my fortune."

I glanced at the note that Mrs V had passed to me when she'd made the appointment. "It says here that you run something called the Double Take Agency?"

"That's right, Jill. Back in the eighties, I used to hire myself out as a Rock Masters lookalike. After a few years, I decided to start my own agency, and I've been running Double Take ever since. I have over fifty lookies on my books now."

"*Lookies*?"

"It's what I call my lookalikes."

"Right. And what exactly is it I can do for you, Mr Double?"

"Call me Rock, everyone does."

"Okay, Rock, how can I be of assistance?"

"I believe that someone is deliberately trying to sabotage my business."

"Sabotage it how? Can you be a little more specific?"

"It all started about six months ago when I took a booking for my Scarlet Jewel lookie."

"Hang on. Scarlet Jewel? Should I have heard of her?"

"She's one of the country's biggest reality TV stars."

"Right. And you have a lookie who resembles Scarlet Jewel?"

"Maggie doesn't just resemble Scarlet. She could be her twin sister."

"Okay, sorry to interrupt. Carry on, please."

"Two days after I'd taken the booking, the client contacted us to cancel. Obviously, cancellations do happen from time to time so I thought nothing of it. But then, about a week later, it happened again. And then again, and that's how things have continued. It's got to the point where every time I take a booking, I expect it to be cancelled."

"And you have no idea why that's happening? Have you asked the customers who have cancelled?"

"Of course. I ask them every time it happens, but they always make some feeble excuse. I'm convinced that someone is deliberately trying to put me out of business."

"What about your competitors, Rock? Do you have any?"

"There was another agency in Washbridge, but they recently went bust."

"Is there anyone else who might have a grudge against you? Any disgruntled ex-employees?"

"Nothing like that. I have always treated my lookies with the utmost respect. Ask any of them."

"Okay. It might be helpful if I paid a visit to your office. Maybe I could speak to some of your—err—lookies?"

"Absolutely."

"I'd also like to see details of some of the bookings that were cancelled."

"No problem. How about tomorrow afternoon? Say one o'clock?"

"That's fine. I'll see you then."

Chapter 2

The lookalike business is a strange one where people get paid just because they look like someone famous. Which got me thinking: Maybe, right now, someone was being paid good money just because they looked like me.

What do you mean, I'm not famous? I'm the most powerful witch in Candlefield—if that's not famous, I don't know what is. If someone is making money by being my lookie, then by rights, I think I should get a share of their earnings. Food for thought, don't you think?

Talking of food, I was feeling rather peckish, so I magicked myself over to Cuppy C where the twins were both behind the counter.

"Hi, Jill." Amber sounded full of the joys of spring.

"Hiya." Pearl flashed me a big smile.

"What's up with you two?" I said.

"Nothing, why?"

"Well, for a start, you aren't arguing, which is a first. And you both look obscenely happy."

"We don't always argue," Pearl said.

"You could have fooled me. So, which one of you two lookies is going to get me a coffee and a blueberry muffin?"

"What makes you say we're lucky?" Amber said.

"Not *lucky*. Lookies. It's what you call lookalikes, and let's face it, you two definitely look alike."

"You're talking in riddles, as usual, Jill."

"It's all to do with my latest case. My client owns a lookalike agency."

"Is it another murder?" Amber said.

"Not every case I work on is a murder. The owner of the

agency thinks he's being sabotaged, and that someone is causing all his bookings to be cancelled. I've got to find out who's doing it and why."

"Where do you start on a case like that?" Pearl said.

"I'm going to pay a visit to his offices tomorrow, to talk to some of his lookies, and I'll take it from there."

"In other words, you're going to wing it."

"Cheek! I do not *wing it*. I'll have you know my methods have been carefully honed over the course of more than a decade."

They looked at each other and laughed. "If you say so."

"Am I going to get my coffee and muffin or not?"

"I'll see to it." Pearl walked over to the coffee machine.

"We were going to call you later today," Amber said. "Pearl and I are taking the two Lilys to the seaside on Sunday. Would you and Florence like to come?"

"Where are you planning on going?"

"Candle Sands of course. Where else?"

"Are the guys going too?"

"No, they both have to work this weekend. What do you say? Do you fancy it?"

"I'd love a day at the seaside, and I know Florence would, but—" I hesitated.

"But what? You can give work a miss for one day, surely?"

"It isn't that."

"What then?"

"It doesn't seem fair because Jack wouldn't be able to come with us."

"I bet if you asked him, he wouldn't mind."

"I'll have to think about it. Can I let you know?"

"Sure. Give us a call."

As Pearl handed me the coffee and muffin, someone called my name. It was only then that I realised Grandma was sitting at the far side of the shop.

"Why didn't you two warn me Grandma was here?"

"We were too busy listening to you talk about lookies."

Somewhat unenthusiastically, I went over to join her. "Sorry, Grandma, I didn't see you over here."

"That's because you were gabbing to those two who, by the way, haven't invited me to go to the seaside."

"Did you want to go?"

"Of course not, but it would have been nice to be asked."

"There haven't been any more altercations between you and Miss Drinkwater since this morning, have there?"

"Of course not. And as long as she keeps her distance, there won't be. Incidentally, did you hear about Gwen Ravensbeak?"

"What about her?"

"She's dead."

"What? How?"

"From what I heard, she'd just taken delivery of a new batch of t-shirts for the bowling team. Apparently, she was trying to carry the box across the road when she dropped it on her toe."

"And that killed her?"

"Of course not. The pain made her take a step back, straight into the path of a bus. She died instantly from all accounts."

"That's awful."

"They think she dropped the box because her nail extensions were so long that she couldn't keep a grip on it. It's just a pity Gwen couldn't see the future instead of the past."

"Grandma! That's an awful thing to say."

"Says the woman who took Gwen to get her nails done." Grandma finished her drink and stood up. "I can't hang around here all day. I have work to do."

I was still feeling guilty about Gwen when a tiny fairy flew into the shop. She looked around and then headed for my table.

"Are you Jill Maxwell?" she said in a teeny voice.

"Yes, I am."

"Good. I was told I might find you here. I'm Melanie."

"Hi, Melanie. It's nice to meet you. I hope you don't mind my asking, but what kind of fairy are you?"

"I'm a sweetheart fairy. I'm hoping you might be able to help my friend, Ursula."

"Is Ursula a sweetheart fairy too?"

"No, she's the queen of the unicorns."

"Really? I've never met a unicorn."

"They're very shy. That's why she asked me to try to set up a meeting between the two of you."

"I'd be delighted to meet her."

"Great. Would Wednesday at one o'clock be okay?"

"Yeah, I can make that. Where?"

"Would it be alright if I took your phone number? Then, I can send you a message on Wednesday with directions."

"Sure." I gave her my number, which she entered into her own teeny-tiny phone.

"Thanks, Jill. I'll be in touch. Bye."

"Bye, Melanie."

Wow! I was going to meet a unicorn. How very exciting! I'd better not tell Florence, though, or she'd want to go with me. She was crazy about them; she had two unicorn soft toys, a unicorn colouring book, and a unicorn duvet cover and pillowcases.

***

I was just about to magic myself back to Washbridge when my phone rang. I was surprised to see that it was Yvonne because she rarely called me.

"Jill, have I caught you at a bad time?"

"No. Is everything alright?"

"Everything's fine, but there's something Roy and I would value your advice on."

"Right. Do the two of you want to pop over tonight to talk to Jack and me?"

"Actually, we'd rather talk to you by yourself if that's okay?"

"I suppose so. When do you want to do it?"

"The sooner the better. Whenever you're free."

"I could pop over now if you like?"

"That would be great."

"Okay. I'll be with you in a minute."

It was a while since I'd been to Ghost Town, and I'd only visited Yvonne's house once before. Fortunately, she and Roy lived on the opposite side of town from my mother and father, so there was no chance I would inadvertently bump into them.

Both Yvonne and Roy came to the door.

"Jill, thanks for coming over." Yvonne beckoned me inside. "Let's go through to the lounge. Would you like a cup of tea?"

"Not for me, thanks. I've just come from Cuppy C. Are you sure there's nothing wrong, Yvonne? Your phone call has left me a little nervous."

"There's nothing to worry about, I promise. Before I get into the reason I asked you over, I really must apologise for what happened on your anniversary."

"Don't worry about it. I'm just sorry we were forced to cut short the dinner. I had no idea Kathy and Peter were coming over." Honest, guv.

"It's probably just as well they did. The way your mother and I behaved was unforgivable."

"My mother can be very difficult."

"It's not fair to lay all the blame at her door. I was just as bad. The two of us will never see eye to eye. I think that's something we'll all have to accept. I must confess I was surprised that Jack had invited us all over that night."

"Not as surprised as I was." I laughed.

"His heart's in the right place."

"I know he meant well, but the outcome was fairly predictable. By the way, is it true what you said about Cakey C and the hygiene certificate?"

"I don't think I should be discussing that, Jill."

"It is true, then."

"I'm sure your mother will have got it renewed since then."

"I'm not sure I share your confidence. I don't think I'll be eating in there for a while. Anyway, what was it you wanted to talk to me about?"

During all of this time, Roy had been listening to the two of us and nodding occasionally.

Yvonne continued, "We thought that it might be nice if we could live some of the time in the human world."

"Do you mean you want to move into our place?"

"Good gracious, no." She laughed. "You wouldn't want

your in-laws living with you."

"I wouldn't mind," I lied.

"That's very sweet of you, Jill, but it would be a nightmare. For all of us. We were thinking more in terms of finding somewhere we could treat as a holiday home."

"Let me make sure I've got this straight. You're talking about haunting this 'holiday home'?"

"Haunting isn't a term I particularly like, but strictly speaking, I guess that's what it would be. Ideally, we'd prefer a sizable house where we could move around without disturbing the occupants too much. We were just wondering what you thought of the idea."

"I don't see why you shouldn't do it. What I don't understand, though, is why you didn't want to include Jack in this discussion."

"It's only an idea at the moment, and we thought it best not to worry him unnecessarily. We weren't sure what he'd think of his parents haunting a house."

"I'm sure he'll be okay with anything that makes you both happy."

"You're probably right, but even so, I'd rather wait until we're sure it's going to happen before we say anything to him. I have no idea how one goes about something like this. I don't suppose you know, do you?"

"I wouldn't know where to start, but I might be able to find out for you."

"We wouldn't want to put you to any trouble."

"That's okay. There's a couple of people I can ask if you like."

"That would be great, Jill, thanks."

"Something else occurs to me. I think I know a house that would be ideal for you."

"Really? Where?"

"I recently completed a case for the woman who owns Tweaking Manor."

"That sounds rather grand."

"It's a large house that's in need of some renovation work, but it might be just what you're looking for. A lot of the rooms aren't even in use, and there are several hidden passageways."

"That does sound good. What do you think Roy?"

"It sounds lovely, dear." He nodded his approval.

"Okay. Why don't I make some enquiries to see what I can find out about the whole haunting thing, and I'll get back to you."

"That would be great, Jill. We really would appreciate it. And you won't mention any of this to Jack?"

"I don't normally like to keep secrets from him, but on this occasion, I'll make an exception until you decide if you're going ahead or not."

***

I'd no sooner walked through the door, than Florence came running up to me.

"Mummy, it isn't fair."

"What's not fair, darling?"

"Wendy can whistle, but I can't." She put her lips together and blew, but no sound came out.

"Not everyone can whistle."

"Can you whistle, Mummy?"

"Err, yeah, but only a little."

"Daddy can whistle too, so why can't I?"

"I'm sure if you keep trying, you'll soon be able to do

it."

"I've been trying and trying, but it doesn't work." She stomped off.

Jack came through from the kitchen. "She's been giving me grief ever since I picked her up from school. I tried to show her how to do it, but it's hopeless. It's something you can either do or you can't."

"She'll get over it."

"I hope so. How was your day?"

"Not bad. I landed a new case involving some lookies."

"What's a *lookie*?"

"It's what they call the people who work at a lookalike agency." I quickly checked to make sure Florence wasn't within earshot, and then said in a hushed voice, "I've also been asked to meet with the queen of the unicorns."

"Seriously?"

"Yeah. Her name is Ursula, and I'm meeting her on Wednesday."

"You'd better not let Florence find out. You know how she feels about unicorns. She'll definitely want to go with you."

"Why do you think I'm whispering? Oh, and I also called in at Cuppy C. Amber and Pearl are taking the two Lilys to Candle Sands on Sunday."

"Didn't they ask you to go with them?"

"They did, but I said it didn't seem fair because you couldn't come too."

"I don't mind. You and Florence should definitely go. In fact, it makes what I'm about to tell you much easier."

"What's that?"

"Tommy Gray asked if I fancied a game of golf on Sunday, and I told him yes."

"Have you joined the golf club?"

"No. He's going to sign me in as a guest, but if I enjoy it, I might just take the plunge."

"Good. You should. I'll go and tell Florence about the seaside. Hopefully, it will take her mind off the whistling."

Chapter 3

The next morning, as I was trying to decide what to have for breakfast, Florence came rushing down the stairs; she was clearly excited about something.

"Listen, Mummy, I can do it. I can whistle."

She put her lips together and blew. Whatever the sound was that came from her mouth, it certainly wasn't a whistle. Not that I was about to tell her that. Obviously.

"That's very good, darling. Well done."

"I did what you said, Mummy. I practised and practised and practised, and now I can do it. I can't wait to tell Wendy."

"Maybe it would be a good idea to keep it a secret. Just between the two of us."

"No, I want to show Wendy."

"Okay. Are you excited about the seaside?"

"Yes, I can't wait. How many days is it until we go?"

"It's Tuesday today and we go on Sunday. So how many days is that?"

She began to count on her fingers. "Tuesday, Wednesday, Thursday, Friday, Saturday. Five days! Aww, that's a long time."

"Not really. It'll fly by."

"I wish Daddy could come with us."

"It's okay, pumpkin," Jack said. "Daddy's going to play golf on Sunday."

"The seaside is much better than golf because there's sand and sea and donkeys."

"There's sand on the golf course too. In the sand traps."

"What's a sand trap, Daddy?"

"It's a hole full of sand. When you hit your ball, you

have to try to make sure it doesn't end up in one of those."

"Can you make a sandcastle in there?"

"No, I don't think the people in charge would like that." Jack turned to me. "What day is it you go and see the unicorn, Jill?"

I glared at him. What on earth was he thinking?

"What unicorn, Mummy?" Florence said.

"Err, I—err—"

"Daddy just said you're going to see a unicorn. Can I go with you?"

Looking very sheepish now, Jack mouthed the word 'sorry'.

"Please, Mummy. I love unicorns. I've got unicorn toys and a unicorn duvet."

"I know you have, darling."

"Can I, pleeeeease!"

"When I visit the unicorn on Wednesday, I'll ask if it's alright for me to take you to meet her."

"What's her name?"

"Ursula. She's the queen of the unicorns."

"I'm going to tell Wendy. She likes unicorns too."

"I don't think that's a very good idea. Humans aren't allowed to know about unicorns."

"But Wendy's not a human, silly billy."

"No, but the other children in your class are, and they might overhear you."

"Can Wendy come to see the unicorn with me?"

"I don't know. I'll have to see what Ursula says."

"Will you tell her that I love unicorns more than anything else in the whole wide world?"

"I will. I promise. Now, why don't you go out in the

garden and play with Buddy?"

"Okay."

Once she was outside, I turned my gaze on Jack. "Thanks for dropping me in it."

"Sorry, the words were out of my mouth before I could stop myself."

"You do realise that she's going to keep pestering now until she gets to see that unicorn."

"Couldn't you just use the 'forget' spell on her?"

"No, I couldn't. I would never use the 'forget' spell on my own daughter. What do you take me for?"

"But it's okay to use it on your husband?"

"Don't be so sensitive. And besides, I haven't used it on you since we were married."

"That's what you tell me, but how do I know it's true?"

"Would I lie to you?"

***

Although I didn't have an appointment, I decided to call on my new accountant, Mr Bacus, in the hope that I'd catch him in. I wanted to talk to him about the upcoming tax inspection that Betty 'the snake' Longbottom had dropped on me.

As I walked by the church, I spotted a squirrel, high up in the tree; those evil eyes of his seemed to be following my every step. What was it about squirrels that made them go nuts like that? I half expected to be hit on the head by an acorn, but he seemed content simply to observe me. Maybe I had just become a little paranoid where squirrels were concerned.

I rang Mr Bacus' doorbell and waited, but there was no

response. I tried again, but still got no response. I'd just started back down the path when the door opened behind me.

"Sorry, Jill," Mr Bacus said. "I was in my brewery."

"*Brewery?*"

"Home brewed beer. It's a hobby of mine. I brew it in the basement. Would you care to try some?"

"It's a bit early for me, Arthur."

"I'll give you a couple of bottles to take away. You and your husband can try them later and let me know what you think."

"Okay. Thanks very much."

"Go and take a seat in the office while I nip downstairs to get the beer."

"Right."

I'd only been seated for a couple of minutes when Mr Bacus returned, with a bottle of beer in each hand.

"Thanks. I see you even have your own labels."

"If something's worth doing, it's worth doing well, don't you think?"

"Absolutely. Bacus Kick? That sounds like it might be strong."

"It is. Very." He grinned. "But I think you'll like it."

"How much do I owe you for these?"

"Don't be silly. Call them samples. If you like it, you can buy some more."

"Okay, thanks."

"Did we have an appointment today, Jill? I don't have anything in my diary and you're not due to bring your books in yet."

"No. I came over because I've just been notified that I'm going to have a tax inspection on Friday."

"How long have you known about it?"

"I only found out yesterday."

"They normally give you more notice than that unless —
" He hesitated.

"Unless what?"

"Unless they suspect there's something amiss. Is there any reason they should?"

"Err — I — err, no."

"You don't sound too sure."

"I've not done anything dishonest, but you know what these tax inspectors are like. They'll always find something. Especially someone like Betty."

"*Betty?*"

"Betty Longbottom. She's a friend of mine, or at least I thought she was."

"Is she the one carrying out the inspection?"

"Yes. I was hoping you'd agree to be there when she comes. I'm sure you'll be able to handle her questions better than I would."

"This Friday you said. What time?"

"Ten o'clock."

"Let me just check my diary. Friday? You're in luck. I don't have any appointments that day. Where exactly are your offices, Jill?"

"In Washbridge City Centre, at the top of the High Street."

"I don't normally do on-site visits these days, but it's a while since I've been to Washbridge and there are a few things I need to get, so why not?"

"That's great. What do you need from me?"

"I'll need your accounts for the last few years, and I think it would be a good idea if I go in early on Friday.

You'll need to give me a lift because I don't have a car."

"No problem. What time were you thinking?"

"The earlier the better. How about we set off at six o'clock?"

"*Six?*"

"Is that too early for you?"

"Err, no. Six will be fine."

"Okay, I'll see you on Friday morning."

"Right, and thanks for the beer."

As I walked back through the village, I noticed a new A-board outside Tweaking Tea Rooms. Clearly, Miss Drinkwater had taken my advice to up her game because the board was promoting her afternoon teas.

Afternoon tea from Tweaking Tea Rooms. With over 30 years' experience.

Do not accept inferior imitations from FIRST TIME amateurs.

Oh dear. If Grandma saw that, she would go ballistic, but there was nothing I could do about it, so I walked on by. I'd not gone much further when I bumped into Barbara Babble.

She glanced at the beer in my hands and said, "It's a little early for that isn't it, Jill?"

"I—err—Mr Bacus gave me these. They're his homebrew."

"I see."

"By the way, Barbara, I thought you should know that the Stock sisters and the vicar aren't romantically involved. They're actually cousins."

"Is that what they told you?"

"Yes."

"And you fell for it? You have a lot to learn about the people in this village, Jill. Anyway, I must be going because I need to pick up my prescription. Don't drive after you've drunk those, will you?"

***

As I walked from the car park to the office, I happened to glance up and I spotted something fluttering in the breeze. There was a flagpole hanging out of my office window, and from it was flying a skull and crossbones flag.

I was going to kill that cat!

I sprinted up the stairs and into the outer office.

"Jill," Mrs V said. "Why do you have a skull and crossbones flag flying from your window? I don't think it projects a very good impression to would-be clients."

"There's been some kind of mistake, Mrs V. Don't worry. I'm going to sort it out."

Winky was sitting on the sofa, dressed in his pirate outfit. "Ahoy, Matey."

"Don't *matey* me!" I snapped. "Why is that flag flying from my window?"

"It looks great, don't you think?"

"No, I do not think. What sort of impression is that going to give to people?"

"They'll think you're cool."

"I don't want them to think I'm *cool*. I want them to take me seriously as a private investigator."

He laughed. "I'm sorry to be the one to have to tell you this, but that particular boat sailed a long time ago."

"I want that flag taken down and I want it taken down now."

"Can't I at least leave it up until after the fancy dress competition?"

"No, you can't. Either you take it down or I'll throw the flagpole and flag out of the window."

"Okay, okay. You're such a spoilsport."

An hour later, Winky had taken down the skull and crossbones flag, but not without much moaning and groaning.

Mrs V popped her head around the door. "Jill, I have Mr Blaze and Mrs Daze to see you."

"Right. Send them in, would you?"

"Are you sure? They're wearing catsuits."

"Positive."

"As you wish."

Daze marched into the office with Blaze a few steps behind her.

"Good morning, you two. Can I get Mrs V to make you a drink?"

"No thanks, Jill," Daze said. "We're really busy at the moment, but we thought it important that we pop in and talk to you."

"I wouldn't mind a drink," Blaze said.

"There isn't time!" Daze slapped him down.

"Is something wrong?" I said.

"I'm afraid there is, and I'm sorry to have to tell you it concerns your grandmother."

"She's okay, isn't she? I only saw her a little while ago."

"She's fine. I'm talking about that hotel of hers."

"You've heard about it, then?"

"We couldn't fail to. It's all the gossip in Candlefield. There's even been a feature in The Candle newspaper. Were you aware that she's targeting her advertising at sups who have never been to the human world before?"

"I didn't know until after the hotel had actually opened, and I only realised then when I noticed the sudden influx of sups into the village."

"Your grandmother has done some pretty outrageous things in her time, but this one takes the biscuit. When a sup visits the human world for the first time, there's always the possibility that something might go wrong. For her to invite them en-masse to the same hotel, in the same village, is just asking for trouble."

"I know. When I found out what she was up to, I tried to persuade her to change her mind, but she wasn't having any of it. I did at least convince her to issue all of her new guests with information packs, to tell them how they should behave in the human world."

"That's something, I guess, but I doubt it will be enough. I have a horrible feeling this is going to end badly."

"Me too, but I'm not sure what I can do about it."

"There's nothing much you can do. This is more by way of a courtesy call to let you know that we'll be keeping a close eye on your village. Please tell your grandmother that if things start to go pear-shaped, we'll be forced to take drastic action."

"I'll have another word with her. And I really do appreciate the heads-up."

Daze and Blaze stood up and were about to leave when I said, "Hey, Daze, what happened to that photo you promised me? Of you in a dress at the awards ceremony?"

"Don't talk to me about the awards ceremony!" She stormed out of the office without another word.

"What did I say, Blaze?"

"Didn't you hear what happened at the awards?"

"No. What did happen?"

"Daze went up to collect her award, but then as she was about to leave the stage, the compere inadvertently trod on her dress and it ripped open at the back."

"Oh no. How bad was it?"

"Very bad. It was gaping wide open, showing everyone her undies. And, of course, all of the press were there to capture the moment for posterity. The photo was in The Candle."

"Poor Daze. No wonder she isn't very happy."

Chapter 4

The offices of the Double Take Agency made mine look palatial. It had taken a while to find them because they were in a building which, at first glance, looked like it had been abandoned. It was only on closer inspection that I realised that, although the offices on the ground floor had been boarded up, there were still some businesses operating out of the first floor.

"Hi, welcome to the Double Take Agency." The woman behind the desk who had bright yellow hair, was wearing a pink scarf, a pink dress and pink fingerless gloves. "I'm Maggie. You must be Jill Maxwell."

"That's right. I'm here to see Rock."

"He told me to expect you. He's just on a call at the moment. Would you like a drink while you wait?"

"Could I get a glass of water, please?"

"Sure. I'll go and get it for you."

She'd no sooner left the room than I heard a little yap from behind the desk, and a Chihuahua appeared at my feet. For a horrible moment, I thought Buddy had somehow managed to follow me, but then I realised it was a lady dog.

"Hi," she said. "I'm Celeste. Who are you?"

"Hi, Celeste. I'm Jill."

"Can you pick me up and put me on the desk, please?"

"I'm not sure if I should. Are you allowed to go on there?"

"Oh yes. Maggie doesn't mind."

"Okay, then." I picked her up, put her on the desk, and gave her a stroke. Her little tail was wagging ten to the dozen. Such a friendly little dog. Why couldn't Buddy be more like her?

She sniffed at my hand. "I can smell Chihuahua on you."

"That's my dog; his name is Buddy."

"Why didn't you bring him with you?"

"I can't. Not when I'm working."

It was only then I realised Maggie had returned with my glass of water. Judging by her puzzled expression, she'd heard me talking to the dog.

"I was just getting to know Celeste," I said, by way of explanation.

"How did you know her name?"

Oh bum!

"I—err—must have seen it on her name tag."

"She isn't wearing one. She lost her collar at the weekend."

"Oh? She just looks like a Celeste."

"Right?" Maggie handed me the water. "And why are you on this desk, Celeste?" She picked up the dog and put her back on the floor. "You know you're not allowed on there."

Rock appeared through the door to my right. "Jill, I'm sorry to have kept you waiting."

"No problem."

"I've brought in three of my lookies for you to talk to. Feel free to ask them any questions you like. They know why you're here, so you can be completely open with them."

"Okay. Thanks."

"Before you do, though, would you come through to my office for a minute?"

"Sure."

His office was tiny or maybe it just looked that way because of the huge desk that filled the room. He took a sheet of paper out of the top drawer and handed it to me.

"This is a list of all the bookings that were cancelled within the last month. Quite a few, as you can see."

"Thanks."

"Okay, let's go and meet my superstars."

We left his office and walked along the corridor to another door. Waiting for us in the other room, were two men and a woman.

"Guys, this is Jill Maxwell, the private investigator I told you about. I want you to answer all of Jill's questions, fully and honestly. Don't hold anything back. Understood?"

They all nodded.

Rock turned back to me. "So, Jill, how does it feel to be in the presence of so many celebrities?"

When Rock had told me I was to meet some of his lookies, I'd expected to recognise at least one of them, but I was wrong. They didn't look like any celebrity that I knew of, but I figured I'd better play along.

"It's quite intimidating," I said.

"There's another small office through there." He pointed to a door at the other side of the room. "You can use that to speak to everyone individually."

"Great."

"Can I leave you to it, Jill?"

"Sure." I turned to the lookies. "Would you come through one at a time, please."

There was a table, four chairs, and nothing else in the small office. I'd just sat down when the first lookie walked in. The young man had jet black hair that was plastered back.

"Take a seat. What's your name please?"

"Can't you guess, sweetheart?" I think he was going for an American accent, but it sounded more like Newcastle-upon-Tyne.

"Err, sorry. It's on the tip of my tongue."

"Leroy Dulce of course."

"Of course. Just remind me, what movies has Leroy Dulce been in?"

"Leroy Dulce isn't a movie star. He's a pop star."

"Oh. You mean *that* Leroy Dulce. Sorry, I was getting mixed up with the *other*, lesser known, Leroy Dulce. What's your given name?"

"Norbert Knowles."

"Which would you prefer I call you today?"

"Everyone calls me Leroy."

"Leroy it is, then. How long have you been on Double Take's books?"

"Coming up for two years now. I don't know if Rock mentioned it to you, but I'm the most popular lookie on his books. And, strictly between you and me, I get paid a higher rate than the others."

"Your secret is safe with me. Have any of your bookings been cancelled recently, Leroy?"

"Yes, three in the last month. I was relieved when Rock told me he was going to bring you in because this is beginning to hit me in my pocket."

"Can you think of anyone who might have a grudge against the agency?"

"You need look no further than Ruby Red out there." He gestured to the door.

"Ruby Red?"

"Don't tell me you haven't heard of her either?"

"Of course I have." Not. "What makes you think she might have something to do with it?"

"I'd have thought that was obvious. Jealousy."

"Jealous of who?"

"Me of course. She can't bear that I get more bookings than she does."

"Right. And if it isn't Ruby, is there anyone else you can think of?"

"It is Ruby." He hesitated. "Unless — no, it couldn't be."

"Go on."

"Mandy Rhinestone."

"I assume she's another of the lookies on the books here?"

"Not any longer. Rock let her go, and good riddance too."

"Was there some kind of problem?"

"She'd got way too big for her boots. She used to turn up late for gigs, and at least once, to my knowledge, she was a total no-show. The last I heard, she was trying to negotiate a contract with a different lookalike agency. Rock found out about it and kicked her out."

"How long ago was this?"

"About six months, I'd say."

"Just before the cancellations started to come in?"

"I guess so, but I still think Ruby is behind this."

When I'd finished questioning Leroy, I asked him to send one of the other two lookies in. It was the young woman who walked through the door next.

"Hi there." She was all red lips and big eyes.

"Come in, Ruby."

"Ooh, you recognise me?" She sounded very pleased with herself.

"Of course. Who wouldn't recognise the famous Ruby Red?"

"I hope Leroy wasn't badmouthing me."

"What makes you think he would?"

"Because he's a horrible person."

"How badly have you been affected by the recent cancellations, Ruby?"

"I've been quite fortunate really. I've only had one in the last month. I know some of the others have had many more than that."

"How long have you been doing this? Being a Ruby Red lookalike, I mean?"

"Nearly five years now. And I've loved every minute of it."

"Can you tell me what a typical gig is like for you?"

"It varies. Sometimes it's a personal appearance—I just have to turn up at a bar or nightclub. I've done a few adverts too—magazines and TV. And once, I was booked to jump out of a cake for this rich guy's birthday."

It occurred to me that the guy couldn't have been all that rich if he'd had to settle for a lookie rather than the real thing, but I didn't share that observation.

"How's the pay?"

"I can't complain. But then, between you and me, I am Rock's biggest earner, so I get a higher percentage than the others. You won't tell anyone, will you? Especially not Leroy."

"Of course not. Tell me, Ruby, do you have any idea who might be behind the spate of cancellations?"

"I would have thought that was obvious."

"Not to me."

"It's Leroy. Who else?"

"What makes you say that?"

"The man is green with envy. He can't bear to think that I get more gigs than he does. He'd love to see me get thrown off the books. I've heard him talking to the other lookies, suggesting that I'm the one behind the cancellations. And I bet he's said the same thing to Rock."

"Is there anyone else apart from Leroy who might have done it? Someone who might have a grudge against the agency?"

"There's Mandy, I suppose."

"Mandy Rhinestone?"

"Yes. Did Leroy mention her to you?"

"He did, but what makes *you* think it might be her?"

"Mandy and I used to be good friends, or at least I thought we were until I discovered that she'd been stabbing me in the back all the time."

"What was she doing?"

"The agency has an online review system where people can leave ratings for each lookie. For a long time, I'd had an average of 4.5, which was better than everyone else. Then, suddenly, within the space of a couple of weeks, I received a load of one-star reviews, which brought my average way down. I told Rock I thought something was off, so he got his IT guy to look into it. He discovered that all the one-star reviews had come from the same computer."

"Were the ratings from Mandy's computer?"

"They weren't able to prove that, but I'm sure it was her. You should definitely talk to Mandy. It's either Leroy or her."

The last of the three lookies was much older than the other two. In his late fifties, he was handsome with the physique of a man twenty years younger. He introduced himself as Wayne Crabtree.

"I'm really sorry," I said. "But I haven't heard of Wayne Crabtree. Is he a movie star or a pop star?"

"Neither." He laughed. "Wayne Crabtree is my real name. I wasn't sure if you wanted me to give you that or my lookie name."

"Both really."

"My lookie name is Alex Wilder. Perhaps you've heard of him?"

"I'm afraid not. Should I have?"

"He's a movie star. Or, at least, he was back in the nineties. His star has rather waned since then. The last few movies he appeared in all bombed at the box office."

"Has that affected your bookings?"

"Unfortunately, yes. Luckily, I'm still quite popular with ladies of a certain age."

"Have the recent cancellations affected you, Wayne?"

"Not particularly, but that's probably because I get so few bookings anyway."

"Have you any thoughts as to who might be behind this?"

"Not really."

"Do you think it could be any of the other lookies?"

"No, I wouldn't have thought so."

"Isn't there any jealousy or backstabbing between them?"

"Not that I'm aware of. Everyone here seems really nice."

"What about Leroy and Ruby?"

"They're darlings, both of them. You couldn't wish to meet nicer people."

"Have you heard of someone called Mandy Rhinestone?"

"Mandy? Yes, of course. She's a lovely girl. She and I often used to go for lunch together."

"I understand she left under something of a cloud?"

"That's what I heard, but I don't know the details because I try not to get involved with the gossip. I thought it was really sad when she left."

***

As soon as I walked through the door, Florence came rushing up to me. "I'm not Wendy's friend anymore."

"Oh dear. Why's that, darling?"

"Wendy says I can't whistle but I *can*." She puckered her lips and blew. "See!"

"Err, yes. Maybe Wendy didn't realise that everybody's whistle sounds a little bit different."

"I'm not going to be her friend ever again."

"Don't say that, Florence. You and Wendy get on so well. You don't want to fall out over something as silly as whistling."

"It's not silly and I'm not her friend." She stomped off into the kitchen.

Jack came to join me in the hallway. "I assume Florence has told you about her altercation with Wendy," he said.

"She has. Poor Wendy." I glanced into the kitchen to make sure Florence wasn't listening. "She's right, though. Florence can't whistle for toffee."

"I wouldn't tell her that, or she won't be your friend either."

Over dinner, Jack asked about my day.

"I spent most of the afternoon at the Double Take Agency."

"Is that the lookalikes place?"

"Yeah. Rock, that's the owner, arranged for me to meet three of his lookies. They're supposed to be lookalikes of famous people, but I didn't recognise any of them. The first one I spoke to was a young guy who was a lookalike for Leroy Dulce. Whoever he is."

"Leroy Dulce? You must know him, Jill. He's really good."

"You've heard of him?"

"Of course. I've got his latest album on Spotify. You must have heard his latest single, Go Love Go."

"I can't say that I have. Then there was a young woman who was supposed to look like a movie star called Ruby Red."

"Don't tell me you haven't heard of her either. She's been in a couple of blockbusters in the last few years, and she's always in the newspapers."

"You're just pretending to know them to make me feel bad."

"No, I'm not. Why don't you call Kathy? I bet she's heard of Leroy and Ruby."

"Kathy will just pretend she's heard of them to annoy me. The other lookie was a much older guy. He was a lookalike for a movie star from the nineties called Alex Wilder. Have you heard of him too?"

"I'm not sure. His name does ring a bell. Have you

come up with any leads so far?"

"Leroy and Ruby both suspect each other of being behind the cancellations. The Alex Wilder lookie was too nice for his own good. He doesn't believe his colleagues would do anything like that. The two young ones mentioned someone called Mandy Rhinestone who got dropped by the agency. I suppose you've heard of her too?"

"No, I can't say I have."

"Incidentally, Daze and Blaze came to see me at the office today. It seems that word has reached them about Grandma's hotel, and Daze is not very happy about it. She asked me to warn Grandma that they'll be keeping a close eye on the village, and on her hotel in particular."

"Do you think speaking to her will do any good?"

"Of course not. When did Grandma ever listen to anyone? I did get one bit of good news today, though. My new accountant has agreed to sit in on the tax inspection on Friday."

"That's good."

"The only problem is that Mr Bacus insists on going in early. He wants us to set off from here at six o'clock."

"Six in the morning?" Jack grinned. "You've never even seen six in the morning."

Chapter 5

The next morning, while Florence and Jack were still eating their breakfast, I sneaked upstairs to our bedroom, and took the spell book out of the wardrobe. I wanted to see if I could identify a few spells that I could teach Florence over the coming weeks.

"What are you up to?"

"Jack! You scared me to death. Why are you creeping around like that?"

"I came up to see what you were doing."

"I thought I'd take a look at the spell book while Florence was eating her breakfast."

"Are you looking for the 'whistle' spell?" He grinned.

"Don't be ridiculous, there's no such thing as a—hang on—what's that?" I'd been running my finger over the index to find suitable spells, and there it was. "I can't believe it. There really is a 'whistle' spell."

"How come you didn't know already? I thought you were supposed to be the most powerful witch in Candlefield."

"That doesn't mean I know every spell in here. There are thousands of them."

"What does it do? Will it help Florence?"

"I'm not sure. Let me take a look." I flicked to the appropriate page and read the instructions. "Yeah, it looks like it might."

"You should cast it on her before she goes to school."

"Why are you suddenly so eager for me to cast spells on our daughter?"

"I just think she'd be happier if she could whistle properly, and it might help to smooth things over with

Wendy."

"You're right. Go downstairs and distract her, and I'll cast the spell while she isn't looking."

"Why do you need to be secretive about it?"

"She might not like it if she knows she can only whistle with the help of magic."

"Okay. How shall I distract her?"

"I don't know. You'll just have to think of something. And be quick about it because I'll be down as soon as I've memorised this."

"Will do." He disappeared downstairs.

The spell was very straightforward and only took a couple of minutes to memorise. After I'd put the spell book back in its hiding place, I went downstairs. Jack and Florence were in the lounge reading a book together. I walked up behind the sofa and cast the spell.

The question now was had it worked?

"What are you two reading?"

"Elly and Smelly." Florence held up her favourite book, which was about an elephant and a skunk who were best friends. It was a book which I had read so many times that I'd come to hate it with a passion. I'd made a promise to myself that if I ever came across the author, I would turn her into a skunk.

"I haven't heard you whistle yet today, Florence," I said.

She puckered her lips and whistled so loudly it made Buddy jump.

"I'm getting better at it, Mummy, aren't I?"

"You certainly are, darling. That was very good. Why don't you try it again, a little quieter this time? You don't want to scare people."

"Okay." She did it again, and this time the whistle was just about as perfect as a whistle could be.

A few minutes later, Florence was out in the garden, whistling and playing with a disgruntled Buddy. Jack was busy stacking the dishwasher when someone knocked at the door.

It was Donna.

"Morning, Jill."

"Hi. Is everything okay?"

"Yeah, I just wondered if I could have a quick word?"

"Sure, come in."

"Would you mind if we spoke out here?"

"O—kay." I stepped outside and closed the door behind me. "Are you sure everything is alright?"

"Yeah, it's just that—err—I don't know if Florence said anything, but she and Wendy had a bit of a falling out yesterday, I think."

"She did mention something about it. Something to do with whistling."

"Wendy's upset because she thinks she was horrible to Florence."

"Tell her not to worry about it. Florence is fine."

"Are you sure?"

"Definitely."

"Will you tell Florence that Wendy is sorry and that she still wants to be her friend."

"I don't think that's necessary, honestly. They'll be best buddies again today, you'll see."

"Okay. Thanks for putting my mind at ease. I know I'm just being silly, but Wendy doesn't find it easy to make friends."

"It'll be fine, I promise."

"Okay. I'd better get back, so I can get Wendy ready for school."

I went out into the garden and called Florence.

"Your whistling is much better now. I bet you can't wait to show Wendy. She'll think you're the best whistler in the whole world."

"But she isn't my friend anymore."

"Of course she is. You want her to know what a good whistler you are, don't you?"

"I suppose."

"There you are, then. You'll be whistling best buddies."

She seemed quite taken by that idea.

Back in the house, Jack had a stupid grin all over his face.

"What?" I said.

"If you ever decide to give up being a private investigator, you'd make a brilliant child psychologist."

I got changed for work, and then gave Jack and Florence a kiss.

"I'm going to have a quick word with Grandma before I go to the office, Jack."

"Good luck with that."

"Thanks. I'm going to need it."

I left the car outside the house and walked across the village to the hotel. En route, I passed a couple of werewolves who looked as though they were headed towards Tweaking Tea Rooms. Little did they know what they were letting themselves in for—Miss Drinkwater would scare them to death.

"Good morning." The receptionist was a witch. "Do you have a room reserved?"

"I'm not a guest. I'm here to see my grandmother."

"Is she staying with us?"

"No, she owns this hotel."

"Mrs Millbright?"

"That's right. Tell her Jill would like to speak to her, would you, please?"

"Right away." She picked up the phone, conveyed my message, then said, "Mrs Millbright says she'll be with you shortly. Would you take a seat over there, please?"

From where I was seated, I had a good view into the restaurant, which was doing a brisk breakfast trade. The guests mainly comprised of vampires, werewolves, wizards and witches. I was a little surprised to see there were also a few elves and fairies.

Ten minutes later and there was still no sign of Grandma. I was getting more and more annoyed because I was convinced she was deliberately keeping me waiting. I was just on the point of going back to the reception desk when she finally made an appearance.

"To what do I owe this pleasure?" she said.

"Can I have a word in private, please?"

"You'd better come through to my office."

There was a jar of green bunion ointment on the desk, and judging by the awful smell, she must have just finished applying it.

"What can I do for you, Jill?"

"Daze and Blaze paid me a visit at my office yesterday."

"That must have been nice for you."

"They've heard about your hotel."

"Good, it's nice to know my marketing campaign is

working."

"Daze isn't very happy about it."

"Oh dear. How awful. Let me think how I feel about that. Err—after careful consideration: I. Don't. Care."

"Daze shares my concern about the impact this hotel will have on the village. She asked me to warn you that the rogue retrievers will be keeping an eye on Middle Tweaking. If there are any problems, they won't hesitate in rounding up your guests and sending them back to Candlefield."

"I've already told you that all the guests will be given information packs with instructions on how to behave in the human world. There won't be any problems."

"I hope you're right. I've done my bit now. I promised Daze that I'd speak to you and I have."

"Is that it? Are we done?"

"Yes, we're done." I started for the door.

"Tell that human of yours he missed his chance."

"I assume you're referring to Jack. Missed his chance at what?"

"To be my bellboy. I couldn't wait any longer, so I had to set on someone else."

"A sup, I suppose?"

"Actually, no. A human. Would you like to meet him?"

"Not really. I have to get to work."

"Come on. It'll only take a minute." She led the way back to reception and pressed the bell on the desk.

"I'm really not all that interested, Grandma."

"Here he is now."

"Mr Ivers?"

***

Was I cursed? That was the only explanation I could come up with. How else did Mr Ivers keep turning up in my life? When I'd moved from my apartment to live in Smallwash, I thought I'd left the annoying little man behind, but then he'd followed me there. Since we'd moved to Middle Tweaking, and I no longer had to use the toll bridge, I'd enjoyed Ivers-free days, and that was a sweet feeling. Grandma must have done this deliberately, just to annoy me.

At first, I couldn't understand how Mr Ivers could be surrounded by sups all day without realising it, but Grandma had explained she'd come up with a potion that caused him to see all of the guests as humans.

That woman was so devious.

As I drove to the office, I was still fuming about the reappearance of Ivers. I'd only travelled a few miles when Henry poked his head out of the glove compartment.

"Why don't you have the radio on, Jill?"

"In a minute. I have a bone to pick with you first."

"Oh?"

"Who was that in there with you the other day?"

"That was my girlfriend, Henrietta."

"Where did she come from?"

"She lives in the boot."

"Of my car?"

"Yes. She used to live in a Volkswagen Beetle, but it was scrapped, so I said she could move in with me."

"That was very generous of you."

"You don't mind, do you, Jill?"

"It would have been nice to be asked."

"She was already living in the boot when you bought the car. We're planning on getting married soon. You won't make her leave, will you?"

"I—err—no, but I'd rather you kept the smooching to a minimum. Preferably, when I'm not in the car."

"I'll do my best, but Henrietta can be quite insatiable."

Way too much information.

"You seem to know a lot about music, Henry. Have you heard of someone called Leroy Dulce?"

"Of course I have. He's one of my favourite pop stars. That track of his, Go Love Go, is brilliant."

"I thought you were a big jazz fan?"

"I am, but I still keep up-to-date with current music."

"How come everybody has heard of him except me?"

"You are getting on a bit."

"What do you mean, *I'm getting on a bit*?"

"I just meant that Leroy Dulce appeals mainly to the younger generation."

"I *am* the younger generation."

"O—kay. So, can I have the jazz channel on?"

"No, you can't. Let's listen to the Latest Hits channel, so I can hear some of the current pop stars."

Henry was soon singing along to the latest tracks. He seemed to know all of them whereas I hadn't heard any of them. And, as it turned out, I hadn't missed much—they were all truly awful. It was almost as bad as listening to jazz.

"These all sound the same," I said.

"That's a sure sign you're getting old, Jill."

Cheek!

By the time I reached Washbridge, I was pleased to leave that awful racket behind. If that was a sample of today's music, they could keep it.

I'd no sooner walked through the door than Mrs V said, "Guess what?"

"You have two trillion followers?"

"Don't be silly. Armi and I got a dog yesterday."

"How come?"

"After spending that time with Polly the poodle, I began to—"

"You mean *Miranda*."

"I still say she looked more like a Polly. Anyway, it got me thinking that we should get a dog. Then, when you brought Buddy in, that sealed it. Armi is at home all day, so it's not like the dog will be lonely. We picked him up yesterday."

"Wow, that was quick. What have you got?"

"A Pekingese called Pepe."

"Aren't they the dogs with no faces?"

"Don't be silly. The reason you sometimes can't see their face is because of all their hair. You'll have to come and meet him, and bring Buddy along, too."

"Err, yeah. I'll see." No chance.

When I walked into my office, a party popper almost hit me on the head. Winky, who was no longer wearing his pirate's outfit, was dancing around on the sofa with what looked like a bottle of champagne.

"What are you doing?"

"Celebrating, of course."

"*Celebrating* what?"

"My win on the feline lottery."

"Pull the other one. It's got bells on."

"It's true. See." He held out what appeared to be a

cheque from the feline lottery, made out to Winky, for one thousand pounds.

"This isn't real."

"I think you'll find it is."

"Do I get half?"

"Are you kidding? I gave you the chance to come in with me, but you turned me down flat."

"That's not how I remember it."

"Listen." He took out his phone and played a recording he'd made of an earlier conversation between the two of us.

"Are you sure about that? Are you really going to turn down the chance to take part in the feline lottery?"

"I don't believe there is such a thing."

I sat down at my desk, feeling quite despondent. I couldn't believe that I'd lost out on a half-share of one thousand pounds. My luck just kept getting worse and worse.

"Hey, Jill," Winky said.

"If you're going to rub it in, don't bother."

"I wouldn't do that. I was just going to ask if you'd made any progress in recruiting your new private investigator."

"I'm interviewing somebody on Monday. They sound very promising."

I'd actually had very few applications for the post, and only one candidate had the right experience. Felix Perkins had, apparently, spent several years in the private investigator arena, so I'd arranged for him to come in for an interview the following Monday. If that went okay and he agreed to join me, that could be the first step in taking my business to the next level.

Chapter 6

Just as she'd promised, Melanie, the sweetheart fairy, had called to arrange my meeting with Ursula, the queen of the unicorns. I magicked myself to a secluded spot on the outskirts of Candlefield where I was to meet Melanie. To my surprise, I found her sitting in a horse and cart.

"Thanks for coming, Jill."

"No problem." I glanced again at the horse because I thought it might be a unicorn, but there was no sign of a horn. "Does the queen live close by?"

"No, her palace is actually some distance from here, but as I mentioned before, unicorns are very secretive, and prefer that no one knows where they live."

"I see. How will we get there?"

"I was hoping you'd agree to travel in this."

"In the horse and cart? Are you serious?"

"Yes, if you don't mind."

"I—err—guess not."

I was just about to climb up and join her on the seat when she said, "I'm sorry to have to ask you this, Jill, but would you mind climbing into the back?"

"You want me to get in there?"

"Yes, please. It takes several of us to control the horse." She tapped on the seat, and another six sweetheart fairies appeared from underneath it, and sat down beside her.

"I see. Okay." I scrambled into the back of the cart and took a seat in one corner.

"There's just one final thing, Jill," Melanie said. "I'm afraid I'm going to have to ask you to wear this blindfold."

Four of the sweetheart fairies held up a strip of cloth.

"Seriously?"

"Yes. Sorry, but like I said, the unicorns really value their privacy."

"Okay, go on then."

The four sweetheart fairies flew over and tied the blindfold over my eyes.

"Can you see, Jill?" Melanie said.

"No. Not a thing."

"Great, we'll get going, then."

"Is it far?"

"Not too far. Just over an hour from here."

"An *hour*?"

The first twenty minutes of the journey were okay, but then the going got much bumpier. I was being bounced up and down and thrown from side to side, to the point where I was beginning to feel quite nauseous.

"Are we almost there yet?" I said.

"Just another few minutes."

Eventually, and much to my relief, the cart drew to a halt and the sweetheart fairies removed the blindfold. It took a minute or so for my eyes to adjust to the light, but then I saw that we were outside a multi-coloured palace with turrets shaped like unicorn horns.

"Do you need a hand to get out of there, Jill?" Melanie offered.

"No, thanks. I can manage." I scrambled out of the cart, and dusted myself down.

"Follow me." Melanie led the way to the huge double doors, which opened automatically as we approached.

The magnificent entrance hall was a feast of colours. Waiting for us, just inside the doors, was a grey unicorn.

"Jill, this is Ronald, the queen's personal assistant,"

Melanie said. "Ronald, this is Jill Maxwell."

"I'm very pleased to make your acquaintance, Jill." Ronald stamped one hoof by way of a greeting.

"Likewise."

"Is it okay if I go now, Ronald?" Melanie said.

"Yes, that's fine. Thank you for bringing Jill here." He waited until Melanie had flown out of the doors, which closed behind her, and then turned to me. "How was your journey?"

"A little uncomfortable if I'm honest. The ground was very uneven."

"I'm sorry you had to go through that, but I'm sure you understand the need for secrecy."

"I guess so."

"Queen Ursula is ready to see you. We'll just need to sort out the horn situation first."

"The *horn situation*?"

"Didn't Melanie explain it to you?"

"No, she never mentioned it."

"Queen Ursula never leaves the palace, which means that, apart from the sweetheart fairies, she only ever sees other unicorns. Because of that, she only feels comfortable in the company of those who have a horn on their head."

"There isn't much I can do about that, I'm afraid."

"Actually, there is. We have plans for just such a contingency." He walked over to a gold cabinet and brought out a conical hat. The sort of thing you might wear at a kid's birthday party.

"If you could just pop this temporary horn on your head."

"That's a party hat."

"No, I assure you these have been specially designed to

resemble unicorn horns. It will put the queen at ease."

"I—err—okay, then." I popped the 'horn' on my head and slipped the elastic under my chin. I felt a bit stupid, but if that's what it took to put the queen's mind at ease, I supposed it would be worth it.

"Right, let's go and meet her majesty." Ronald led the way across the hall to another set of double doors where he stopped and knocked twice.

A voice from inside shouted, "Come in."

Inside the enormous room, the queen, who was wearing a crown over her horn, was seated on a beautiful throne. On seeing us, she stepped down and trotted over to meet me. I was just about to introduce myself when she began to laugh hysterically. I had no idea what was going on.

When she eventually managed to compose herself, she said, "Ronald, how could you do that to our guest?"

"I'm sorry, your majesty." He chuckled. "I just couldn't help myself. Witches and wizards are all so very gullible."

"Hold on a minute." I grabbed the 'horn'. "Is this a wind-up?"

"I'm afraid it is," the queen said. "Ronald fancies himself as some kind of practical joker."

"Does he indeed?" I pulled off the horn-hat and thrust it at Ronald.

"You must accept my apologies," the queen said.

"That's okay."

This wasn't the first time I'd been made to look a fool like this. I'd been the butt of a similar practical joke when I'd visited King Dollop, the king of the pixies.

"It's Jill, isn't it?" the queen said.

"That's right. Jill Maxwell, your majesty."

"Forget the, *your majesty* nonsense, you must call me

Ursula. Would you care for some tea?"

"Is it a special unicorn brew?"

"Actually, no. It's Earl Grey, which we import from the human world."

"Oh? Okay. Yes, please."

"Ronald, go and make us some tea, would you? And bring in the biscuits."

"Yes, your majesty." He turned and left, still chuckling to himself.

The queen led the way to a huge circular table, around which all the chairs, apart from one, had been designed to accommodate unicorns. I took the other chair, which had clearly been provided for my benefit. The queen sat directly opposite me.

"It was good of Melanie to make contact with you and bring you here. She's such a *sweetheart*." The queen laughed at her own joke. "Did she explain the problem we've been having, Jill?"

"No, she didn't."

"It's a nasty business. I'm sorry to say that someone has been stealing our horns."

"Isn't that painful?"

"Fortunately, or unfortunately, depending on how you look at it, it isn't. Whoever is doing it is removing them while the unicorns are asleep."

"That's terrible. Will they grow back again?"

"Yes, but it can take several weeks. A similar thing happened about seven years ago, but fortunately that episode was short-lived."

"Do you know who was behind the thefts back then?"

"No. They stopped as suddenly as they had started. No one was ever caught and charged."

"Why would anyone want the horns?"

"Your guess is as good as mine. My brother, Devon, believes they're being sent to Candlefield."

"What makes him think that?"

"I don't actually know, but he seems convinced of it. I wanted to bring in a professional some time ago, but he persuaded me to let him carry out his own investigation. But here we are two months later, and he doesn't seem to be any closer to figuring out what's going on. That's why I asked you to come and see me."

"Where is your brother?"

"He's been conducting the investigation from Candlefield."

"How is he managing to do that? I understood that unicorns preferred not to be seen."

"That's true, but our scientists recently developed a potion that can make our horns invisible for up to twenty-four hours at a time. That allows us to pass ourselves off as horses. Devon has been living in Candlefield undercover."

"As a horse?"

"That's correct."

Ronald returned with the tea and biscuits which he placed in the centre of the table.

"Do help yourself to a biscuit, Jill," Ursula said.

Although there were custard creams on the tray, they had been mixed in with the other, inferior biscuits, so I had no option but to decline.

"I'll just stick with the tea, thanks."

"So, Jill, are you willing to take the case?"

"Of course. I'll be happy to help if I can."

"Good. I'll ask Devon to contact you. He can tell you

what he has uncovered so far. If anything."

"Thanks. It might also be useful if you were to tell me where I can contact him in Candlefield."

"I'll do that."

Over tea, we made small talk, but when we'd finished, Ursula suddenly became much more serious.

"Before you leave, Jill, I think it's important you understand the gravity of the situation. I'm going to ask two of my ladies-in-waiting to come through, so you can see for yourself the damage that is being done."

"Okay."

She rang a bell, and moments later, the door behind her opened, and in clomped two unicorns: a yellow one and a pink one. The very first thing I noticed was that they were both missing their horns.

"Lydia, Bella," the queen addressed them. "Come a little closer so that Jill can see you."

They were both clearly embarrassed to be seen without their horns.

"This is Jill Maxwell. She's going to try to get to the bottom of who's been doing this dreadful thing. Lydia, would you tell Jill what happened to you, please?"

"I was staying at my parents' house. When I woke up that morning, something just didn't feel right, and when I realised my horn was gone, I was devastated."

"And you didn't feel anything during the night?"

"Nothing. I'd had a nightmare, but that's not all that unusual."

"So, there was no pain?"

"None. Not then or since, but you can see how horrible it looks. I'd prefer to stay at home until it's grown back, but it takes such a long time that's simply not practical."

"What about you Bella?" Ursula said.

"My story is much the same as Lydia's. I woke up one morning and found my horn had been stolen. Whoever did it must have been very quiet because I'm a light sleeper. I can't believe someone would do such a terrible thing. I hope you find out who's behind it."

"Thank you, ladies," Ursula said. "You may go now." She waited until they were out of the room and then turned to me. "Do you see what I mean, Jill? It's such an awful thing to happen to a unicorn because their horn is part of their identity."

"I could see how upset they were. Don't worry. I'll do my best to find out who's behind this and put a stop to it."

"Thank you. That's very reassuring."

"Before I go, Ursula, can I ask, do all the unicorns live in this palace?"

"Goodness, no." She laughed. "The palace is very large, but it's not nearly big enough to accommodate all the unicorns. Behind this palace is U-City. That's what everyone calls Unicorn City. Come on. I'll show you." She led the way out of the throne room to an oversize lift.

"We'll go up onto the roof. You'll get a good view from there."

From the rooftop, I could see the city, which extended as far as the eye could see. It looked much like any other city, except all the inhabitants were unicorns who were going about their business. Even from that height, I spotted a number of them whose horns were missing.

"This really is a beautiful place, Ursula. Do you get many visitors from Candlefield?"

"Not many. Just a few traders."

Fifteen minutes later, Ursula accompanied me back downstairs to the main doors.

"Before I leave, Ursula, I do have one request."

"Of course. Name it."

"I'm not sure I could face that journey in the horse and cart every time I come to see you. Is there any other way that—"

"Say no more. Just wait there." She disappeared back into the throne room, and returned a few minutes later with a slip of paper. "These are the map co-ordinates for the palace. You can use them to magic yourself here."

"That's great, thanks."

Chapter 7

The good news was that Florence and Wendy had made up and were best friends again. The bad news was that Florence was now whistling nonstop.

She'd spent most of the previous evening doing it. It wouldn't have been so bad if it had been a recognisable tune, but it wasn't—not even close. And, as soon as she got up the next morning, she'd picked up where she left off. It was driving Jack and me crazy. So much so that we'd both escaped to the lounge.

"You've got to do something about this," Jack said. "It's driving me mad."

"I don't know what you expect me to do."

"You're the one who cast the 'whistle' spell on her."

"Only because you told me to."

"Can't you reverse it?"

"What good would that do? You know how upset she was before. It'll be even worse if she suddenly finds out she can't do it again."

"Okay, but one of us has to tell Florence that she doesn't need to whistle all the time."

"Are you volunteering?"

"I think it would be better coming from you. You are the child psychologist, after all."

"I'll give it a go, but don't blame me if it doesn't work."

Jack escaped into the garden, leaving me to do his dirty work.

"Florence, can I have a word, please?" She nodded but carried on whistling. "Do you think you could stop whistling while we talk?"

"Okay, Mummy."

"I want to talk to you about your whistling."

"I'm really good at it now, aren't I?"

"Yes, you are."

"Me and Wendy are the best whistlers in the school, and I'm even better than Wendy."

"I'm sure you are, but you have to be careful not to overdo it or you might run out of whistle."

"You can't run out of whistle. That's silly."

"What I meant was that you might tire out your lips, and then you won't be able to whistle properly. Why don't you save your whistling so you can do it at school when you're with Wendy?"

She thought about that for a moment. "Okay, Mummy. Can I go and play with my dolls' house before school?"

"Of course you can. Off you pop."

Jack had obviously been listening from just outside the door because as soon as Florence had gone upstairs, he walked back into the kitchen. "Very impressive. You should definitely consider a career change."

"Talking of career changes, you've blown your chance to be a bellboy at Grandma's hotel."

"Oh no. Don't say it's so."

"I was up there yesterday, and you'll never guess who she's set on."

"I've no idea."

"I'll give you a clue: Toll bridge."

"*Toll bridge*?"

"Another clue: Movie newsletter."

"Not—"

"Yep."

"Mr Ivers? But won't he notice the hotel is full of paranormal creatures?"

"That's what I thought, but apparently Grandma has come up with a potion, so that he sees them all as humans."

"I bet you were thrilled when you heard the news."

"Oh yeah. I just can't shake that guy." I glanced around. "Have you seen Buddy?"

"He's out in the garden."

The dog was sitting by the fence, looking up at the tree, clearly transfixed by something.

"What are you doing, Buddy?"

"Watching that thing."

"What *thing*?" I followed his gaze to a squirrel, which was sitting on a branch high up in the tree.

"He's been watching the house for ages," Buddy said.

"Are you sure you're not imagining things?"

"I'm telling you. He's spying on us."

"Don't be ridiculous. Come on. I've put your food out."

"Why didn't you say so before?" He dashed past me into the house.

As I made my way back inside, the squirrel's gaze followed my every step.

"What was Buddy looking at out there?" Jack said.

"There's a squirrel in that tree. Buddy reckons it was spying on the house."

"A squirrel? Spying?" He laughed.

"It might not be as crazy as it sounds. When I went to see the accountant, there was a squirrel in the tree at the rectory, and it was definitely watching me. For all I know, this could be the same one."

"You've definitely been overdoing it, Jill. You need a holiday."

"Maybe. Or maybe the squirrels around here have all

gone nuts."

***

I was just about to get into my car when Barbara Babble appeared.

Great! She was the last person I wanted to see.

"Hi!" she shouted.

"Morning, Barbara. Sorry, I can't stop. I'm just on my way to work."

"Awful business at the tea room, isn't it?"

"What's happened?"

"Haven't you heard about Marcy?"

"Miss Drinkwater? What about her?"

"She's dead."

"How terrible. What was it? A heart attack?"

"No, someone murdered her."

"Are you sure?"

"Go and see for yourself. The police are there now."

Should I believe her? Her intel so far hadn't been very reliable—she'd been the one who misled me into believing that the vicar and the Stock sisters were having a ménage à trois.

But it turned out that Barbara was right this time because the area outside the tea room was cordoned off with yellow tape. A young police officer was standing in front of it.

"What's going on, officer?"

"I'm sorry, madam, I'm not at liberty to say."

"I heard Miss Drinkwater has been murdered?"

"Like I said, I'm not at liberty to say. Now, if you wouldn't mind moving on."

The guy clearly wasn't going to tell me anything, so I made my way back to the car.

***

Raymond Double, AKA Rock Masters, had given me Mandy Rhinestone's address, which turned out to be an apartment not far from where Mad and her husband, Brad, lived.

I hadn't called in advance, and when I rang the doorbell, there was no response. I was just about to leave when the door of the apartment opposite opened, and a woman appeared; she had a ginger cat in her arms.

"Are you looking for Christine?"

"Err, I'm not sure."

"How can you not know who you're looking for?"

"The woman I'm after goes by the name of Mandy Rhinestone, but I don't know her real name."

"That's Christine."

"You don't happen to know when she'll be back, do you?"

"No, but I know where you can find her."

"Great. Where?"

"She works in a coffee shop not far from here called Full Of."

"*Full of?*"

"Yeah, when you leave this building, turn left."

"Okay."

"Then take the first right."

"Right. Okay."

"Then you want the second right, then left. Or is it right? No, left. Then another right."

"Err, right."

"Then a left and you're there."

"Okay. Thanks very much."

There was precisely zero chance that I'd remember those directions, so I found the coffee shop by using the map app on my phone. The shop was very small and not one that I'd come across before; the only customers were sitting at a table near the back of the shop. The young woman on duty looked bored, but she managed a smile when I approached the counter.

"Welcome to Full Of. What can I get for you today?"

"Could I get a caramel latte, please?"

"Sure. Would you like anything to eat with that?"

"No, just the coffee, please." Once I had my drink, I said, "Are you by any chance Christine?"

"Yeah, that's me."

"Do you also go by the name of Mandy Rhinestone?"

"I do, yes, but not so much these days. Who are you, anyway?"

"My name's Jill Maxwell. I'm a private investigator."

"I haven't done anything wrong, have I?"

"No, of course not. I wonder if you could spare me a few minutes for a quick chat."

"Why not?" She shrugged. "It's not like I've got much else to do. It's been dead in here all day, but I'll have to stop if someone does come in."

"Of course. I've been hired by Raymond Double."

"Rock? How is he?"

"He's okay, but there have been problems at the agency recently, which is why he's hired me."

"What kind of problems?"

"They've been getting lots of cancellations, and Rock

suspects someone is trying to deliberately sabotage his business."

"I hope he doesn't think I did it, does he?"

"No, I don't think so. He never actually mentioned you."

"So how come you're here?"

"Some of the other lookalikes mentioned you in passing."

"Did they, now?" She grinned. "I can guess who that was. Leroy, right?"

"Leroy did suggest I talk to you."

"I bet he did. Who else? Astrid?"

"I didn't speak to an Astrid."

"Ruby, then. It must have been Ruby."

"Yeah, I did speak to Ruby. How was your time at Double Take?"

"I loved working there."

"So why did you leave?"

"Although the work was great, I got tired of all the backstabbing and gossiping that went on. Leroy and Ruby were among the worst of them."

"Someone said that you'd had an offer from another agency?"

"That's right. I never should have left Double Take, though. Rock was really good to me; he got me loads of work. But then, another offer came along, and I told Rock that unless he improved my pay, I was going to leave. I thought it would convince him to give me a bit more money, but I totally misjudged it. He got really angry, called me ungrateful, and told me to get out."

"Did you go to the other agency?"

"Yeah, and it was okay at first. I got tons of work, more

than I used to get at Double Take, but then things started to go downhill. The same sort of thing happened there as is happening to Double Take now. They got loads of cancellations too. So many that eventually they went bust which left me without an agency."

"Couldn't you have gone back to Double Take?"

"I wanted to, but I felt like I'd burnt my bridges with Rock because when he asked me to leave, I gave him a mouthful, and told him what I thought of him. It's not like I really meant it; I was just trying to hurt him because I was angry. That's how I ended up working in this place. People still say I look like Mandy Rhinestone occasionally." She turned her head to give me a side profile. "What do you think?"

"Can I be honest?"

"Sure."

"Until I went to Double Take, I'd never even heard of Mandy Rhinestone."

***

Ever since I'd spoken to Yvonne and Roy, I'd been trying to get in touch with the colonel and Priscilla, but I'd been unable to reach them because they were somewhere on the high seas. On the off-chance that Mad might be able to help, I called in at Vinyl Alley on my way back to the office.

Both she and Brad were behind the counter; he was busy serving a customer.

"I see you've got rid of the buckets, Mad," I said.

"Yes, thank goodness. We've not had any problems since you sorted out those roof sprites. And there hasn't been a single theft as far as we know. We really owe you, Jill."

"Funny you should say that because I'm after a favour."

"Anything. Just name it."

"I've been talking to Jack's parents. They've got it into their heads that they'd like to divide their time between GT and the human world."

"Do you mean they want to go into the haunting business?"

"Apparently, but they don't have the first clue how to go about it, so they asked if I knew anyone who might be able to help. I tried to get hold of the colonel and Priscilla because they've been doing just that for some time now, but they're on a cruise ship somewhere and I can't reach them. I don't suppose you know who I could ask, do you?"

"They need to get in touch with the Haunting Society."

"Are they in Ghost Town?"

"Yeah, they should be able to find them in the phone book."

"Do you have any idea how it all works?"

"Essentially, there are two ways you can get into haunting. There's the official route, which is through places like the Haunting Society. Then, there's the unofficial route."

"What's the difference between the two?"

"In theory, everyone should use the official route, but not everybody does. Anyone found haunting in the human world unofficially can, in theory, be brought back to Ghost Town and fined."

"Like when my mother and father pop over to see me?"

"No, that sort of thing is okay. Short visits like that are

not considered a haunting. I'm talking about situations where ghosts move into a property and stay there for long periods of time. In those cases, you need to be granted a licence."

"Is it difficult to get one?"

"Provided that you don't have any kind of criminal record, it's pretty much a formality. I'm sure Yvonne and Roy won't have any problems."

"Could there be an issue with Yvonne because she used to be a witch finder when she was alive?"

"Definitely not. The application is judged purely on someone's record since they became a ghost."

"That's great. Just one more thing. If they get a licence, will they be able to choose where they haunt? I did some work recently at Tweaking Manor. It's a lovely old place, even though it needs a lot of work doing to it. I mentioned it to Yvonne and Roy, and they thought it sounded like just the sort of place they might want to haunt."

"I'm not sure if that's possible or not, but the Haunting Society will be able to advise them."

"Okay, thanks again. I'd better get going."

I was just about to leave when Brad said, "Jill, I didn't get the chance to thank you properly for sorting out the roof sprites."

"No problem."

"Mad and I would like to treat you and your husband to dinner one day next week."

"There's really no need to do that."

"We'd like to."

"Okay, but I'll have to check with Jack to see which days we can make. I'll give you a call."

Once I was outside, I called Yvonne to find out when

would be a convenient time to go and see her.

"I'm free now if that works for you, Jill."

"Great. Are you at home?"

"Actually, I'm in town. I've been doing a bit of shopping."

"In that case, why don't we meet at Cakey C?"

"I—err—okay, sure. I'll see you there."

As soon as I walked into Cakey C, I realised it had been a mistake to meet there because Yvonne and my mother were already locked in a staring match with one another.

"Hello, darling." My mother came around the counter to greet me. "You didn't tell me you were going to pay us a visit."

"Actually, I'm here to see Yvonne."

"Well that's just charming. You don't have time to visit your own mother, but you can make time for—" She turned towards Yvonne. "*Her*."

"I have some information for Yvonne, that's all."

"Hmm. I suppose you'll be wanting a drink, though."

"If it isn't too much trouble. Just a small caramel latte, please."

Still grumbling under her breath, she went back behind the counter and I went to join Yvonne.

"Meeting here wasn't one of my better ideas," I said.

"Your mother has been giving me the dead-eye ever since I walked in."

"There you go!" My mother put the drink down with such force that most of it ended up on the table.

"How much do I owe you?"

"That's okay." She grinned. "I'll put it on Yvonne's bill."

"Sorry about that," I said, once my mother was out of earshot.

"It's not your fault. You said you had news for me."

"Yeah. I didn't manage to get hold of the colonel and Priscilla, but I've spoken to Mad, and she reckons you need to get in touch with the Haunting Society. Apparently, they handle all the paperwork for this type of thing."

"Thanks, Jill, I appreciate you taking the time to do this. Have you said anything to Jack?"

"No, not yet. I promised you that I wouldn't until it was definite."

"How do you think he'll take it?"

"I'm sure he'll be fine about it. As long as you and Roy are happy, that's all that matters to him."

Chapter 8

Mrs V was flat out on the desk, with her head resting on a giant ball of wool. For a horrible moment, I thought she must have passed out, but when I got closer, I could hear her snoring. All that knitting must really take it out of you. I didn't have the heart to wake her, so I crept past her desk and into my office where Winky was sitting on the windowsill, staring at something.

"What are you looking at, Winky?"

"We were being spied on."

"What do you mean, *spied on*?"

"He was over there, on the other side of the road."

"Who was?"

"A squirrel. And I know what you're thinking, but I'm not going crazy."

"I believe you."

"You do?"

"Yeah, this is the third time it's happened. He was watching me as I walked through the village the other day. He was at it again yesterday in our back garden. But I never thought he'd follow me into the city."

"How do you know it's the same squirrel?"

"It looked like the same one to me, but I suppose that might just be my imagination. Either way, it's starting to give me the creeps."

"You should report it to the police."

"And what exactly am I supposed to tell them? That I'm being stalked by a squirrel? I don't think so. They'll think that I'm the one who's gone nuts."

I spent the next hour digging out all my books in

advance of the following day's tax inspection. I'd just finished when Mrs V popped her head around the door.

"Jill, I'm awfully sorry. Why didn't you wake me when you came in?"

"I didn't have the heart; you looked so peaceful. Didn't you sleep very well last night?"

"Quite the contrary. I slept like a log, but that was because I'd taken a sleeping draught."

"Really?"

"Yes, it's called U-Sleep."

"Do you often take that?"

"No, but I haven't been sleeping well lately. One of the yarnies suggested I try it, and it did the trick—it completely knocked me out. It took Armi all his time to wake me up this morning. It must have been strong because I still feel half asleep."

"Do you need to go home?"

"No, I'm going to make myself a coffee. That'll wake me up. Do you want one?"

"Not right now, thanks." Just then, my phone rang. "Sorry, Mrs V, I'll have to take this. It's my grandmother."

"Alright, dear."

"Grandma, hi."

"I need you to come and pick me up. I'm at the police station."

"What are you doing there?"

"These idiots brought me in for questioning."

"About what?"

"What do you think? Miss Drinkwater's murder of course."

"You haven't been arrested, have you?"

"No, they were just questioning me, but it's obvious

they're treating me as a suspect. Why are you wasting time, gabbing? I need to get back to the hotel."

"Okay, I'll be there in a few minutes."

I hurried out of the office.

"Mrs V, I have to go. My grandmother needs picking up from the police station."

"What has she done this time?"

"Nothing." Fingers crossed. "She was just helping with their enquiries."

Grandma was waiting outside the police station.

"It took you long enough, didn't it?" She climbed in beside me. "Where were you?"

"I got here as quickly as I could. Why didn't you just magic yourself to the hotel?"

"Aren't you always telling me that I shouldn't use magic in the human world?"

"I—err—yes, but since when did you take notice of anything I say?"

"Come on. Can't this thing go any faster?"

"I'm not getting a speeding ticket just for you."

We hadn't gone far when Henry popped his head out of the glove compartment. "Jill, can you put on some music?"

Before I could reply, Grandma had pushed him back inside, and slammed the glove compartment closed. "Stay in there, young elf. We're busy."

Poor old Henry. He didn't know what had hit him.

"What did the police actually say to you?"

"They asked lots of stupid questions: When was the last time I saw Miss Drinkwater? What were we arguing about the other morning? That sort of thing. I told them they were wasting their time talking to me, and that they should be out looking for the murderer."

"The police don't really think you did it, do they?"

"Who knows what those fools are thinking."

"You didn't do it, did you?"

"Of course I didn't, but I need you to find out who did."

"I'm not getting involved. The police can deal with it."

"It'll take them forever. I can't afford to have the police hanging around the village. It'll be bad for business. No one will want to stay at First Time if they know Middle Tweaking is swarming with police."

"I'm already busy working on two cases."

"You'll just have to drop one of them, then, won't you? This is clearly more important."

"There's no way I'm dropping one of my cases, but I'll see what I can find out about Miss Drinkwater's murder."

"Good, and I need a quick result otherwise people will start to cancel their bookings. You should start by talking to Marian."

"Who's Marian?"

"The young waitress who works there. Apparently, she was the one who found the body."

"I will if I can track her down. It might not be easy now the police are involved."

"This is her phone number." Grandma handed me a slip of paper.

"How did you get that?"

"Are you going to give me the third degree too, or are you going to do something useful, like talking to the waitress."

"Okay, I'll speak to her."

After I'd dropped Grandma off at the hotel, I tried calling Marian's number but there was no reply, so I sent her a short text message, asking her to get in touch with me. Whether she would or not, was anyone's guess.

"You're early, aren't you?" Jack said.

"I had to bring Grandma home from the police station."

"What was she doing there?"

"They took her in for questioning about Miss Drinkwater. I assume you heard she was murdered?"

"Of course. There's been talk of nothing else around the village all day. They don't suspect your grandmother, do they?"

"I don't think so, but she's demanding I solve the murder because she's worried the police presence will affect her business."

"I hope you told her to get stuffed."

"Something like that."

"Mummy! Mummy!" Florence came running in from the garden. "Did you come home early to teach me the 'faster' spell?"

Oh bum! I'd forgotten all about that.

"I—err—"

"You said you were going to teach me it today if the weather was nice, and it is. It's sunny."

"You might as well go now," Jack said. "I haven't even started dinner yet."

"Okay. Florence, you have to learn the spell before we go because we can't take the book with us to Tweaking Meadows."

"Mummy, can I come and get the spell book with you?"

"No, you can't, you little monkey. You can stay down here."

I went upstairs, got changed, and took the spell book from its hiding place in the wardrobe. Back downstairs, Florence and I sat at the kitchen table.

"Take your time. You have to be sure you know it."

She studied the page. "This spell is really easy. I've learned it already."

"Are you sure? We don't want to get all the way down there and find you've forgotten it. Why don't you take one more look?"

"Okay." She studied the page for another minute. "I know it now. It's easy peasy."

After I'd put the spell book back in its hiding place, Florence and I set off for Tweaking Meadows.

"Florence, listen to me for a minute."

"Yes, Mummy?"

"If there are any humans there, we'll have to go home and try another day."

"But you said I could do it today."

"And you can, but not if there are any humans around."

"Couldn't you use magic to make them go to sleep or forget?"

"No, I can't. You'll just have to keep your fingers crossed that the meadow is deserted."

"Why?"

"That's what you do when you hope for something." I crossed my fingers to demonstrate.

"My fingers won't do that."

Oh no! What had I done? First the whistling, now this.

"Give me your hand." I gently put one of her fingers

over the one next to it. "See! You can do it."

"How does crossing your fingers work, Mummy?"

"I don't know." I was beginning to regret having mentioned this, but then I spotted that the meadow was deserted. "Look, we're okay, there's no one here."

"Is that because we crossed our fingers?"

"Probably."

"Shall I cast the spell now, Mummy?" She was clearly eager to get started.

"Not just yet. Why don't you run to that tree over there, touch it, and run back, and I'll time how long it takes. Then, after you've cast the spell, you can do it again and we'll see how much quicker you are."

"Okay. Are you going to say *go*?"

"Yes. Ready? One, two, three, *go!*"

And off she went as fast as her little legs would carry her. After touching the tree on the other side of the meadow, she ran back to me.

"That was very good! That took you thirty-six seconds. Now, cast the spell and do it again."

"Okay, Mummy." She closed her eyes and I could see that she was focusing as hard as she could. "I've done it. I've cast the spell."

"Okay. Ready? One, two, three, *go!*"

This time, she ran so fast that I could barely see her. She had no sooner touched the tree on the other side of the meadow than she was back by my side.

"How long did it take me this time, Mummy?"

"Five seconds."

"That's super-fast, isn't it?"

"It certainly is."

"I wish I could use the 'faster' spell on sports day at

school."

"Well, you can't. You know you can't."

"But I always come last in races. If I used the spell, I'd be first."

"It doesn't matter. You can't use it and that's all there is to it. Okay?"

"Okay. Can I run again?"

"Yes, off you go."

No sooner had she set off than I heard a voice behind me.

"Hi, Jill." It was Olga. "I thought I saw Florence with you."

"I—err—" Florence suddenly appeared at my side. "Yes, she's here."

Olga did a double take. "I don't understand. She was here, then she wasn't, and now she is again."

I was such an idiot. Why hadn't I checked the meadow was still empty before telling Florence she could go for another run?

"She was here all the time, weren't you, Florence?" I said. "She was standing behind me."

"Oh?" Olga was clearly still puzzled. "What are you two doing here? Have you brought your little doggy for a walk?" She glanced around.

"No, Buddy's back at the house. He's already had his walk today and he's tired out."

"We came to practise—" Florence blurted out.

I jumped in before she could say too much. "Practise, err—making daisy chains. Didn't we, Florence?" I winked at her.

"Yes, Mummy." Winking was another thing that Florence hadn't quite mastered, so she blinked both eyes.

Olga glanced around. "But I can't see a single daisy in the meadow."

"I know." I sighed. "It's so disappointing. Florence had been so looking forward to it too. Oh well, we'd better get back for dinner."

"Before you go, Jill, I'd intended coming to see you later. I wanted to invite you to—" As soon as I heard the word *invite* my heart sank. "—come to the meeting of the Middle Tweaking Basket-weaving Society on Saturday. You said you thought you might enjoy it."

I was pretty sure I'd said no such thing. "Saturday? How disappointing. I would have loved to come, but I take Florence to her dance class on Saturday."

"Don't worry. You'll still be able to make it. The dance class is in the morning. I know that because we use the village hall too. The meeting doesn't start until two."

"Right. That's great. Oh, wait a minute. Oh no. I've just remembered that we've already arranged to do something on Saturday afternoon. Maybe next time." I grabbed Florence's hand. "Come on, darling. Our dinner will be ready. Bye, Olga."

As we walked back to the old watermill, Florence said, "I didn't get chance to practise the 'faster' spell very much, Mummy."

"I know, but we couldn't do it while Olga was there, could we?"

"Can we go back there another day, so I can practise some more?"

"I have a better idea. You'll be able to do it at the seaside on Sunday. You can run up and down the beach as often as you like in Candle Sands."

"Do you think the two Lilys know how to do the 'faster' spell?"

"I don't know, darling. Probably not because the twins haven't taught them much magic."

"I could show them, couldn't I?"

"That's a great idea."

"You two weren't gone very long," Jack said.

"Florence managed to try the spell a couple of times, but then Olga appeared, so we had to call it a day."

"I ran really fast, Daddy, didn't I, Mummy?"

"You did. She was like a cheetah."

"I didn't cheat!" Florence sounded quite put out.

"I didn't mean that, darling. A cheetah is a really fast wild animal."

"I'm a cheetah. I'm a cheetah." She ran outside and began to chase Buddy around the garden.

"Olga invited me to her basket-weaving club on Saturday, but I told her that we'd already planned to go out."

"Oh dear."

"What do you mean, *oh dear*?"

"While you were out, Oscar came around to ask if I'd like to see more of his stamp collection."

"Lucky you." I grinned.

"On Saturday afternoon while Olga is at her basket-weaving club."

"You told him no. Please tell me you told him no."

"I wanted to, but I didn't have the heart because he seemed so keen."

"Well that's just dandy. Now Olga will know we're not going out, and she'll expect me to go to the stupid basket-weaving class."

"Why don't you tell her that you can't leave Florence alone?"

"Good idea. That's what I'll do."

"I'm a cheetah! I'm a cheetah!" Florence came running into the house.

Just then, there was a knock at the door.

"Olga?"

"I've just seen Oscar. He told me the good news."

"Did he?"

"Now you aren't going out on Saturday afternoon, you'll be able to join us at basket-weaving."

"I really wish I could, but I have to stay here and look after this little one." I gave Florence a gentle pat on the head.

"She can come too. We have a kid's group. You'd like to learn how to make baskets, wouldn't you, Florence?"

"Yeah! Can I, Mummy? Please?"

"Err, yeah, of course."

"Great!" Olga said. "We'll see both of you on Saturday."

Chapter 9

"Jill? What are you doing?" Jack rolled over in bed. "Are you alright?"

"I'm fine. Go back to sleep."

"It's still dark."

"I have to pick up Mr Bacus, remember?"

"Oh yeah." He yawned. "See you tonight, then."

When I left the house, toast in hand, Jack and Florence were still in bed. Although I was grateful that Mr Bacus was going to be there for Betty's visit, I wished he hadn't insisted on going in so early.

I'd just got in the car when the glove compartment opened, and Henry stuck his head out; he had a small plaster on his forehead.

"I wish to register an official complaint," he said.

"Not now, Henry. I'm really not in the mood for this. I'm too tired."

"Just look at my head." He pointed to the plaster. "That woman with the wart on her nose did this to me. She could have killed me."

"Don't exaggerate."

"Who is she, anyway?"

"That, Henry, is my grandmother."

"I've a good mind to sue her."

"If you'll take my advice, you'll let it drop. You really don't want to go up against that woman. You'll only live to regret it."

"The least she could do is to reimburse me for the cost of the plasters."

"I'm sorry, Henry, but you'll have to get back in the glove compartment because I have to pick up my accountant."

"What about my head? I have a blinding headache."

"Take some tablets and sleep it off." I closed the glove compartment.

What do you mean, where was my compassion? I'd left it back in my bed where I should have been.

Mr Bacus was waiting for me by his gate.

"Good morning, Arthur." I opened the door. "I hope I'm not late."

"No, you're dead on time." He climbed in beside me. "I do appreciate punctuality; it's so rare these days. I'm sorry I had to ask you to get up so early."

"No problem. I'm an early riser, anyway."

"I'm looking forward to spending some time in Washbridge. It's a while since I was there."

"When you buy your lunch, make sure to get a receipt and I'll reimburse you."

"That's very generous of you, Jill, but there's no need." He opened his briefcase and took out a Tupperware box. "I always bring my own sandwiches."

Mrs V wasn't due to arrive for at least another couple of hours, so I had to unlock the offices.

"My office is through here."

He followed me in, but then stopped dead in his tracks.

"Is everything alright, Arthur?"

"Err, yes. I was just wondering why your cats are dressed in pirate outfits."

I glanced across at the sofa where Winky was seated next to a small female cat. They were both dressed as pirates.

"I—err—show cats," I said. "It's a hobby of mine."

"Dressed as pirates?"

"That is a little unusual, granted, but there's a good reason for it."

"There is?"

"Err, yeah. There's a competition coming up in a couple of weeks for cats wearing fancy dress."

"I see." He scratched his chin. "It takes all sorts, I suppose. Is there a toilet close by, please, Jill?"

"Yes, it's back out the way we came, across the landing, down the corridor, and it's on your left."

"I won't be a minute, then I'll make a start on your books."

As soon as he was out of the door, I turned on Winky. "What's going on here?"

"We're preparing for the fancy dress competition, obviously."

"Well, you can't do it in here."

"How was I supposed to know you were going to choose today to come in at the crack of dawn? You're never here at this time."

"I had to come in early because my accountant's going through the books before the tax inspection later. Anyway, why on earth am I explaining myself to you?"

The female cat coughed. "Seeing as no one else is going to do it, I suppose I'd better introduce myself. I'm Mimi. Winky is my boyfriend."

"It's nice to meet you, Mimi, but I'll have to ask you to leave, I'm afraid."

She turned to Winky for support, but he just shrugged. "Sorry, babe, it's out of my hands."

"That's just great." She huffed. "And after all the effort I made to get here so early."

"I said I was sorry, babe. See you later?"

"You might. You might not." And with that, she disappeared out of the window.

"See what you've done now?" Winky said. "You've upset Mimi."

"I don't care. I've got more than enough on my plate with the tax inspection, without having to explain why there are two cats dressed as pirates in my office. Now take that stupid outfit off."

He moaned and groaned, and then disappeared under the sofa.

Moments later, Arthur came back. I'd expected him to ask me lots of questions, but he simply got his head down and began to work his way through my books. Every now and then, he made a disconcerting tutting sound, and occasionally said things like, "Oh dear."

I felt a bit like a spare part, so to pass the time, I started messing around on my phone. I sent Kathy a couple of messages, but she didn't respond. She was no doubt still tucked up in bed.

About an hour later, I heard the door in the outer office open. It was clear Arthur didn't need me, so I went out to greet Mrs V.

"Good morning, Jill. I'd forgotten you were coming in so early. Have you filled the kettle?"

"No, sorry. I never thought about it."

"Not to worry. I'll do it in a minute."

"You look a lot brighter this morning, Mrs V."

"I feel much more awake. I've stopped taking that sleeping draught. It was way too strong. In fact, I heard that a couple of yarnies have been hospitalised after taking it."

"That doesn't sound good."

"I'm glad I only took it the once. Would your accountant friend like a drink?"

"I'll go and ask him." I stuck my head around the door. "Arthur, I'm sorry to disturb you, but would you like a drink?"

"Yes, please."

"Tea or coffee?"

"Tea would be lovely."

"Milk and sugar?"

"Milk and one and five-eighths teaspoons of sugar, please."

"Right, you are." I turned to Mrs V. "Arthur would like a cup of tea please. Milk and one and five-eighths teaspoons of sugar."

She grinned. "That brings back memories."

"Mrs V, would you be able to do a little job for me this morning?"

"Of course, dear. What is it?"

I took out the sheet of paper that Raymond Double had given to me.

"This is a list of the clients who cancelled their bookings with the Double Take Agency. Would you get in touch with them, starting with the most recent, and see if you can arrange for me to go and talk to them? I want to try to find out the reason for the cancellation."

"I'll be glad to. Just drop it on my desk."

Arthur was still busy going through the books while tutting to himself, so I sat on the sofa and played around with my phone some more.

Thirty minutes later, Mrs V popped her head around the door.

"Jill, Betty Longbottom is here."

"Okay. Excuse me, Arthur, the tax inspector is here. Are we ready for her?"

"As ready as we're ever going to be."

"Okay. Send her through, please, Mrs V."

"Good morning, Jill." Betty was full of smiles; she was clearly a woman who enjoyed inflicting pain on others.

"Morning. Can I introduce you to my accountant, Mr Arthur Bacus? Arthur, this is Betty Longbottom."

"I'm very pleased to make your acquaintance, Betty." Arthur stood up and offered his hand.

"Likewise, Arthur. Is it alright if I sit here?"

"Of course. We're all ready for you."

"I'd like to go through the last three years' accounts, if that's alright?"

"Absolutely." Arthur nodded. "Shall we start with the oldest first?"

Mr Bacus, who had always struck me as rather timid, seemed much surer of himself in the presence of Betty.

I was happy to leave the two of them to get on with it, so I took a seat on the sofa again. As I did, a voice came from underneath it. "The end is nigh."

I glanced under the sofa to find Winky grinning. "It's all over now that the taxman has caught up with you."

"Be quiet."

"Sorry, Jill?" Betty said. "Did you say something?"

"Err, no. I've just got a tickly throat."

As the two of them went through my books, Betty asked a number of questions. Every time she did, Arthur seemed to come up with an answer that satisfied her. This was going much better than I could have hoped.

An hour later, and I was bored out of my brain, and feeling quite peckish.

"I'm sorry to interrupt, but I have some urgent work that I need to attend to. Would it be alright if I nipped out for a while and left you to it?"

"That's fine by me," Arthur said. "What about you, Betty?"

"Yes, but I will need to talk to you this afternoon, Jill. Can you be back by three o'clock?"

"Of course. Right, I'll be off, then."

"How's it going in there?" Mrs V asked as I was on my way out.

"Swimmingly. The accountant seems to have it all under control. I'm going to nip out for a while, but I'll be back by three."

"Okay, dear. I've rung some of the people on the list you gave me, but I haven't had any joy yet. No one wants to talk to you, but I'll keep at it."

"Okay. I'll see you later."

I was headed down the high street when my phone rang.

"Is that Jill Maxwell?"

"Speaking?"

"This is Marian from Tweaking Tea Rooms. You sent me a message."

"Hi. Thanks very much for getting back to me. I'm investigating the murder of Miss Drinkwater."

"Are you the police?"

"Not exactly. I—err—I work alongside them."

"I see. I've already talked to one of the detectives working on the case."

"Yes, but as I said, my work complements theirs. When would be a good time for me to talk to you?"

"With the tea room closed, I've no work to go to, so you can come over anytime. Right now, if you want to."

"Err, okay." I was dying for a blueberry muffin, but I didn't want to risk missing the opportunity to speak to the person who had discovered Miss Drinkwater's body. "What's your address, Marian?"

The address she gave me was only a few minutes' walk away.

"Okay, I'll be straight over."

Marian lived on the second floor. She answered the door wearing a baggy track suit and fluffy slippers.

"Come in. I'm sorry for the mess; my flatmates are rather untidy."

"Are they here now?"

"No, they're both at work. This has all been rather a shock for me. I still can't quite believe it's happened."

"I understand you were the one who discovered her body."

"That's right. Miss Drinkwater gave me a key to let myself in if ever she was running late, but she rarely was, so I was surprised to find the door locked."

"And that's when you found her body?"

"Not immediately. The first thing I did was go into the back to turn down the heating. It was like a furnace in there. It was only when I came out and went into the tea room that I found her. It was horrible. I'll have nightmares about that forever."

"I know this is difficult, but can you tell me exactly what you saw?"

"She was just lying there, face-down in a pool of —" Her words drifted away.

"Blood?"

"No. Water. There was a pool of it on the floor. I think she must have spilled it when she fell."

"Could you see her injuries?"

"I've already told the other officer all of this."

"I know, and I really do appreciate your patience."

"The side of her head —" Marian touched her temple. "It was caved in, like someone had hit her with a hammer or something."

"Did you see anything like that on the floor?"

"No. Nothing." She seemed to study my face for a minute. "Haven't I seen you in the tea room?"

"Yeah, I live in Middle Tweaking. You served us the day that I came in with my husband and our little girl."

"I remember. She had a strawberry milkshake."

"That's right. Can I ask, how did you get on with Miss Drinkwater?"

"If I'm honest, I didn't like her very much. You've seen how she could be. Even so, I would never have wanted anything like this to happen to her."

"Can you talk me through the day of her murder? Did anything unusual happen?"

"Miss Drinkwater did have a couple of run-ins that day, but that wasn't particularly unusual."

"Tell me about them, anyway."

"Okay. The first was with a couple who had come in for

breakfast. They were a bit noisy, and Miss Drinkwater was getting angrier and angrier. Eventually, she lost her temper, and went over to tell them to be quiet. There was a big argument, and for a while there, I was worried it might get out of hand. They were both well-built, like they were bodybuilders or something, and they both towered over Miss Drinkwater."

"Did it get out of hand?"

"No. In the end, they just told her where she could stuff her breakfast and walked out."

"This couple, do they live in the village?"

"I don't think so. I'd never seen them before that day. I reckon they must have been staying at the new hotel. We've had quite a lot of people in the tea room recently who were staying there."

From the description Marian had given me, I suspected the noisy couple were the two werewolves I'd seen going into the tea room that morning.

"You said Miss Drinkwater had a couple of run-ins?"

"Yeah, she also had a blazing row with the vicar. I was really surprised because he's a regular customer and he's usually very quiet, but they were really going at it."

"Did you happen to hear what they were arguing about?"

"No, I stayed well clear."

"Were you the only waitress working that day?"

"No. Elizabeth was working there too. Until Miss Drinkwater sacked her, that is."

"Why did she sack her?"

"Miss Drinkwater was always being nasty to us. I just took it and kept my mouth shut, but Elizabeth often talked back to her. She answered back once too often that day, and Miss Drinkwater completely lost it and sacked her on the spot."

"What will you do now, Marian?"

"I don't know. I need to find a job to pay the rent on this place. I suppose it depends on what Miss Drinkwater's brother decides to do."

"I didn't realise she had a brother."

"Yeah. Ryan. He's a part-owner of the tea room."

"I didn't realise. Does he work there?"

"No. He used to come in about once a month for a meeting with his sister."

"Did you ever hear what they talked about?"

"No, because they always went into the back."

Chapter 10

Ursula, the queen of the unicorns, had said she would get her brother, Devon, to contact me. She was going to ask him to update me on his investigation into the stolen horns. That was a couple of days ago and I still hadn't heard from him, so I magicked myself over to the farm on the outskirts of Candlefield where he was living undercover as a horse.

Whoops!

If I'd thought it through, I would have realised that my footwear wasn't exactly suited for visiting a farm. Wellingtons would have been much more appropriate than the flats I was wearing, which were already covered in mud.

There were four horses in the field behind the stables. After squelching my way over there, I leaned on the fence and tried to work out which one of them was Devon. After a couple of minutes, the black horse stopped eating grass, looked my way, then walked over to me.

"Hi, Devon, I'm Jill Maxwell. I believe your sister may have been in contact with you. She's asked me to investigate the missing unicorn horns."

He continued to stare at me but didn't say a word. Perhaps he resented me being brought in on the investigation. Undaunted, I continued, "I was hoping that you might be willing to share whatever information you've uncovered so far."

He stared at me in silence for another minute or two, then turned around and walked away.

How very rude!

"Devon!" I called after him. "It would be really helpful

if—"

"I think you must be looking for me." The voice came from behind me.

I spun around to find a much smaller grey horse standing there.

"Devon?"

"That's right. You must be Jill. I'm sorry I haven't been in touch, but I've been rather busy here on the farm. Why don't we go into the stables in case the farmer happens to come by?"

"Sure." I squelched my way back across the yard. "Your sister told me that you've been investigating the missing horns."

"That's right, and I don't mean to cause any offence, but I'm not really sure why Ursula felt the need to bring you in. I'm confident that I'm going to get a result any time now."

"Obviously, I don't want to tread on your—err—hooves, but if you're willing to tell me what you've done so far, it will save me covering the same ground. Maybe you could start by explaining why you're so sure the horns have been brought to Candlefield?"

"I would have thought that was pretty obvious. Although sups know that unicorns exist, they rarely, if ever, get to see us. I'd venture that most sups will go through their whole life without ever having seen one. For that reason, there's a certain fascination about everything unicorn. I believe whoever is stealing the horns is bringing them to Candlefield and selling them. Because they're so rare, they're bound to fetch a high price."

"Your theory is sound enough, but do you actually have any proof?"

"Nothing concrete as yet, but it's only a matter of time. I've been working with a number of sweetheart fairies. I've asked them to keep an eye on all the collectibles shops in and around Candlefield. I'm convinced, sooner or later, the horns will show up in one of those shops, and when they do, we'll bring in the authorities. They should be able to trace them back to whoever's stealing them. We just need to have some patience."

"Is there anything I can do to help speed up the process?"

"You're welcome to check some of the collectibles shops yourself. Maybe you'll strike lucky."

"Okay. I appreciate you sparing me your time. If anything crops up that you think I should know, will you give me a call?"

"Of course."

I wasn't particularly impressed with Devon or his so-called investigation. Based on no evidence whatsoever, he seemed to have decided that the stolen horns would eventually turn up in collectibles shops in Candlefield. He could be right, but it seemed reckless not to at least consider other possibilities.

That would be my job, I guess.

My shoes were caked in mud, and there was no way I could go back to the office looking like that, so I magicked myself over to Cuppy C, where I'd be able to get cleaned up and get a well-deserved blueberry muffin and coffee.

I'd just stepped into the shop when Pearl yelled at me, "Hey! Stop there! You're treading mud into the shop."

"Sorry, but I've just come from a farm."

"I don't care where you've been. You can't come in here

with those shoes on. Go back outside."

"Will you bring me something to clean them with?"

"Okay, but wait out there."

Pearl appeared a few minutes later with a bucket of water and a scrubbing brush. "There you go."

"Thanks, Pearl."

"If you were visiting a farm, why on earth didn't you wear wellies?"

"That's a very good question." I took off my shoes and cleaned all the mud off them. "Is it okay to go in now?"

"Yes, they're fine. Why don't you come and meet Jill Maxwell?"

"Sorry?"

"I said, come and meet Jill Maxwell."

"What are you talking about, Pearl? You're making even less sense than usual, and I wouldn't have believed that was possible."

"Come inside." She grinned. "I'll show you."

I followed her into the shop where Amber was behind the counter.

"I think your sister's cracking up, Amber," I said. "Could I get a blueberry muffin and a caramel latte, please?"

"Sure. Are you here to meet Jill Maxwell?"

"Don't you start." Whatever craziness was going on inside Pearl's head was clearly contagious.

Pearl walked to the back of the tea room. "Come over here, Jill." She gestured to a table which was surrounded by a small crowd of people.

As I got closer, I could see they were all holding books or posters; they appeared to be waiting for the woman seated at the table to autograph them. I assumed the woman must be a celebrity, but I couldn't see her face because she was leaning forward, signing a poster.

Pearl turned to me and said, "Jill Maxwell, meet Jill Maxwell."

The woman looked up, and I could see that she bore a remarkable resemblance to me.

"Excuse me, everyone," Pearl said. "I'm sorry to interrupt the signing, but I thought you might like to meet this lady."

All the people crowded around the table looked up and stared at me.

"Who is she?" a wizard said.

"Should we know her?" The witch standing next to him shrugged her shoulders.

"This is the *real* Jill Maxwell," Pearl said.

They stared at me for a while longer, and then the wizard said, "That's not the real Jill Maxwell."

"She doesn't look anything like her," said another witch.

Then, to my astonishment, they all turned back to the woman seated at the table.

Somewhat bemused by the encounter, I went to sit at another table. Amber brought over my coffee and muffin, and the twins joined me.

"That was a bit surreal." I took a bite of muffin.

"You have to admit Linda does look a lot like you," Amber said.

"You know her?"

"Yeah. I'm surprised you haven't come across her before. She's a full-time lookalike."

"Hang on. Are you telling me that she makes her living by looking like me?"

"Yeah, it appears so."

When the autograph hunters had dispersed, Linda walked over to our table. "Is it okay to join you?" She looked a little sheepish.

"Sure." I gestured to the seat next to me.

"It's such a pleasure to meet you at last, Jill. I'm really sorry about what happened back there. I was so embarrassed. I tried to tell them that you are the real Jill Maxwell, but they wouldn't believe me."

"It's alright." I laughed. "It's actually quite funny. Do you use the 'doppelganger' spell to make yourself look like me?"

"No, I've always looked like this."

"The twins tell me that you do this for a living."

"I do now. I used to work in a sewing factory, making cushions. When you first appeared on the scene, everyone kept telling me how much I looked like you. I didn't think much of it at the time, but then one day I was having a coffee, and this guy approached me. He owned a talent agency and he asked if I'd like to be signed onto his books. I thought he was joking, but he persisted, and in the end, I decided I didn't have anything to lose. I assumed I might make some extra pocket money, but pretty soon it turned into a full-time job."

"You should pay Jill royalties," Amber said.

"I suppose I ought to." She turned to me. "I could start to send you a percentage of my earnings."

"Don't be ridiculous. I wouldn't hear of it."

"That's very kind of you. Incidentally, I have a little girl too. She's a couple of years older than Florence."

"How do you know my daughter's name?"

"I've made it my business to learn everything I can about you. I find it makes my act more realistic. My daughter's name is Eliza. It would be lovely if the two of them could meet sometime."

"That sounds like a great idea. I can't wait to see Florence's face when she meets you. Why don't you give me your number, Linda, and I'll give you a call to arrange something?"

"That would be great, thanks." She took out her phone and gave me her number. "Sorry, Jill, I have to go because I have a gig in about twenty minutes."

***

I arrived back at the office just before three o'clock.

"Is Betty Longbottom still here, Mrs V?"

"She is. She went out for about half an hour for lunch. Other than that, she and Arthur have been hard at it."

"I suppose I ought to go through and find out what the damage is."

"Before you do, Jill, I'm afraid I've drawn a complete blank with the list of names you gave me. I spoke to everyone on the list, but no one is willing to talk to you. I don't understand it. I've never known such resistance."

"Okay, thanks for trying, anyway. Give me the list, and I'll try to work out what to do."

Betty and Arthur had obviously finished working on my books because they were talking about dolphins. The atmosphere certainly seemed cordial, which I hoped was a good sign.

"Jill, you're back," Betty said.

"I promised I would be. How did it go?"

"Absolutely fine," she said. "You have a completely clean bill of health."

"I do? I mean, of course, that's what I expected. I always do my best to make sure that I abide by all current HMRC legislation."

"Well, you passed with flying colours." She picked up her books and put them into her briefcase. "I have another appointment in thirty minutes, so I'd better be off. Thank you again for your assistance, Arthur."

"My pleasure, Betty."

"Bye, Jill."

"Bye, Betty." And off she trotted. "Arthur, you're a genius. How did you manage that?"

"There was nothing to it. Your previous accountant did an excellent job."

"But I kept hearing you tutting and saying things like *oh dear*. I assumed that meant you'd found lots of discrepancies."

"Not really. Although Luther Stone did a first-class job, he did miss a few things that I thought you could have claimed back. I pointed them out to Betty, she agreed, and she's going to issue you with a small rebate."

"I'm going to get a *rebate*?"

"Don't get too excited. It'll be less than a hundred pounds."

"Who cares? I was expecting to be landed with a big bill. I'm so grateful to you, Arthur. When you're ready, I'll drive you back home."

"There's no need. I'm going to stay in Washbridge for a while."

"Are you sure? How will you get home?"

"I'll take the bus. I quite enjoy a bus ride. And besides, I want to do a little shopping. I also thought I might check out that coffee shop called Coffee Animal. It sounds quite intriguing."

Not long after Arthur had left, Winky came out from under the sofa, stood in the middle of the floor, and began to shake his head.

"What's wrong with you now?" I asked.

"I can't believe it. You must have bribed her."

"Bribed who?"

"That tax inspector woman of course. It's the only explanation for why she'd give you a clean bill of health."

"Don't be ridiculous. I knew my books were in order."

"Don't give me that," he scoffed. "You were terrified."

"Nonsense."

"Anyway." He turned his back to me. "I'm not talking to you."

"What have I done now?"

"You've probably ruined my chances with Mimi." He turned back around. "She got up early especially so we could practise for the fancy dress competition. Then you show up and kick her out."

"I explained why she had to leave. Mr Bacus needed to prepare for the tax inspection. I couldn't have him distracted by a couple of pirate cats. And, anyway, she seemed like a nasty piece of work to me."

"Rubbish. Mimi's a little darling."

***

As I walked to the car park, I gave Grandma a call.

"Yes? What is it?" she snapped. "I'm very busy."

"So am I. Working on the Miss Drinkwater murder case *for you*."

"Have you found the murderer yet?"

"Not yet, but I want to interview those two werewolves who are staying at your hotel."

"Why do you want to talk to them?"

"Because I have a witness who saw them having a blazing row with Miss Drinkwater that morning."

"Did your witness see them kill her?"

"Of course not, but I still need to talk to them."

"How will it look if I allow you to start interviewing all my guests?"

"I don't want to interview *all* of your guests, just those two werewolves. Either you organise it or I drop the case altogether."

"Very well. When?"

"Jack and I will be taking Florence to her dance class tomorrow morning at ten. I can nip out for a few minutes to speak to them then. Make sure they're available from ten onwards."

"Okay, but don't go giving them the third degree."

***

"How did the tax inspection go?" Jack said.

"Brilliantly. Arthur Bacus is an absolute diamond. Not only did Betty Longbottom give me a clean bill of health, but she's going to issue me with a small tax rebate."

"Really? That's great. How much?"

"Don't get too excited. Arthur said it will be less than a hundred pounds."

"Still, it's better than a kick in the teeth."

"It'll pay for our dinner with Mad and Brad next week. Which reminds me, have you thought about where we should go?"

"Why don't we get them to come to Middle Tweaking? They could drop in at the house first and meet Florence, then we could go to The Middle. They do some nice food over there."

"That's not a bad idea. If we go to The Middle, we could have a drink because we won't be driving. I'll call Mad later and suggest it. Speaking of Florence, where is she?"

"Upstairs, practising her dancing for tomorrow."

"She doesn't normally bother practising."

"It's her exam in the morning."

"I'd forgotten all about that. Is she nervous?"

"She doesn't seem to be. In fact, she sounds quite confident."

"That's because she takes after her mother; we're both natural dancers."

For some unfathomable reason, Jack found that hilarious.

Chapter 11

For once, the three of us were having the same thing for breakfast: toast and jam. I'd gone for raspberry, Jack had chosen apricot, and Florence had insisted on her favourite, strawberry. Most mornings, we had to cajole Florence to hurry up because she could be glacially slow eating her breakfast. Not this morning, though, because she'd finished her second slice of toast while Jack and I were still on our first.

"Is it okay if I go upstairs to practise my dancing, Mummy?"

"Of course, darling. You've got an hour or so before we go."

"Okay." She got down from the table and dashed upstairs.

"Florence is very keen, isn't she?" Jack said.

"It's probably because she has that exam today."

That morning, Jack and I both took Florence to the dance class. After we'd been there for a few minutes, I told Jack that I needed to nip to the hotel to interview the two werewolves.

"You'll miss Florence's exam."

"No, I won't. I've just checked the schedule, and she's the last one on."

"Okay, but make sure you're not late. She'll be upset if you aren't here to watch her."

"I'll be back."

"Was that supposed to be your Arnie impression?"

"It was good, wasn't it?"

"No, not really." He laughed. "You sounded more like

Elmer Fudd."

I hurried out of the village hall, and over to the hotel, where the receptionist clearly recognised me.

"Mrs Millbright said to expect you. She told me to ask you to go to the Thunder Room. It's the one directly behind you. I'll let her know you're here."

"Okay, thanks."

The so-called *Thunder Room* was just a meeting room with a table and half a dozen chairs in it. The decor was all red and black and if I'm honest, a little overpowering. I'd just taken a seat when Grandma walked in.

"Where are the two werewolves?" I said.

"They'll be here in a moment. What are you planning on saying to them?"

"Maybe I'll give them the Spanish Inquisition. Nobody expects that."

"Don't try to be clever, Jill. I don't want you interrogating them."

"You can sit in on the interview if you don't trust me."

"I'm far too busy." She started for the door. "They'll be with you in a couple of minutes."

"Grandma, I suppose a cup of tea would be out of the question, would it?"

"You're right, it would." And with that, she disappeared out of the door.

A couple of minutes later, the two werewolves joined me. Surprisingly, they both seemed rather nervous.

"Hi, my name's Desmond." He shook my hand. Fortunately, I'd had the good sense to cast the 'power' spell, otherwise I might have ended up with a couple of broken fingers.

"Hi, I'm Dolly." Her grip was almost as strong.

"Please take a seat. Did my grandmother tell you why I wanted to speak to you both?"

"Yes, she did, but we didn't have anything to do with the lady's death," Desmond said.

"I'm not suggesting you did, but I understand that you had a blazing row with Miss Drinkwater that morning."

"We did," Dolly said. "But only because she was being totally unreasonable. We were just sitting there, eating our breakfast, when she came over and tore into us."

"I understood you were being a bit rowdy."

"We definitely weren't being *rowdy*," he said. "We were just talking and having a laugh. Perhaps we were a little loud, but nothing out of the ordinary."

"That's right," Dolly agreed. "It wasn't like there were any other customers in there, so we weren't disturbing anyone. That woman came storming over, thumped the table, and told us to be quiet. Who goes off like that?"

"What did you do?"

"I told her she was being unreasonable," Desmond said. "And that she should leave us alone. With hindsight, that was clearly a mistake because it made her even madder. She said we had to leave, so I told her where she could shove her breakfast and we walked out."

"Did you pay?"

"Yes, although I don't know why, after the way we were treated."

"How was Miss Drinkwater when you left?"

"She was red in the face and looked as though she might explode at any moment, but other than that, she was fine."

"Where did you go after you left?"

"We took a walk around the village, then out into the

countryside, and came back to the hotel for lunch."

"Okay. Thank you for talking to me today. How long are you staying in Middle Tweaking?"

"We leave today. We would have left already but your grandmother said that you wanted to speak to us."

"I appreciate you staying on. Thanks again for your help."

I had a few questions I wanted to ask Grandma, but that would have to wait because Florence's exam was in five minutes' time.

When I got back to the village hall, Florence had just been called from her seat.

"I didn't think you were going to make it," Jack said.

"No way I was going to miss this."

The dance teacher nodded to the woman at the piano. As she started to play, Florence began her little routine, which I'd seen her practise a dozen times. It was short and very simple. So simple in fact, that even I could have done it.

What? I'll have you know I could have been a ballerina if I'd put my mind to it.

The whole routine lasted less than three minutes and as far as I could tell, Florence had not put a foot wrong. When she'd finished, the dance teacher told her to go back to her seat. Florence came running over, full of smiles, and sat next to me.

"Was I good, Mummy?"

"You were very good, darling."

"Do you think I'll pass the exam?"

"I think there's every likelihood you will."

The dance teacher disappeared out of the room for

fifteen minutes. When she returned, she called for silence.

"The examinations are now complete. I will call out the names of the successful students one at a time. If I call your name, please come forward to receive your certificate. Parents, we'll be sending you a form, which you need to return with your payment for the medals."

She worked her way through the list, calling each girl to come forward. I was just starting to panic that Florence might have missed out when her name was called. Florence shot out of her chair and rushed over to collect her certificate.

"Look, Mummy! Look, Daddy! I passed."

"Well done, pumpkin." Jack gave her a kiss on her forehead.

"Congratulations, darling," I said. "You did really well."

The dance teacher called for silence again. "That concludes today's examinations. We'll see you all next Saturday at the usual time for our regular classes."

As we walked out, Jack said to me in a hushed voice, "Did you notice that every one of the girls passed the exam?"

"I did, yeah. I can't say I'm surprised because that means all of the parents will have to fork out for the medals. Still, Florence enjoyed it and that's all that matters. Are you okay to take her home because I need to nip back to the hotel."

"Didn't you get to speak to the werewolves?"

"I did, but I need to ask Grandma a few questions. I couldn't do it before because I didn't want to miss Florence's exam."

"Okay, we'll see you back home."

I rushed back to the hotel where the receptionist looked surprised to see me.

"Can you tell my grandmother I need another quick word with her, please?"

"I'm sorry, but she left a message that she wasn't to be disturbed."

"I don't care. Call her, please. You can blame me."

She hesitated but then made the call. "Mrs Millbright, I—err—yes, I know what you said but it's your granddaughter. She's in reception and she insisted I call you. Yes, okay." She put down the phone. "Mrs Millbright says she can spare you two minutes. Do you know where her office is?"

"Yeah, I know my way."

Grandma was looking at napkins.

"This had better be urgent, Jill. I have to choose new napkins and I can't decide which design to go with. Did you speak to the werewolves?"

"Yes, I did. They were very helpful."

"Are you satisfied now that they had nothing to do with the murder?"

"I think so. They seemed genuine enough."

"What brings you back here, then?"

"I want to ask you some questions."

"Me? Don't tell me you think I did it. Do you really think I'd hire you to find the murderer if I had?"

"What do you mean, *hire me*? You haven't hired me; you asked me to do you a favour."

"Don't quibble. It's the same difference."

"No, it's not. If you'd hired me, you'd have to pay for

my time. Do you intend to pay me?"

"Of course not. I'm family."

"That's what I thought. When was the last time you saw Miss Drinkwater?"

"You know when it was. You saw us arguing out in the street."

"And you didn't see her again after that?"

"No. I didn't trust myself to be in her company for another minute. I might have done something rash."

"Like killing her?"

"I did not kill that woman!"

"Okay, I believe you."

"Good, so stop wasting my time and go and find out who did."

***

"You realise that this is all your fault, Jack," I said.

"How is it my fault?"

Jack was going to Oscar Riley's house to look at his stamp collection. Florence and I were going back to the village hall. This time, to the basket-weaving society with Olga Riley.

"It's your fault because I'd told Olga we were already doing something this afternoon, but then you went and told Oscar that we weren't."

"I don't know what you're complaining about. I'd much rather make a basket than have to spend two hours looking at stamps."

Florence came running into our bedroom. "Is it time to make a basket yet?"

"Yes, darling, I'm afraid it is."

"I'm really excited, Mummy, aren't you?"

"Thrilled to bits."

"What kind of baskets do you think we'll make?"

"I honestly don't know. We'll have to wait and see. Why don't you say goodbye to Daddy."

"Bye, Daddy." She gave him a hug and a kiss. "I hope you like the stamps."

"Thanks, pumpkin. Enjoy your basket-weaving." Florence went running downstairs. "I hope you enjoy basket-weaving too, Jill."

"I'm going to get you back for this. You see if I don't."

As soon as Florence and I stepped into the village hall, Olga came running over to greet us.

"Hi, Jill. Hello, Florence. Are you both excited to make your first basket?"

"I am." Florence beamed.

Olga turned to me. "Jill?"

"Absolutely. I can hardly wait."

"The group is divided into two sections: Michelle is in charge of the children. Shall we go and join them, Florence?"

"Yes, please."

Michelle, who looked about thirteen or fourteen, greeted Florence with a smile. "Hi, Florence. Is this your first time at basket-weaving?"

"Yes."

"Why don't you take a seat next to Rachel and we'll get you started?"

Olga turned to me. "Come on, Jill, I'll introduce you to the other ladies." At the opposite side of the room, four tables had been pushed together to create one large one, around which were seated about a dozen women, the youngest of whom was at least ten years older than me. "Everybody, please welcome our new member."

Member? I didn't remember anyone mentioning anything about becoming a member?

"Hi." I forced a smile.

Olga continued, "Some of you probably already know Jill. She lives in the old watermill. Okay, Jill, I'm going to hand you over to Suzanne who looks after all our newbies. Suzanne, can you get Jill started?"

"Of course." Suzanne gestured for me to sit next to her. "So, Jill, have you done any basket-weaving before?"

"No, never."

"Don't worry. It's very easy. Basically, the basket comprises of two parts: these long thin strips of reed, which act as spokes. And this round reed which you weave around the spokes. To get you started, I've already cut the spokes to size, and pinned them together. I've also woven in some yarn to give the basket shape." She handed it to me. "All you need to do now is weave the round reed in and out of the spokes. It goes behind one, and then in front of the next. Does that make sense?"

"Yeah, that sounds straightforward enough."

But it wasn't.

For some reason, I just couldn't get the hang of it. My reed ended up behind the spoke when it should have gone in front. And vice versa.

"Are you okay, Jill?" Suzanne asked.

"Err, yeah. Fine."

I undid the reed and started again, but it was just as bad the second time.

About an hour later, Olga stood up and said, "Okay,

everybody, that's all we have time for today. How did Jill get on, Suzanne?"

Suzanne glanced at the thing on the table in front of me. "Not too bad for a first attempt. I'm sure she'll get the hang of it next time."

Next time? Not if I had anything to do with it.

"Right, Jill," Olga said. "Shall we go and see how Florence did?"

"Sure."

I was hoping Florence wouldn't be too disappointed with her first attempt at making a basket. I was only too aware of how difficult it was.

When we got over to the children's table, Olga said to Michelle, "How did Florence get on?"

"Brilliantly. In fact, I've never known anyone take to it so well. Hold up your basket, Florence."

Florence held up an almost perfect basket, which put mine to shame.

"That's excellent, Florence," Olga said. "Are you sure you haven't done this before?"

"No, I haven't, have I, Mummy?"

"No, I can vouch for that."

Olga nodded her approval. "You're clearly a natural, Florence. I hope you'll both come back again."

"Can we, Mummy?"

"Err, yeah. Sure."

As we made our way home, Florence said, "Where's your basket, Mummy?"

"Oh dear. I must have left it behind."

"Shall we go back and get it?"

"No, it's okay. It'll still be there the next time we go."

As soon as we walked through the door, Florence ran

over to Jack with her basket held high. "Daddy, look what I made."

"That's fantastic, pumpkin. Did you need much help?"

"No, I did it all by myself."

He turned to me. "Where's yours?"

"Mummy forgot to bring hers home."

"Did she now?" Jack eyed me suspiciously.

Chapter 12

"What on earth are you wearing?" I laughed.

"These are my plus fours." Jack was checking his appearance in the wardrobe mirror. "I think I look rather dapper."

"Couldn't you find any to fit you? They barely reach below your knee."

"That's how they're supposed to look."

"But I can see all of your socks."

"I'll have you know this is the last word in golf attire."

"More like the last word in golf *dire*."

"I don't care what you say because I think I look good. I'm going to ask Florence for her opinion. I bet she likes them."

While Jack went downstairs in search of approval from his daughter, I looked through my wardrobe, trying to decide what to wear for our trip to Candle Sands. As I did, I noticed that the boxes, which I'd used to hide the spell book, had been moved around. I removed a couple of them and saw that the spell book was face down. And yet, I distinctly remembered putting it in the wardrobe face up.

When I took it out and placed it on the bed, I noticed that the edge of some of the pages had a red hue. What was going on? I opened the book and flicked to the pages with red edges.

That's when I spotted it: A spell called 'perfect baskets'.

No wonder Florence's basket had turned out so well — she must have used magic. The red marks on the edge of the pages were clearly strawberry jam. That also explained why she'd gobbled down her breakfast and disappeared upstairs. She hadn't been practising her dancing. She'd been looking for a spell to help her with the basket-weaving.

The crafty little madam!

What should I do about it? I couldn't just turn a blind eye, but neither did I want to spoil today's trip to the seaside. I replaced the spell book and put the boxes back on top of it. I would talk to that daughter of mine when we got back home.

When I got downstairs, Florence came running up to me. "Mummy, I don't have a bucket and spade for the seaside."

"Don't worry about it, darling. We'll be able to buy them when we get there."

"But they might not sell them."

"They will, I promise. Why don't you go and say goodbye to Daddy."

She ran over to Jack. "Bye, Daddy. We're going to the seaside now."

"Before you go, pumpkin, tell Mummy what you said about my trousers."

"I think Daddy's trousers are super nice. I like the way they look all puffy."

"I'm guessing you bribed her to say that. Come on, Florence, take my hand, and I'll magic us to Candlefield."

We'd agreed to meet at Aunt Lucy's house. When we arrived, they were all waiting by the gate.

"We're not late, are we?" I said.

Aunt Lucy checked her watch. "No, you're dead on time. Hi, Florence. Are you excited about going to the seaside?"

"Yes. Mummy says we can buy a bucket and spade."

The two Lilys came over and gave their cousin a hug.

"How are we getting there?" I asked. "On the train, like last time?"

"No, we've booked a minibus," Amber said. "In fact, it should be here any minute."

Sure enough, two minutes later, it came up the road and pulled up in front of us. The doors opened and the wizard behind the wheel shouted, "All aboard for Candle Sands."

"Come on, girls," Aunt Lucy said. "Go and pick your seats."

Florence and the two Lilys rushed onto the bus and headed straight for the bench seat at the back. The twins sat on one side of the aisle, and Aunt Lucy and I sat on the other.

"Is everyone ready to go to the seaside?" the driver shouted.

"Yes!" the girls all chorused.

"Right, off we go, then."

"What's Jack doing today?" Aunt Lucy said.

"Wearing stupid trousers."

"Sorry?"

"He's bought himself a pair of plus fours to go golfing in."

"I hope you didn't tell him they looked stupid."

"Of course I did. You would have thought so too if you'd seen them."

After we'd been on the road for about an hour, the twins began laughing; very soon they were hysterical.

"What's the matter with you two?" Aunt Lucy said.

"We were just thinking back to the last time we all went

to Candle Sands," Amber managed to say through her tears. "Do you remember? Jill spent all day looking for sand demons."

"Those sand demons can be really vicious," Pearl said.

Even Aunt Lucy laughed at that.

On a previous visit to Candle Sands, some years earlier, Grandma had warned me to watch out for sand demons. She had told me they lived just under the sand and were very dangerous. Like an idiot, I'd believed her, and I'd spent most of the day on my guard, in case we were attacked. Of course, it turned out there are no such things as sand demons.

"Very funny," I said. "You lot are truly hilarious."

The minibus dropped us in a car park close to the beach.

"Mummy, look over there." Florence pointed to the shop just beyond the car park. "They sell buckets and spades. Can we buy some?"

"Let's go and see what they've got."

We bought a bucket and spade for each of the girls and hired four deckchairs for the grown-ups.

No sooner had we picked our spot on the beach than Aunt Lucy and the twins had put their deckchairs up, and they began to sunbathe. Meanwhile, I was still struggling with mine. For some reason, I'd never been able to master deckchairs.

"What are you playing at, Jill?" Amber laughed.

"Don't just sit there. Come and give me a hand."

"I'll do it." Pearl jumped up, came over, and had it up in a few seconds. "There you go."

She'd made it look so easy.

"Thanks."

The four of us relaxed in the sunshine while the girls raced to see who could make the most sandcastles.

I was almost asleep when I heard all three of the girls shout out. I looked up and saw a young boy running away. He had kicked over several of the sandcastles.

He was some distance away when Aunt Lucy said, "Jill! How could you?"

I had no idea what she was talking about, but when I followed her gaze, I could see that the boy had disappeared. In his place, a snake was slithering across the sand.

"He's only a kid," Amber said.

I was just about to tell them that I hadn't turned the boy into a snake when I noticed the grin on Florence's face. She must have cast the spell on him. There was no way I was going to tell Aunt Lucy and the twins that she was responsible, so I quickly reversed the spell.

"Sorry, I overreacted. He's okay now."

I glared at Florence who rather sheepishly went back to her sandcastles. I'd already planned to talk to her about the basket-weaving spell, but now we would need to have a much more serious conversation.

Florence had decided to teach the two Lilys the 'faster' spell. The three of them were running up and down the beach. Florence was moving so fast you could barely see her, but the other two seemed to be running at a normal pace. After about twenty minutes, they grew bored with that game and came back to join us. The Lilys went back to their sandcastles. Florence came up beside me and whispered in my ear. "I showed the Lilys how to do the 'faster' spell, but they couldn't do it. They're rubbish at magic."

"Shush, you mustn't let them hear you."

"But they are. Why can't they do it? They're older than me."

"We'll talk about it when we get back home."

An hour later, the beach was much busier.

"What's that, Mummy?" Florence pointed at something behind us.

I glanced around and saw that someone had set up a Punch and Judy stand. I hated those things. The stupid voices drove me insane, and who cared about a few sausages anyway?

"I love Punch and Judy," Amber said.

"Me too." Pearl was already out of her deckchair. Come on, kids, let's go and get a seat on the front row."

The three girls didn't need telling twice.

"Come on, Jill," Pearl said.

"Actually, I think I'll go and fetch some drinks."

"You'll miss the show."

"That's okay."

"I'll come with you to help carry them," Aunt Lucy offered.

"No, it's alright. I can manage. You stay here and watch our bags."

I didn't want Aunt Lucy to accompany me because I didn't plan on going directly to the refreshment stall. I was going to take my sweet time, so that when I returned, the stupid puppet show would be over.

After wandering aimlessly for about fifteen minutes, I made my way to the refreshment stall where there was a long queue. By the time I got served, the beach was really packed, and I wasn't sure where the others were, but then I spotted Aunt Lucy waving to me. The Punch and Judy show must have finished because the twins were back in their deckchairs, and the kids were making more sandcastles.

"We thought you'd got lost," Amber said. "You've been gone for ages."

"There was a long queue at the shop. I had to wait."

"Punch and Judy were really funny, Mummy," Florence said. "The dog stole the sausages."

"That sounds fantastic. I'm really sorry I missed it." Not! "Come and get your can of pop, girls."

I'd no sooner settled back into the deckchair than one of the Lilys yelled, "Look! Donkeys!"

Soon, all three girls were pleading for a donkey ride.

"They look dangerous," I said. "Probably better to stick with the sandcastles."

"Rubbish," Pearl said. "Donkeys are great fun."

"Yeah, come on kids." Amber was already out of her deckchair.

"Please, Mummy!" Florence grabbed my hand.

"Okay, we'll go and see what the man says."

The donkeys were walking up and down the beach, near the sea's edge.

"They look awfully big," I said when we got closer.

"Not all of them. There are some smaller ones." Pearl pointed out.

Amber went up to the man in charge and asked if it was okay for the girls to ride on them.

"Yes, it's perfectly safe. Maureen will accompany the youngsters."

"What about us adults?"

"You're fine too. These bigger ones can carry adults quite easily."

"Hold on." I took a step back. "I'm not going on one of those things."

"Come on, Mummy." Florence tugged on my hand.

"Yes, come on, *Mummy*," Pearl said. "Don't be a spoilsport."

Before I knew it, I was seated astride a donkey called Trudy.

Maureen, the man's partner, took the reins of the kids' donkeys and led them slowly down the beach; our donkeys followed them. When we'd gone about a hundred yards, Maureen turned around and started back the way we'd come. Amber and Pearl's donkeys followed suit, but mine kept on going.

"Hey, Trudy," I said. "You should have turned around back there."

"Why? I want to walk down here."

How come *I* got the donkey with attitude and an independent streak?

"Come on, Trudy. Please!"

She ignored me and carried on. Eventually, after another hundred yards or so, she stopped dead in her tracks.

"What now?" I said.

"This is where you get off."

"Can't you take me back?"

"No, I'm done."

"Great!" As I dismounted, I saw Maureen running down the beach towards us.

"Why didn't you turn Trudy around?" she said.

"I don't know how to steer a donkey. She just kept on going."

"I should charge you double."

"You'll be lucky."

"That was fun, wasn't it, Mummy?" Florence said when I re-joined them at the deckchairs.

"It was great."

"You had a longer ride than everyone else."

"That's because my donkey wouldn't turn around."

"A bad workman blames his donkey," Pearl quipped.

**

It was mid-afternoon when Jack arrived home. Florence was outside in the garden, playing with Buddy.

"I see you've still got your clown trousers on," I said.

"I'll have you know that several people commented on my plus fours."

"I just bet they did."

"They said how smart I looked."

"They were definitely lying. So, how did the golf go?"

"Not so great, I'm afraid." He sighed. "I need a lot more practice. I managed to lose six balls."

"How on earth do you lose *six* balls in one round of golf?"

"Some of the holes on that course are very challenging. On the fourth, for example, you have to get over a stream to get to the green."

"I take it you didn't manage to get over the stream?"

"It took me four attempts. That's where I lost three of the balls. At this rate, it's going to cost me more in golf balls than the monthly membership."

"Couldn't you have just paddled in the stream and retrieved them?"

"In my plus fours? Certainly not."

Florence came rushing in. "Daddy, Daddy, I had a brilliant time at the seaside."

"Did you, pumpkin? I wish I could have been there with you. Did you make any sandcastles?"

"Yes, I made lots more than the Lily's, didn't I, Mummy?"

"I don't know, darling, I didn't count them."

"I did. I made tons. And I'm much better at magic than they are. They're rubbish. They couldn't even do the 'faster' spell. Me and Mummy went on the donkeys too."

Jack turned to me. "*You* went on a donkey?"

"It wasn't my idea. The twins bullied me into it."

"Mummy's donkey wouldn't turn around." Florence giggled. "It just kept on going."

Jack looked to me for an explanation.

"It's like Florence said. All the other donkeys turned around and walked back up the beach, but my stupid donkey refused to. It just kept going in the same direction."

"I'm going outside to play with Buddy again," Florence said.

"Okay, darling."

"It sounds like Florence enjoyed herself," Jack said.

"She definitely did." I quickly checked that she was out of earshot. "Guess what I discovered today?"

"That you don't know how to control a donkey?"

"I'm being serious. I found out that Florence has had her nose in the spell book again."

"How do you know?"

"You know that basket she brought home yesterday?"

"Yeah, it was really good."

"I'm not surprised, seeing as how she used magic to make it."

"Are you sure? She might just have a natural talent for basket-weaving."

"I'm positive because I found her jammy fingerprints on the page for that spell."

"Oh dear." He grinned. "Still, if it's only the once."

"That's just it. It isn't. If it were just the basket-weaving spell, I wouldn't be too concerned, but while we were at Candle Sands, a young boy kicked over some of the girls' sandcastles."

"Little boys are so horrible, aren't they?"

"No kidding. When he ran off, Florence turned him into a snake."

"She did *what*?"

"You heard. She turned him into a snake."

"What did Aunt Lucy and the twins make of that?"

"Luckily, they didn't realise she was the one who'd done it. They all assumed it was me. I didn't correct them because I didn't want them to know it was Florence. It's one thing for her to use magic to weave baskets, but quite another to turn someone into a snake. That's a very advanced spell."

"It sounds like she's going to be a powerful witch, just like her mother."

"I know, and that's all well and good, but she could end up getting into serious trouble."

"What do you think we should do about it?"

"I really don't know. I'll need to give it some thought

overnight."

Chapter 13

It was Monday morning and Florence was much slower at eating her breakfast, so when Jack and I had finished, I caught his eye, and gestured that we should go through to the lounge.

"Have you decided what you're going to do about Florence and her magic?" he said.

"I'm going to call Aunt Lucy later. I want to set up a meeting with her and Grandma."

"Your grandmother? Why on earth would you involve her? This is all her fault, anyway."

"You can't blame Grandma for what's happened in the last few days."

"Why not? If she hadn't gone behind our backs, we wouldn't be in this position."

"Going over old ground won't get us anywhere. I want to hear as many opinions as possible before I decide what to do."

"But *we're* her parents, Jill."

"I know that, but it can't do any harm to talk it over with Aunt Lucy and Grandma. We'll still be the ones who make the decision."

"I wish I could be involved in the discussion."

"What good would it do? This is primarily about magic, and with the best will in the world, there's not a lot you can offer on that subject."

"Okay. But you mustn't agree to anything until you've run it by me."

"I won't. I promise."

I didn't want Florence to hear, so I waited until I was

out of the house before calling Aunt Lucy.

"Morning, Jill. You're up bright and early this morning. Did you and Florence enjoy yourselves at the seaside yesterday?"

"Yes, we both had a lovely time. Florence has talked about nothing else since we got back. The reason I called is to ask if I could get together with you and Grandma for a chat."

"What about?"

"I want to talk to you both about Florence and her magic."

"Are you sure you want your grandmother there?"

"Much as it pains me to say so, I think she needs to be. Will you see what you can arrange?"

"Of course I will. I'll get hold of her as soon as possible, and I'll call you back."

***

I'd just walked into the office building when who should I see, sitting on the landing, staring down at me, but that pesky squirrel.

This was getting beyond a joke. I was going to have it out with that squirrel once and for all. I was just about to start up the stairs when the door behind me opened, and a woman with a Jack Russell came in. As soon as the dog saw the squirrel, he pulled so hard on the lead that it slipped out of the woman's hand. Seeing the dog charging towards it, the squirrel bolted down the corridor in the direction of Bubbles. The woman and I both rushed up the stairs.

"Come here, Malcolm," she shouted. "Come back here

right now!"

The woman managed to grab the dog.

"Did you see where that squirrel went?" I said.

"No, it's disappeared. What was it doing in here, anyway?"

"Your guess is as good as mine."

"I'm sorry about Malcolm. He's usually so well behaved."

"No problem."

I went through to my office where Mrs V was looking down in the dumps.

"What's the matter, Mrs V?"

"I've had some terrible news. You know I mentioned that two of my yarnie friends had been hospitalised after taking that sleeping draught? Well, one of them, Sue Cumber, has been moved to intensive care. It's touch and go whether she'll make it or not."

"Oh dear. I'm really sorry to hear that. I hope she pulls through."

"What was all that noise out there, Jill?"

"A Jack Russell. He was on his way to Bubbles, but he managed to slip the lead and run up the stairs."

I thought it best not to mention the squirrel because I didn't want to blow Mrs V's mind.

There was no sign of Winky, which came as something of a relief because I was due to hold an interview for the post of private investigator. As I walked across the room, Bertie and Bobby, my resident pigeons, landed on the ledge outside the window.

"Hi, boys. The last time I saw you two, you were just

about to go on a double date. How did it go?"

"We *thought* it had gone well," Bertie said.

"That's good, isn't it?"

"Not really." Bobby sighed. "We haven't heard from Bianca or Briana since."

"Have you tried contacting them?"

"We can't because, like idiots, we didn't take their phone numbers."

"That was a bit silly, wasn't it?"

"They took ours, and we just assumed they'd call us, but there's been no word. We've taken to hanging around the fountain in the park, in the hope that they'll show up, but there's been no sign of them so far. It's like they've disappeared off the face of the earth. We're not sure if they're avoiding us or if something's happened to them."

"You need to give it more time, boys. I'm sure they'll be in touch. We ladies don't like to appear too keen, you know."

"I hope you're right, Jill, because we really enjoyed our date. Anyway, it's breakfast time. We'd better get going."

Poor Bobby and Bertie. Those guys weren't having much luck in the dating stakes.

It was almost ten o'clock and my interviewee was due to arrive at any moment. If he was half as good as his CV suggested, then he should be an ideal fit. Hopefully, he'd be able to start immediately, in which case I thought I might run a small advertising campaign to try to generate more business. But I was getting ahead of myself. I needed to see how the interview played out first.

Just then, Winky came through the window, and for reasons known only to him, he was wearing a suit.

Great! I'd been hoping he'd stay away until the interview was over. Having a cat in the office wouldn't give my prospective new employee a good impression.

"Are you going somewhere?" I said hopefully. "You look like you're dressed for a wedding."

"Nope." He jumped down from the windowsill, hurried across the room, and then hopped onto the seat opposite me. "Okay, I'm ready."

"You can't sit there. I'm due to interview someone for the post of private investigator in a couple of minutes."

"Yeah, I know."

"Move then."

"It's me you're interviewing."

"What? But I was expecting someone called Felix Per—" That's when the penny dropped. "Hold on a minute. *Felix*? *Purr*—kins? It's you, isn't it?"

"None other. I knew if I used my real name, you wouldn't give me the time of day. But when you saw my CV, you couldn't wait to offer me an interview."

"I am *not* interviewing you."

"That's understandable. After all, you already know about my many qualities, so we can dispense with the formality of an interview. Let's just talk terms of employment."

"I'm not interviewing you, and I'm certainly not employing you as a private investigator."

"Why not?"

"For a start, you're a cat."

"You can't discriminate on that basis. That's animalism."

"There's no such thing, and what's all this rubbish you

put on the CV about spending eight years in the private investigator arena?"

"It's true. I've been in this office for that long, and if this isn't the private investigator arena, I don't know what is."

"You're wasting my time. And, where did you get that suit from?"

"I hired it especially for today. It cost me an arm and a leg. Come on, you could at least give me an interview."

"It would be a waste of time because there's no way I'm employing a cat as a private investigator." I stood up and started for the door. "I have to go out."

"What about the suit? Aren't you at least going to reimburse me for that?"

"No, I'm not. You can whistle and flute for it."

Mrs V shot me a puzzled look. "I thought you had an interview arranged for this morning, Jill. Mr Perkins, wasn't it?"

"He phoned earlier to say he's withdrawn his application."

"It was rather inconsiderate of him to leave it until the last minute to tell you. Do you have many more interviews lined up?"

"No, I've given up on the idea of recruiting anyone. I work better alone."

"You're probably right. What with you being a control freak."

***

I wanted to know what progress, if any, the police had made with their investigation into Miss Drinkwater's murder. I had considered asking Jack to talk to one of his ex-colleagues, but he would more than likely have refused. And, besides, I shouldn't need to rely on him to do my job for me.

To find out what the police knew would require a visit to the incident room at Washbridge Police Station—something that didn't pose any particular difficulties for me these days. It had been a different matter the first time I'd done it. That had been many years earlier when I investigated the 'Animal' serial killer case. The murderer had been targeting women with 'animal' surnames such as Lamb and Fox. Jack had been the detective in charge of that case. Back then, he and I couldn't stand the sight of one another.

At the time, magic had all been very new to me, and I was nothing like as powerful as I am now. I'd used the 'invisible' spell, but it had only lasted for a short period of time, so I'd been forced to hide underneath the desk. That's when I got my first glimpse of Jack's Tweety Pie socks. Even now, the thought of it brought a smile to my face. How could I have known then that I'd end up marrying the man with the stupid socks, and that we'd have a child together? Life sure was strange.

Fortunately, Washbridge Police Station hadn't changed much over the years, so I was able to use the same MO to get inside: I made myself invisible and waited at the side door until someone let themselves in using the access code, then I sneaked in behind them. The interior of the police station was more or less the same as the last time I'd been there, except that it had been given a much-needed lick of paint.

Once inside, I made my way to the incident room on the

first floor. Stuck to the top of the whiteboard was a photograph of Miss Drinkwater. Below that, were other photos of the crime scene, including one of her body, which was on the floor near to the counter. Just as Marian had said, Miss Drinkwater was lying in a pool of water. There was no sign of broken glass, which I found curious. Surely the glass would have smashed when she dropped it. There was a horrific injury on the side of her head.

It only took a quick scan of the notes on the whiteboard for me to realise that the police knew little more than I did. There were arrows linking the two waitresses, Marian and Elizabeth. Another of the arrows pointed to a photo of Miss Drinkwater's brother, Ryan, who was the spitting image of his sister. The vicar was on there too, as were the couple who had been staying at Grandma's hotel. At the very bottom of the whiteboard, in big letters, were the words: *Murder Weapon?* Clearly the police had yet to identify what had been used in the attack.

It was time to take my leave. This had been a colossal waste of time because I'd learned nothing that I didn't already know. As I walked along the corridor towards the stairs, I heard footsteps coming up them. It was Big Mac and another officer, and they were obviously discussing the Drinkwater case.

"I think we should take another look at the old bird who owns the hotel," Big Mac said.

"I agree, sir. She's got a terrible attitude. Maybe she lost her temper and lashed out."

"If we don't come up with any other leads soon, we'll bring that old witch back in for questioning."

***

Mrs V had drawn a blank in her attempts to arrange for me to visit any of the businesses who had cancelled their lookalike bookings with Double Take. If I wanted to talk to them, I was going to have to take the direct approach.

I have never really understood the game of squash. In most racquet games, you face your opponent across a net, which is how it should be. That way, you get to see the whites of their eyes as you do battle. In squash, though, you're either standing in front of or behind your opponent. It has always struck me as a dangerous game because if you're not careful, you could get hit on the back of the head with a ball or even with the other player's racquet. Worst of all, whenever I've watched a game of squash, the players are always so sweaty.

I mention this only because I was on my way to Wash Squash, the only squash club in Washbridge. There used to be squash courts at the Lilac Leisure Centre, but they closed some years ago. Wash Squash had booked Leroy Dulce, one of Double Take's top lookies, for their twenty-fifth anniversary celebration. Then, only a few days before the event, they'd cancelled the booking without any explanation.

There seemed to be little point in turning up at reception and asking about the lookalike cancellation because I'd no doubt be given the brush-off like Mrs V had. I would have to take a more subtle approach.

What do you mean, I don't know the meaning of the word subtle? I'll have you know that subtle is my middle name.

The young man behind the reception desk was wearing a white tennis shirt and blue shorts. "Hi, do you have a court reserved?"

"Actually, no. I'm new to the area, and I was just wondering whether you're accepting new members at the moment."

"Yes, we are. Would you like me to get the paperwork for you?"

"Would it be okay if I take a look around before I make up my mind?"

"Of course. I'll try and get someone to give you the tour."

"Actually, I'd prefer to look around by myself if that's alright."

"That's fine. If you have any questions, please pop back here and I'll do my best to answer them for you."

"Thanks."

"Would you mind if I took your name?"

"Sure. It's Jill Subtle Maxwell."

I followed the signs to the viewing gallery, from where I was able to look down onto the five squash courts. I'd clearly picked a quiet time because only one of the courts was in use. Two middle-aged men, both with beer bellies, were chasing around whilst sweating profusely. The taller of the two reached for a shot, missed it, and sprawled head-first across the court. I'd seen more than enough, so I went downstairs to the coffee shop, which was also very quiet. The young man behind the counter, who was also wearing white tennis shirt and blue shorts, looked bored.

"Hi. What can I get for you?"

"Can I get a caramel latte, please?"

"Sure. Coming right up."

I sat on a stool at the counter while I drank my coffee.

"Have you worked here long?"

"A couple of years now. Are you a member? I don't think I've seen you in here before."

"No, I'm just looking around to decide whether or not to join."

"The facilities are very good. I take it you've seen the courts."

"Yes. There's only one in use at the moment."

"It gets busier around lunch time. Do you play?"

"Yes, at quite a high level, actually."

"Really?"

"Oh yes. I've won a few tournaments. Only local competitions, you understand. Down south, before we moved up here."

"We hold regular competitions. You'll be able to join those if you sign up as a member."

"I read somewhere that it was recently your twenty-fifth anniversary."

"That's right."

"Did you do anything special?"

"We had a disco for the members. We also hired a celebrity lookalike."

"It's strange you should say that because my husband recently booked someone from the Double Take agency. Did you use them?"

"The manager made all the arrangements, but from what I understand, they booked someone from Double Take originally, but then they changed to another agency."

"Any idea why?"

"I was told the other agency offered to provide any lookalike at half the price of Double Take."

"Really? I don't suppose you know the name of the other agency, do you?"

"I don't, but my manager will. Wait there and I'll see if I can find him."

A few minutes later, a man in his sixties, red in the face, came storming into the room, trailed by the young man.

"Are you the one who's been asking about Double Take?"

"Yes. I was just wondering if—"

"You rang yesterday, didn't you?"

"I—err—"

"I thought as much. I've already told you that we have nothing to say on that subject. I'm afraid I'm going to have to ask you to leave."

"Can't you at least tell me the name of the agency you used instead of Double Take?"

"That's none of your business. Now, if you wouldn't mind, I'd like you to leave."

Chapter 14

My visit to Wash Squash had been a total waste of time. I couldn't understand why the manager had refused point blank to discuss his decision to cancel the Double Take booking. There was definitely more to this than met the eye.

Another business which had cancelled its booking with Double Take was a women's clothes shop called Young and Stylish (which if you think about it, describes me to a tee). As it was only a ten-minute walk from the squash club, I decided to try my luck there. The only person in the shop was the young woman behind the counter.

"Good morning. Is there anything in particular you're looking for today?"

"No, thanks. I'm just browsing. I didn't realise this shop was here. Is it new?"

"Yes, we've only been open for a few weeks."

"I guess I missed out on all the opening day offers, then?"

"I'm afraid so, but there are still plenty of bargains to be had."

"Were you busy on opening day?"

"Very, but I think some of that was down to the lookalike we booked. She was very popular."

"It's funny you should say that because my husband is opening his new shop soon, and he's been talking about hiring a lookalike to generate publicity, but I thought it sounded like a naff idea."

"Not if you get the right lookalike. We had Ruby Red, and like I said, she was very popular."

"That just shows what I know. I don't suppose you

remember the name of the company you hired the lookalike from, do you? I could let my husband know."

Before she could answer, another woman came through from the back. "Excuse me. I couldn't help but overhear you talking to my assistant. I'm the owner. Can I help you?"

"I was just asking her who you booked your lookalike from?"

"Why do you want to know?"

"As I told your assistant, my husband is opening a shop soon, and he's thinking of hiring a lookalike for the launch day."

"I'm sorry, but I don't remember who it was."

"Might you still have the paperwork?"

"No, I'm sorry. I didn't keep it."

"Right. Okay, thanks anyway."

This was getting weird. Why was no one willing to discuss their reasons for cancelling with Double Take, or to tell me which agency they'd used instead? I needed to take a different approach. Luckily, I had a super-cunning plan, so I called Kathy.

"It's me."

"Don't tell me you're going to cry off Friday's launch, Jill."

"No, I'll definitely be there. I'm looking forward to it."

"What do you want?"

"What makes you think I want something?"

"Because you're being nice. That's always a sure sign."

"Actually, I was hoping you might do me a teeny, tiny favour."

"I'm listening."

"I need you to book a lookalike to appear at your shop on opening day."

"A *lookalike*? Aren't they a bit naff?"

"Definitely not. In fact, they're considered very cool right now."

"Says who?"

"Says everyone. Plus, you'd really be helping me out."

"How so?"

"I've been hired by the Double Take agency. They've had a ridiculous number of cancellations. No sooner do they take a booking than it's cancelled."

"How come?"

"That's the sixty-three-thousand-dollar question."

"Sixty-four."

"What?"

"It's the sixty-*four*-thousand-dollar question. Not sixty-three."

"Says who?"

"Says everyone except you, apparently."

"The owner of the agency is convinced someone is deliberately sabotaging them. I'm trying to find out who. I had Mrs V call everyone who cancelled a booking, but no one is willing to talk to me. I've even tried calling in at a couple of the places that cancelled, but they refused to discuss it. There's definitely something fishy going on. I thought if you made a booking with Double Take, we might find out what's happening."

"I don't mind doing it, as long as you're going to pay for the lookalike."

"No problem. I can charge it to Double Take when I present them with my bill."

"I suppose a lookalike might generate a bit of interest.

Which ones do they have?"

"I know they have Leroy Dulce and Ruby Red."

"Leroy Dulce? That might work. I'm a big fan."

"You've heard of him?"

"Of course I have."

"Right, so give them a call, and if Leroy is already booked, I'm sure they'll be able to set you up with someone else."

"Okay. By the way, Jill, you didn't let me know how the interview for your new PI went. Did you offer him the job?"

"No, I didn't. It was a total *cat* – astrophe."

"The search goes on, then?"

"No. I'm not going to bother. I work better alone."

"You're probably right. What with you being a total control freak."

Sheesh!

I'd no sooner finished on the call to Kathy than my phone rang.

"Jill, it's Yvonne. I called to let you know that Roy and I went to see the Haunting Society this morning."

"That was quick. How did it go?"

"Really well. It was all very straightforward. They took our details, checked them against their database, and then issued us with a licence."

"That's fantastic. What happens now?"

"We have to find somewhere that we'd like to haunt. You mentioned Tweaking Manor?"

"Yeah. It's definitely worth checking out. It could be ideal for you."

"We'll do that. In fact, we'll probably go over there this

weekend."

"What about Jack? Now you've got your licence, don't you think you ought to tell him?"

"Can you talk to him first? Then, once we know where we're going to be haunting, we'll come over and have a proper chat with him."

"Sure."

***

I was desperate for a cup of coffee and a cupcake, so I magicked myself over to Cuppy C.

"If it isn't the horsewoman of the year." Pearl laughed.

"Giddy up, donkey!" Amber shouted.

"I suppose you two think you're funny. Just because I got the disobedient donkey, doesn't make me a poor horsewoman."

"What's all this about?" Daze said.

I hadn't noticed her and Blaze sitting at the table to one side of the counter.

"Take no notice of these two," I said. "They're talking nonsense as usual."

"I'll tell you what happened, Daze." Amber jumped in. "We went on the donkeys at Candle Sands on Sunday—the three of us and the kids. We all rode them up and down the beach. Except for Jill, that is. Her donkey didn't turn around; it just kept on going and going. In fact, if it hadn't got tired and decided to stop, she'd probably still be riding it now."

The twins once again dissolved into laughter.

"Hilarious, I don't think." I turned to Pearl. "Can I get a caramel latte and a cupcake, please?"

"Which flavour cupcake do you want?"

"I'll have a lemon one for a change. Can you bring it over, please? I'm going to have a chat with Daze and Blaze."

"Okay, but make sure to stop when you reach the table." She laughed. "Don't keep on walking."

"Ha, ha. You crack me up."

I took a seat next to Daze. "I'm glad I've bumped into you two because I'm being followed by a squirrel."

Now it was Daze and Blaze's turn to laugh at me.

"Sorry, Jill, but you do sound a little crazy," Daze managed eventually.

"You can laugh, but for the last few days, the same squirrel has turned up wherever I go."

"How do you know it's the same one?" Daze said.

"I just do. I saw it in the village and then again in my back garden."

"That doesn't sound all that extraordinary."

"I know, but the other day, it was across the road from my office building."

"Are you sure?" Blaze said. "Could it have been a small dog?"

"I'm positive. You haven't heard the best yet. This morning, when I walked into the office building, it was looking down at me from the top of the stairs."

"Did you confront him?"

"I didn't get the chance because a dog came into the building and ran up the stairs after it. By the time I got up there, the squirrel had disappeared."

"That is weird."

"Tell me about it. I've started to wonder if it might be one of those shapeshifters who were farming acorns for Ajuice?"

"I highly doubt it. They're all behind bars."

"There goes that theory, then. Maybe it's just this one squirrel that has gone nuts."

I'd just taken a bite of cupcake when my phone rang.

"Hi, Aunt Lucy." I managed to say through a mouthful of cake.

"Jill? Is that you? You sound strange."

"Yes, it's me. You caught me mid-cupcake."

"Grandma is here with me. Can you come over?"

"Yes, I'll be right there."

I shoved the rest of the cupcake into my mouth and washed it down with coffee.

"Sorry, everyone, I have to go."

Aunt Lucy and Grandma were seated at the dining table.

"Lucy tells me you're in need of some parenting advice," Grandma said.

"That's not what I said at all, Mother." Aunt Lucy shot her a look.

"So *why* am I here?" Grandma sighed.

"I wanted to talk to you and Aunt Lucy about Florence's magic—err—education. If you recall, my original plan was to take it slowly and teach her a small number of spells, and then wait until she was older before teaching her any more. But then you, Grandma, persuaded me that I should allow her to learn more spells now."

"And have you?"

"Yes, I've gradually increased the number of spells I've taught her."

"Good. So, what's the problem?"

"The problem is that Florence has been teaching herself more magic without my knowledge."

"Good for her." Grandma burst out laughing. "She's a chip off the old block."

"It's not funny, Grandma. Florence went behind my back. She shouldn't have done it."

"Why not? She's a witch, isn't she? Witches are supposed to learn magic."

"Yes, but I should be the one to teach her, so that I can control which spells she learns."

"Nonsense. She has every right to learn any spell which takes her fancy."

"Not at five years old, she doesn't."

Suddenly, Aunt Lucy thumped the table, making both Grandma and me jump. "That's enough, you two." This wasn't like Aunt Lucy at all. Normally, she was so reserved and quietly spoken. I wasn't sure who was most shocked, me or Grandma. We both sat back and waited for her to continue. "You're both missing the point. You're assuming that this problem is about magic, but it isn't. It's about child psychology."

"What are you talking about?" Grandma said.

"If you understood anything about raising children, you'd know that whenever you tell a child they can't have something, or that they can't do something, they'll want it all the more. The more you try to restrict Florence's access to magic, the more she'll want to do it."

"What are you suggesting, exactly?" I said.

"That if you allow her unrestricted access, she'll soon get bored."

"But there are some dangerous spells in that book, Aunt

Lucy."

"You'll still have to keep an eye on her, obviously, but I think you'll find that the novelty will soon wear off. It wouldn't surprise me if, after a short time, you have to twist her arm to learn more spells."

"That all sounds like psychobabble to me," Grandma said.

Aunt Lucy turned on her. "And do you have any better ideas, Mother?"

"Well, I—err—think Florence should be able to learn magic whenever she wants."

"Isn't that precisely what I've just advocated?"

"Err, I suppose so."

"So, you agree?"

Grandma nodded.

I was gobsmacked. I'd never known her back down like that before.

"What about you, Jill?" Aunt Lucy said. "What do you think?"

"What you said makes sense, but I need to talk this through with Jack."

***

"Mummy!" Florence came running up to me as soon as I walked through the door. "Bill's here."

"Bill *who*, darling?"

"She means this." Jack handed me a sheet of paper. "It's the bill for her dance medal."

When I saw the amount, I did a double take. "Are they serious?"

"Yeah. I saw Donna at school, and she's received one for

exactly the same amount."

"Are the medals made of solid gold? I would hope so for this sort of money."

"You have to send them the money, Mummy," Florence said. "Or they won't give me my medal."

"Don't worry, darling, we will. Now, why don't you go and give Buddy some food?"

"His food smells horrible." She screwed up her nose.

"We've been through this before, haven't we? Buddy is your dog, so you have to feed him. You don't want him to starve, do you?"

She hesitated, clearly weighing the pros and cons. "Okay, Mummy, I'll feed him." And off she ran into the kitchen.

"How did you get on with your grandmother and Aunt Lucy?" Jack said.

"I'll tell you tonight after Florence has gone to bed. Incidentally, I got a call from Yvonne today."

"From Mum? What did she have to say?"

"She and your father have decided they'd like to divide their time between GT and the human world."

"How do you mean?"

"It seems that they fancy the idea of haunting somewhere."

"Are you serious?"

"Yeah, they've already been granted a licence."

"They need a licence?"

"Apparently. I had no idea until Mad told me."

"Hang on. How long have you known about all this?"

"Yvonne called me last week to ask how they should go about it. That's when I contacted Mad."

"And you didn't think to tell me?"

"Your mother asked me not to say anything until it was definite. She said she didn't want to worry you."

"You should have told me anyway. Where are they going to haunt? Our house?"

"Of course not. They're considering Tweaking Manor."

"That's not a bad idea."

It was my turn to take Florence to bed. She must have been tired because she was fast asleep before I reached the last page of her bedtime story.

"That didn't take long," Jack said when I joined him in the lounge.

"I didn't even make it to the end of the book."

"Come and sit down and tell me what happened in Candlefield."

"You should have seen Aunt Lucy. She thumped the table and put us both in our place."

"I didn't think she had it in her."

"Neither did I, but what she had to say did make sense."

"Which was?"

"According to her, our problem doesn't have anything to do with magic. She said it's a child psychology problem."

"I don't understand."

"Basically, she reckons kids always want the things they can't have, and they want to do the things that they aren't allowed to do. By forbidding Florence from looking at the spell book, all we've done is make it even more attractive. Aunt Lucy's theory is that if we were to allow Florence free rein with magic, she'd soon get fed up with it."

"That sounds dangerous to me. What if she learns a

spell that could cause herself or someone else harm?"

"She's already turned a little boy into a snake, Jack. It doesn't get much worse than that."

"What are you suggesting, then?"

"That we should only do this if we're both on board with the idea."

"It scares me, but like you said, how much worse can it get? I say we give it a try."

"Okay, I agree. And as for how much worse it can get, I guess we'll soon find out."

Chapter 15

The next morning, I got up early and took the spell book from the bottom of the wardrobe. Then, later, after we'd all finished breakfast, I asked Florence to follow me into the lounge.

"Come with me. There's something I want to show you."

"What is it, Mummy? Have we got a cat?"

"No. Why would we have a cat?"

"A cat would be a nice friend for Buddy."

"I don't think that would work, darling. Dogs and cats don't really get on."

"You could bring home the cat from your office. He could be Buddy's friend."

"That definitely wouldn't work out. Winky would scare Buddy."

"What did you want to show me, Mummy?" She looked around the room.

"Look over there." I pointed to the bookcase. "Do you see what's on the middle shelf?"

"The spell book! Why isn't it hidden in the wardrobe anymore?"

"How did you know it was in the wardrobe?"

"I just guessed." She looked down at her feet.

"I know you found it and used magic to make that basket on Saturday, didn't you?"

"Maybe."

"And when we were at Candle Sands, you used magic to turn that little boy into a snake."

"He kicked our sandcastles over. He's a naughty boy."

"You're right. He was naughty, but that doesn't mean

you can turn him into a snake."

"He smashed our sandcastles."

"That's still no excuse."

"I'm sorry, Mummy. I won't do it again. Is the spell book going to stay down here forever?"

"Yes, that's what I wanted to talk to you about. From now on, you can look at it whenever you like."

Her face lit up. "Can I learn lots of spells?"

"Yes, but you have to promise that you won't use magic in the human world."

"What about here in the house?"

"That's alright as long as no one else is here."

"What about Daddy?"

"You can do it if Daddy's here, but if there is anyone else in the house, then you mustn't."

"What if Buddy's here?"

"Yes, that's okay too. But if there is anyone here apart from you, me, Daddy or Buddy, you mustn't use magic. Do you promise?"

"I promise. I can still use magic when I'm in Candlefield, can't I?"

"Yes, but you mustn't go around turning people into snakes."

"What about rats? Can I turn them into rats?"

"No, you mustn't turn them into any kind of animal. Okay?"

"Okay. Can I look at the spell book now?"

"Yes, you can."

She grabbed it from the bookcase, lay on the floor, and began to flick through the pages.

I went back through to the kitchen to join Jack.

"The deed is done," I said.

"Do you think we're doing the right thing?"

"I don't know. I hope so, but only time will tell. We'll both have to keep a close watch on her because the more spells she learns, the more potential for trouble there'll be. I've already told her that she can only practise magic in the house and garden, and then only when there's no one else around. I just hope Aunt Lucy's theory proves to be correct and that she soon gets tired of it."

Florence was still studying the spell book when it was time for me to go to work. As I kissed the top of her head, I glanced to see which spell she was looking at. I was relieved to find it was the 'take it back' spell, which she'd learned some time ago. She couldn't do any harm with that at least.

I'd just stepped out of the door when Oscar came through the gate. For once, he wasn't wearing his postie uniform.

"Morning, Oscar. It's a little early for the post, isn't it?"

"I'm not working today, Jill. It's my day off. Did Jack tell you he looked through my stamp collection the other day?"

"He did. He told me he found it absolutely fascinating."

"That's what I thought." He held up a small box. "So, I brought him this starter kit so that he can begin his own collection."

"That's really thoughtful of you, Oscar." I opened the door. "Jack! Oscar's here."

Jack came out of the kitchen and mouthed the words, "What does he want?"

"He's brought you a stamp collector starter kit. Isn't that

kind of him?"

Jack's face fell like a lead weight. "Yeah. Very."

"Go in, Oscar." I stepped to one side. "I'm sure Jack can't wait to get started."

Poor Jack. Snigger.

***

I was just about to get into the car when Kathy rang.

"Jill, I just wanted to let you know that I managed to book a lookalike for Friday."

"That's great. Did you get Leroy Dulce?"

"No, he's booked up well in advance, but I did manage to get a Lucinda Lazenby lookalike. She should bring in the crowds, don't you think?"

"Err, yeah, I guess so."

"You don't know who Lucinda Lazenby is, do you?"

"Of course I do. She's a—err—actually, no. I have no idea."

"She was runner-up in Rock Singer Search the year before last."

"Oh, right. *That* Lucinda Lazenby. Nope, still never heard of her."

"You're showing your age, Jill. You've lost touch with what's happening today."

"If by that, you mean that I don't watch trash TV, you're right. I have more discerning tastes."

"Says the woman who has watched every episode of Greenside Place."

"Greenside is a classy series."

"If you say so. Anyway, according to the lady at Double Take, the Lucinda Lazenby lookalike has a voice just as good as the real Lucinda."

"I can't wait to hear her. In the meantime, I need you to let me know if anyone contacts you about the booking."

"Will do. And I'll see you on Friday for the opening."

I'd just started the car, when the glove compartment opened. I was expecting Henry to appear, but it was his lady friend. "Hi, Jill."

"Hi. You must be Henrietta."

"That's right. I really must apologise for the other day. Henry and I got a bit carried away."

"Water under the bridge. Where is Henry, anyway?"

"He has bad toothache, so he's had to go to the dentist in Candlefield. I think it's one of his molars."

"Poor old Henry. I suppose you'd like to listen to some jazz?"

"Good gracious, no." She pulled a face. "I hate jazz."

"That's a bit unfortunate, isn't it? What with Henry being such a big fan."

"I don't allow him to listen to that awful stuff when I'm around. I'm into soul music myself."

"That's more like it. I'll see if I can find a station for us to listen to."

I tuned into Soul City Radio, and Henrietta and I sang along as we drove into Washbridge.

Mrs V had emptied all the coins from her purse onto the desk.

"What are you doing, Mrs V? Have you lost something?"

"Didn't you see the local news last night, dear?"

"No, I rarely get the chance to watch it."

"There's a very rare ten-pence piece in circulation here in Washbridge."

"What's rare about it?"

"It has the year 2045 stamped on it. Apparently, it's worth twenty-thousand pounds."

"Twenty grand? Wow! How do they know it's here in Washbridge?"

"I've no idea, but you should check all your coins."

"Don't worry. I will."

Winky was lying on the sofa with his head resting on his paws, looking very sorry for himself. He barely registered my arrival.

"Good morning, Winky."

"Not from where I'm lying, it isn't."

"Whatever's the matter with you, Mr Grumpy?"

"If you must know, Mimi came over here a little while ago, to tell me she was dumping me. And it's all your fault."

"How do you work that out?"

"She only did it because of the way you treated her the other day."

"There's plenty more *cat*fish in the sea." I laughed.

"Very amusing, I don't think."

"I don't understand why you're so upset. It's not like you haven't been dumped a thousand times before. You always bounce back."

"It's not losing Mimi that bothers me. We'd entered the couples' pirate costume competition, so now I don't have a partner."

He looked so miserable, I actually felt sorry for him.

Big mistake!

"I'm sorry, Winky, I didn't mean to scare Mimi off. If there was something that I could do to make things right, you know I would."

"There is." He sat up. "You can be my partner in the pirate couples' competition."

"Don't be ridiculous. I'm not a cat."

"Turn yourself into one using magic. You've done it before."

"I—err—I would, but I don't have a pirate costume."

"No problem. Mimi threw her costume at me when she dumped me. You can wear that."

"I don't think so."

"You said you'd do anything to make things right."

"I did say that, didn't I? When is the competition?"

"On Thursday. It'll be great."

Somehow, I doubted that.

"I'll get it for you." He disappeared under the sofa for a few seconds. "Here, try it on."

"Not in here."

"Why not? Just turn yourself into a cat and put it on."

"I am not turning myself into a cat in the office. I'll take it home with me."

"But I need to see you in it. I want to know that you look alright, and that we have a good chance of winning the competition."

"I'm not putting it on in the office, and that's final. I'll take a selfie of me wearing it tonight. You can see that tomorrow."

"I suppose that will have to do."

***

It seemed pointless to follow Devon's suggestion that I check collectibles shops in Candlefield. He'd been doing just that for some time with zero results. Instead, I planned to take a different approach by speaking to some of the unicorns who'd had their horns stolen.

In common with most other unicorns, Missy lived in Unicorn City, on a pleasant little street called Mountain Dew Road. Other than the queen's palace, this would be my first time inside a unicorn's home, and I was intrigued to see what it looked like.

"Hi, you must be Jill." Missy met me at the door. She was pink with sparkly yellow hooves; there was a white stump where her horn should have been. "Do come in."

The building was part house, part stable. Although the furniture was similar to that found in a human house, it was much larger and had been designed specifically for unicorns.

"You have a lovely home, Missy."

"Thank you. Lola, is just having a nap, so I'll have to keep an eye on this." She nodded to the baby monitor on the table.

"Could I take a look at her?"

"Of course. Come and see." The image on the monitor was crystal clear. Lying on a bed of hay was the cutest little unicorn you ever did see. She was yellow with pink sparkly hooves, and unlike her unfortunate mother, had a shiny red horn.

"She's beautiful."

"Thanks." Missy sighed. "My horn is going to take ages to grow back. I feel naked without it. I really hope you find out who's responsible before they do the same thing to other unicorns."

"I'm going to do my best."

"It's not just me who it affects. It's Lola too."

"Sorry, I don't follow. They didn't touch her horn, did they?"

"No, thank goodness, but young unicorns love to fall asleep nuzzled up to their mother's horn. Just after giving birth, the horns develop an aroma which seems to soothe the little ones."

"Really? I had no idea."

She walked over to me and lowered her head. "Take a sniff."

"Err, okay." It felt a bit weird, but I did as she said.

"Can you smell it?"

"I think so."

"Because my horn is only just starting to grow back, it's very weak. That's why I'm having such an awful time trying to get Lola to sleep at night. I always read her a story of course, but she keeps reaching out for the horn that isn't there. It makes me so sad."

"Poor little mite. I understand that your horn was taken during the night?"

"That's right. I was in bed, fast asleep. When I woke up the next morning, I couldn't believe my eyes."

"Do you have a partner, Missy?"

"Yes, my husband, Brock. He was asleep beside me. He didn't hear anything either."

"Did they take his horn too?"

"No, just mine."

"And you didn't feel anything?"

"No, but then there are no nerves in our horns."

"I assume someone must have broken in?"

"I guess so, but there was no sign of a break-in."

"Nothing?"

"No. The doors were still locked and none of the windows had been broken."

"Apart from yourself and your husband, does anyone else have access to your house?"

"No. No one."

Just then, a sound came from the monitor.

"It looks like Lola is awake. I'm sorry, Jill, but I'll have to go and see to her."

"No problem. I won't take up any more of your time. If you think of anything that might help my investigation, will you give me a call?"

"Of course. I hope you find out who's behind this. I wouldn't want anyone else to have to go through what I'm going through."

The next name on my list was Sam, a unicorn who lived on Greenacre Lane. His house was considerably smaller than Missy's, but the decor and furnishings were exquisite. Sam, a navy-blue unicorn with yellow hooves, had a large plaster on his head where his horn should have been.

"Hi." He greeted me at the door. "Do come in, Jill. I was just about to have some lemon tea, if you'd care to join me."

"Not for me, thanks."

Once he'd finished his drink, we went through to the lounge area.

"I'm really sorry for what happened to you, Sam."

"Thanks. It's been very difficult. It's not just my appearance, although goodness knows that's bad enough. It's also affected my career because I'm a model for horn accessories. I had three months' work booked, but of course it's all been cancelled. No one wants a unicorn without a horn."

"That must have cost you a lot of money."

"It did. I had hoped I might be able to make a claim against my insurance, but you know what those companies are like. They have a loophole for everything. They insist that my health cover doesn't include the loss of a horn because, technically, I'm not unwell."

"When exactly was it stolen?"

"Some time during the night. When I went to bed, everything was fine. I always clean my horn just before I retire. When I woke up the next morning, I couldn't believe my eyes. I broke down and cried for over an hour, then I called the police. They told me there had been a spate of similar thefts."

"Was there any sign of a break-in?"

"No, nothing."

"Do you live here alone?"

"Yes. My girlfriend used to live with me, but we split up about three months ago."

"Were there any bad feelings over the split?"

"No. Judy and I are still the best of friends."

"Who else has access to the house?"

"No one."

We talked a little longer, but it soon became clear that Sam was as much in the dark about what had happened as everyone else.

Chapter 16

I was on my way to speak to Elizabeth Wilson, the waitress who had been sacked from Tweaking Tea Rooms on the day that Miss Drinkwater had been murdered. I'd only been driving for a couple of minutes when the glove compartment opened, and Henry stuck his head out. The side of his face appeared to be a little swollen.

"Are you alright, Henry?"

"Just about, Jill. The dentist had to extract a tooth."

"It must have been very painful."

"It's my own fault. I've not been flossing nearly enough."

"I met Henrietta while you were at the dentist."

"Yes, she told me. She said you were very nice."

"I have to say, Henry, your girlfriend has much better taste in music than you. The two of us listened to some soul classics."

"Not really my thing, I'm afraid. Henrietta and I like the same food, and the same books, but not the same music. Speaking of Henrietta, it's her birthday tomorrow. I was wondering if you might have any suggestions as to what I could buy her?"

"I can tell you what *not* to buy her. Don't get her a jazz album."

"I won't." He grinned. "What about chocolates?"

"You could, I suppose, but it's rather impersonal. What kind of books does she like?"

"Modern classics, mainly."

"There you are, then. Why don't you get her a book?"

"That's a good idea. I might just do that."

"Where do you do your shopping? Do you have to go

back to Candlefield?"

"No. One of the main reasons I moved to the human world was so that I could order stuff online." He took out his phone. "It's so much more convenient. If I order it today, it'll be delivered tomorrow."

"Where do you have your parcels delivered to? Not my car, surely?"

"No, I rent a locker. Whenever I order stuff, I just pop over there and pick it up. Ouch." He winced and held his jaw. "It's still a bit sore."

"I shouldn't go eating any humbugs if I were you."

***

Elizabeth Wilson lived in a flat, roughly halfway between Middle Tweaking and Washbridge. She greeted me at the door, wearing PJs.

"Sorry about the pyjamas. I had a late night." She rubbed the sleep from her eyes. "I need a coffee. Would you like one?"

"Yes, please."

Once we had our drinks, we took a seat at the breakfast bar.

"Marian told me that you were sacked on the day that Miss Drinkwater was murdered."

"That's right." She took a sip of coffee. "Although, I didn't find out that she'd been murdered until the next day. I heard about it on the local news."

"Can you tell me what happened that day to get you the sack?"

"It was my own fault. I'm much too mouthy. My mother has always said so. When I was at school, I was always getting in trouble for talking back to the teachers. I'm just not very good with authority figures, I guess. It's not like I mind hard work. Marian will tell you that I always pulled my weight, but nothing was ever good enough for Miss Drinkwater. She would always find fault with something: My apron wasn't on straight, or I was slouching, or I hadn't taken an order quickly enough. In the end, I snapped."

"Do you remember what exactly happened that day to cause you to snap?"

"Miss Drinkwater had told me to clear a table. There had been five people sitting at it, so there was a ton of pots and cutlery. I'd just taken them through to the kitchen when she tore a strip off me because I hadn't wiped the table. I told her that I'd intended to go straight back out to do it. She said what if somebody came in and saw the table looking like that? That's when I lost it. I said no one's going to come into this place because you've scared them all away."

"Oh dear." I grinned.

"She told me to get out and never to come back. To tell you the truth, it came as a relief. I'd been thinking of resigning for some time, but it would have been better if I'd found another job first."

"Did anything else out of the ordinary happen that day?"

"Not really. Miss Drinkwater was arguing with some of the customers, but that wasn't particularly unusual."

"Do you remember who they were?"

"Yeah. There was a couple having breakfast. It's not like they were doing anything wrong; they were just laughing and talking. They might have been a bit loud, but nothing outrageous."

"Who else did she argue with?"

"The vicar. That was a bit more unusual because he's one of the few people she didn't hate."

"Any idea what they were arguing about?"

"No clue. She also had a blazing row outside with that woman who's opened the hotel. Miss Drinkwater was fuming because the hotel is going to offer afternoon tea. I heard her call the woman an ugly old witch."

"That's awful." Even if it is accurate.

"I know. At one point, I thought they were going to come to blows, but then someone stepped in and stopped them."

"That was me. Did anything else of note happen that day?"

"Apart from me getting sacked, you mean? Not really."

***

When I arrived home from work, there was no sign of Florence, which was rather unusual. Normally, as soon as I walked through the door, she came running to greet me.

Jack came out of the kitchen.

"Where is she?" I said.

He gestured towards the lounge and said in a hushed voice, "She's had her nose in that spell book ever since she got back from school."

"Oh dear. Has she actually been casting any spells?"

"No. At least, I don't think so."

"Don't you *know*?"

"How can I be sure? If Florence has learnt the 'forget' spell, and she's used it on me, I wouldn't remember what she's been up to, would I?"

Oh bum! I hadn't even considered that.

"I doubt she'll have learnt that because it's very complicated."

"You said that about the 'invisible' spell. And what about the spell she used to turn that young boy into a snake? Wasn't that complicated too?"

"I'd better check on her." I went through to the lounge where Florence was still studying the spell book. "Hello, darling."

"Mummy." She jumped up from the sofa. "I didn't know you were home." She came over and gave me a big hug.

"I see you're still reading the spell book."

"Yes, I've learnt lots of spells already."

"Have you? That's — err — great."

Aunt Lucy's advice was beginning to look more and more suspect with every passing minute.

"Is dinner ready yet, Mummy?"

"Not yet, darling. It'll be another hour at least."

"Good, I can learn more spells." She jumped on the sofa and went back to her book.

Back in the kitchen, Jack was seated at the table. Spread all over it, were hundreds of stamps.

"What are all those?" I laughed.

"It's the starter kit that Oscar brought over for me. He said I have to sort through these and put them into different categories, according to subject matter or country. He's going to come back later in the week, to help me arrange them in my stamp album."

"That's hilarious."

"It's not funny, Jill. I couldn't care less about stupid

stamps, and I certainly don't want to collect them."

"Do you know your problem, Jack?"

"No, but I suspect you're going to tell me."

"You need to be more assertive. When Oscar brought you the starter kit, you should have told him that you had no interest in stamps. Then you wouldn't have been in this position."

"How could I do that? He would have been offended."

"Better to offend someone than to saddle yourself with this lot forever."

Just then, there was a knock at the door.

"Hello, Jill."

"Mr Ivers. What a surprise. How did you know where I live?"

"After I saw you at the hotel the other day, I asked your grandmother. She told me you lived in the old watermill."

"That was good of her. Actually, we were just about to have our dinner."

"That's okay. I won't take up more than a minute of your time. I have something for you." He opened his bag and took out a pile of movie newsletters, which he handed to me. "When you moved house, you forgot to give me your forwarding address, so I wasn't able to send these to you. I knew you wouldn't want to miss out, so I kept hold of them on the off chance that we'd bump into each other again."

"That's—err—fantastic. Thanks."

"You don't need to pay me right now if you're about to eat. You can give me the money later in the week."

"I thought you would have cancelled my subscription when I moved."

"Why would I do that? You would have missed out on all of these. And, of course, I'll make sure you get all the new issues from now on."

"Great."

"I'd better go, Jill. I'm due back at the hotel."

"Right. Okay. Thanks."

I closed the door and turned around to find Jack grinning at me.

"You really must learn to be more assertive, Jill."

"What could I do? He'd saved them for me."

"Better to offend someone than to saddle yourself with that lot."

Before I could respond with a clever rejoinder, my phone rang.

"Yes? What is it?" I snapped.

"Charming," Kathy said. "Here I am trying to help you, and you bite my head off."

"Sorry, Kathy, it's Jack. He's being a smarty-pants, as usual."

"I've just been contacted by someone about the booking I made with Double Take."

"Already? That was quick. Who was it? What did they say?"

"His name, if you can believe it, is Boris Charming. He says that his lookalike agency, Charming Lookalikes, can provide any lookalike at half of Double Take's prices."

"Did you ask him how he knew you were in the market for a lookalike?"

"That was one of the first questions I asked him, but he never really gave me an answer. He just kept pressing me to change my booking over to his agency."

"What did you tell him?"

"That I needed to think about it, but he was very pushy. He asked if he could come and see me tomorrow."

"I hope you said yes."

"Of course I did. He's coming over at two o'clock."

"That's brilliant. Which shop is he going to?"

"The new one. I said I'd meet him there."

"Okay. I'll be there by one-thirty, and we'll see what Mr Boris Charming has to say for himself."

***

Florence had gone to bed, and Jack was so engrossed in one of his favourite TV programmes that he didn't notice me sneak out to the car. I didn't want him to see me as a cat, dressed in a pirate costume; I would never live it down. I took the costume out of the car boot, crept back into the house, and hurried upstairs to our bedroom.

After placing the pirate costume on the bed, I took off my clothes, and then turned myself into a cat. Getting into the costume was a real struggle, but I eventually managed it. Now, all I needed to do was take a photo of myself, but like an idiot, I'd left my phone in my trouser pocket. I was just about to jump on the bed to retrieve it when Jack walked into the bedroom and stopped dead in his tracks.

"Jill!" he shouted. "There's a cat in our bedroom, and it's dressed as a pirate."

I had no choice but to reverse the spell. As I did, I ripped the costume in several places.

Jack did another double take. "What's going on? Why are you naked?" He looked around. "And where's that cat gone? It was dressed as a pirate."

"That was me."

"What was you?"

"The cat. I turned myself into one."

"Why? And what's with the pirate costume?"

"I promised Winky that I'd enter a contest with him."

"What kind of contest?"

"It's a long story. Let me get dressed, and I'll tell you all about it."

Chapter 17

Jack and I were enjoying a fry-up for breakfast. Florence had opted for a boiled egg with toast soldiers. Every so often, for no apparent reason, Jack kept chuckling to himself.

"What's tickling you?" I said.

"Nothing."

"Come on. Share the joke."

"I was just thinking about cats dressed as pirates."

"That's silly, Daddy." Florence laughed. "Cats can't dress as pirates."

"Yes, that's silly, *Daddy*." I shot him a look.

"And you said *I* wasn't assertive enough." Jack laughed again. "At least I don't get ordered around by my cat."

"Eat your breakfast."

I'd just taken a bite of sausage when I noticed that Florence seemed to have zoned out. I was about to ask her what the matter was when I realised that she was about to cast a spell. Before I could say anything, she had disappeared. Jack dropped his fork and stared at the toast soldier as it dipped itself into the egg.

"Florence!" I said.

"Yes, Mummy?" The voice came from the direction of her chair.

"We do not turn ourselves invisible while we're eating breakfast, do we?"

"Sorry, Mummy." She reversed the spell and reappeared. "I like being invisible. It's fun."

"I know it is, but you mustn't do it while we're eating a meal. You nearly made Daddy choke on his sausage."

"Sorry." She giggled. "Don't you wish you were a sup,

Daddy?"

"I've never really given it any thought."

"It's lots of fun because we can do magic. I can make myself invisible, I can make plants grow and I can do lots of other things."

"It does sound like fun." Jack put his knife and fork down on the empty plate. "Mmm, I could eat that again."

He'd no sooner said the words than his fry-up reappeared. He stared at it in disbelief, but I was looking at Florence.

"Did you just use the 'take it back' spell, Florence?"

"Yes. Daddy said he could eat his breakfast again, so I brought it back for him."

"You can't keep using magic spells willy-nilly. That spell is for when you break something, and you want to mend it."

Apparently unconcerned by this turn of events, Jack was already tucking into his sausages again.

After breakfast, Florence went out into the garden to play with Buddy.

"By the way, Jack, you've not forgotten we're going for dinner with Mad and Brad tonight, have you?"

"Of course not. I spoke to the babysitter yesterday to confirm she's still available. She's coming around at seven-thirty. Is that okay?"

"Yeah. Mad said they'd be here by seven, so that'll give them time to meet Florence before Sarah arrives."

***

According to Marian and Elizabeth, the two waitresses from Tweaking Tea Rooms, Miss Drinkwater had been arguing with the vicar on the day she was murdered. Both of them had expressed their surprise at this turn of events because the vicar was one of very few people that Miss Drinkwater had got along with.

Although I'd walked past the rectory several times, this would be my first visit. The property was beautiful, and one of the largest houses in Middle Tweaking. I was just about to knock on the door when someone shouted.

"Hello there."

I turned around, expecting to see the vicar, but instead I was confronted by a man dressed in wellingtons, baggy trousers and an even baggier jumper. Wearing a straw hat that had seen better days, the man had ruddy cheeks and a huge smile.

"Are you here to see the vicar?" he said.

"Yes, I am. Is he in, do you know?"

"I believe so. I'm Wilberforce, the gardener."

"It's very nice to meet you, Mr Wilberforce. I'm Jill Maxwell."

"Do you live in the village, Jill?"

"Yes, with my husband and daughter, in the old watermill."

"Ah, right. Turtle's old place."

"What about you, Mr Wilberforce, do you live in the village?"

"No, I live in Lower Tweaking, but I've always looked after the gardens here. It's not a paid position. Purely voluntary."

"I see. I must say you're doing a marvellous job."

"It's very kind of you to say so, Jill. If you'd like to wait here, I'll go and see if the vicar is around." He disappeared into the house and returned a few minutes later with the vicar at his side. "I'll leave you to it. I must get back to my gardening."

The vicar studied me for a moment. "We've met before, haven't we?"

"Yes, you gave me a flyer for Freaking Tweaking."

"Of course. Now I remember. And didn't I see you in the village store too? You were buying cheese for the barber, I seem to recall."

"Err, yeah. That was me. My name is Jill Maxwell. I live in the old watermill."

"Was it your husband who came to my rescue the other day when I was trying to catch Donovan?"

"The Labrador? Yes, that was Jack."

"That was very kind of him. What can I do for you, Jill?"

"I was hoping we might have a chat."

"Actually, you've caught me in the middle of preparing my sermon, but I can spare you a few minutes. Can I get you a drink?"

"Not for me, thanks."

"Let's go through to the study. We can talk there." The study was enormous and smelled of vinegar. "So, Jill, how exactly can I help you?"

"I'm afraid it's a rather delicate matter, Vicar."

"Please don't be embarrassed. I'm sure it's nothing I won't have heard before."

"I'm actually a private investigator. I'm—err—sort of assisting the police with their enquiries into Miss Drinkwater's murder."

"A terrible business. Marcy was a pillar of the community."

"Indeed. I was told by the two young ladies who

worked at the tea room that you and Miss Drinkwater were arguing on the day she was murdered."

"I'm afraid they're right, and I feel awful about it. We'd been good friends for such a long time. For our relationship to finish on such a sour note saddens me deeply."

"Would you be prepared to tell me why you were arguing?"

"It all seems so silly now." He sighed. "It's the annual church fete in a couple of weeks' time. Marcy has always provided the refreshments, and she has always done so at cost. I'd gone over there to discuss this year's arrangements, and out of the blue, she said she'd have to double her charges. I told her I thought she was being unreasonable, and she said if I could do better, I should go elsewhere. I was flabbergasted because she'd always been such a steadfast supporter of the church."

"Do you have any idea what caused her change of heart?"

"None, but I did get the feeling that something or someone had really upset her."

"How did you leave things?"

"I could see there was no point in pursuing the matter because she was in no mood for compromise, so I walked out. I had planned to go back another day after she'd had time to calm down. But, well, I guess it's too late for that now."

***

As I approached the office building, I noticed a young boy scout, standing near to the door. When I walked past him, he held out a bag.

"Would you like to buy some cookies, Mrs?" He had a tray full of the small bags. "We're raising money for a new scout hut."

"How much are they?"

"Seventy-five pence for a bag of two."

"Sure, if I have enough change." I felt in my pocket and took out all the coins I had. "You're in luck. I've got eighty-pence. You can keep the change."

"Thanks very much." He passed me the cookies.

"Good morning, Mrs V."

"Morning, Jill."

"Would you like a cookie?"

She hesitated. "Did *you* make them?"

"No, I bought them from a boy scout outside."

"In that case, I don't mind if I do. Thanks."

"Can I have a cookie?" Winky said when I went through to my office.

"No. I only have one left."

"Give me half, then. Please."

"Oh, okay." I broke the remaining cookie in two and handed half to him.

"Mmm, that was delicious."

"Did you seriously eat that all in one go?"

"It was only a small piece. Anyway, never mind about the cookie. Where is it?"

"Where's *what*?"

"The photo of you in the pirate costume of course. I've been dying to see it."

"Yeah, there's a bit of a problem there."

"What kind of problem?"

"I had a bit of an accident." I took what was left of the pirate costume from the carrier bag.

"What did you do to it?"

"I was trying it on when Jack startled me. It ripped when I changed back from being a cat."

"Well, that's just great. Why didn't you use that spell of yours? The back it up spell?"

"It's called the 'take it back' spell."

"So, why didn't you use it?"

"I don't know. I didn't think about it at the time and it's too late now. I'm really sorry. I guess you'll have to drop out of the couples' competition."

"No chance." He took out his phone. "Sid? It's Winky. Yeah, not bad, thanks. I need an urgent favour. I don't care if you're busy; you owe me one after the pompom incident. That's what I thought. I'll be over in a few minutes." He turned back to me. "Give me that costume."

"Who was that you were speaking to?"

"Sid the Stitch. He'll have this sorted in no time."

"But look at it. It's ruined."

"Sid is a magician with a sewing machine. You'll see."

"What was the pompom incident?"

"I could tell you, but then I'd be forced to kill you." And with that, he disappeared out of the window.

Not long afterwards, two pigeons landed on the window ledge. I assumed it was Bobby and Bertie, but when I looked closer, I realised these pigeons were much smaller.

"Hi there," I said.

"Oh? Hi." They were clearly surprised that I'd spoken to them.

"Are you two new to the area?"

"We're not new to Washbridge, but we haven't been to this particular building before. We're actually looking for someone."

"Oh?"

"We met a couple of handsome guys the other day in the park, near the fountain. In fact, we went on a double date with them. We had a great time and my friend here took down their phone numbers, but then the silly moo lost her phone."

"I didn't lose it," her friend protested. "I dropped it when we were flying, and it broke."

"Now we have no way of contacting them, so we've been visiting all the buildings in Washbridge, in the hope that we might bump into them. But to be honest, we've more or less given up now."

"Are you Bianca and Briana by any chance?"

"Yes, how did you know?"

"I assume you're looking for Bobby and Bertie."

"That's right. Do you know them?"

"Yes, they live on this ledge, but I don't know where they are at the moment."

"Really? That's fantastic."

"Why don't you wait here for them? I don't imagine they'll be very long."

"We can't. I promised to visit my mother. If we leave our phone numbers with you, would you pass them on?"

"Of course. I'm sure the boys will be delighted."

***

My phone rang.

"Jill, it's Ursula."

Although it wasn't particularly unusual for me to receive a phone call from someone in Candlefield, there was something a little bit weird about being called by a unicorn.

"Hi, Ursula."

"Is there any chance you could pop over to the palace now? There's something rather important that I'd like to discuss with you."

"Sure, I'll be straight over."

I magicked myself to the gates of the palace. I'd no sooner arrived than they opened, and Ronald was waiting inside to greet me.

"Hello again," he said. "The queen is expecting you. Please follow me."

Ursula was on her throne, next to which stood her brother, Devon. There was something different about him, and it took me a couple of minutes to work out what it was: His sparkly green horn was on display today. The last time I'd seen him, he'd been masquerading as a horse and had used a magic potion to hide it.

"Is there anything I can get you, your majesty?" Ronald asked.

"Jill, would you like a drink?" Ursula said.

"Not for me, thanks."

"We're okay, thanks, Ronald." Ursula waved him away.

"Wait! Get me some iced tea," Devon demanded. "And not that horrible stuff you made last time."

"Yes, sir."

"And make it quick. I'm parched."

"Very well, sir." Ronald managed an insincere smile. He clearly wasn't a fan of Devon, and I couldn't say I blamed him.

"Thanks for coming over, Jill," Ursula said.

"No problem. You said you had something important to tell me?"

"Devon has made an exciting breakthrough in his investigation."

"Really?" I found that hard to believe.

"Why don't you tell Jill, Devon?"

"Certainly." He picked up the bag next to him, walked over to the table, and emptied out the contents: at least a dozen unicorn horns.

"Where did you find those?"

"I told you it was just a matter of having patience. My suspicions proved to be correct. These turned up in an antiques and collectibles shop, close to the market square in Candlefield."

"Devon received an anonymous tip-off," Ursula said.

"How very fortuitous." Not to mention, highly unlikely.

"I did. From someone who had heard about my investigation." Devon looked remarkably pleased with himself. I was beginning to really dislike the smug git.

"Did you find out who had supplied the horns to the shop?"

"I'm afraid not. The owner bought them as part of a job lot, along with a load of other stuff, all for a knockdown price."

"But he must know who he bought them from."

"He did have a name and address, but it turned out to be false. Still, it proves we're on the right track, don't you think?"

"Maybe."

"Of course it does." Devon was clearly frustrated by my

lack of enthusiasm. "Surely it's obvious. The fact that these were found in a collectibles shop means there's every chance they'll be in others too. I'm confident that we'll be able to track down the supplier, given enough time."

"I guess it's possible."

"I've told Ursula that there's very little point in you pursuing a separate investigation because it's only a matter of time until I have this all tied up."

I turned to the queen. "Ursula, what do you think?"

"I—err—I suppose Devon is right, Jill. I just feel bad that we have wasted your time."

"Are you sure you wouldn't like me to continue with my investigation? It's not like it can do any harm."

"It's not necessary," Devon snapped. "It would be a total waste of time and money."

"Devon is right," Ursula said. "You'll be paid for the time you've already spent on the case, obviously. If you send me your bill, I'll make sure it's paid straight away."

They had clearly made up their minds, so I said my goodbyes and made my way out of the palace. At the gates, I bumped into Ronald who was enjoying a drink of tea.

"I hope that's not the *horrible stuff*, Ronald." I grinned. "How do you put up with Devon?"

"It isn't easy." He rolled his eyes. "It's a good job I like her majesty, otherwise I'd have handed in my notice long ago."

"Devon seems to have a lot of sway with his sister."

"Too much. I don't know why she listens to him, particularly with his track record."

"What do you mean?"

"I really shouldn't say."

"Come on, Ronald. You owe me one for that trick you played on me with the horn hat."

"Fair enough, but you didn't hear this from me. Okay?"

"I give you my word."

"Our friend Devon almost bankrupted the monarchy a few years ago with one of his ridiculous business schemes."

"What happened?"

"I'm not supposed to know the details because it was hushed up."

"Something tells me you know anyway."

He glanced around to make sure no one was within earshot. "He was selling love potions."

"Are you serious?"

"I'm afraid so. By all accounts, he was charging a small fortune for them until it all came crashing down, and his sister had to bail him out."

"What went wrong?"

"I don't know. Like I said, it was all hushed up."

"I'm surprised Ursula puts up with it. She's seems a smart lady."

"She is, but she has a blind spot when it comes to her brother."

"I really am grateful to you for sharing that."

"No problem. Will we see you back here soon?"

"Probably not. Devon has apparently solved the case all by himself."

"Hmm. I very much doubt that, but it's been nice to have made your acquaintance, Jill."

"Likewise."

There was something about all of this that simply didn't

ring true. The horns were rare and extremely valuable, so why would someone go to the bother of stealing them, only to sell them as part of a job lot, at a knockdown price? And as for the anonymous tip, I didn't buy that at all. I didn't trust Devon as far as I could throw him, and although I'd said I would drop the case, I felt I owed it to the queen to discover the truth. To do that, I would need to find out what Devon was really up to, but I didn't have time to tail him. I did, however, know someone who might be able to help, so I made a call to my old friend, Edna the surveillance fairy. It was some time since I'd used her services, and I wasn't sure if she was still in business, but I'd no sooner made the call, than she appeared on my shoulder.

"I wish you wouldn't do that, Edna. You made me jump."

"Do you have a job for me or not?"

"Yes, but I'd need you to start straight away."

"You're in luck. I'm between jobs. What do you need?"

I told her all about the unicorns and the stolen horns.

"You want me to follow the unicorn queen's brother?"

"That's right. His name is Devon. I want to know where he goes and who he sees."

"Am I looking for anything in particular?"

"No. Just keep tabs on him."

"Okay, I should warn you that my rates have gone up since the last time I worked for you."

"By how much?"

"Ten percent."

"*Fairy* enough." I laughed.

"Was that supposed to be funny?"

"I thought so. Do you still require payment in custard

creams?"

"Of course."

"Okay, it's a deal. Follow Devon and report back to me in a couple of days."

***

I had intended to get to Kathy's shop thirty minutes before the man from the lookalike agency was due to arrive, but what with one thing and another, I made it there with only five minutes to spare.

"I didn't think you were coming," Kathy said.

"I'm sorry. It's been a heck of a day. Where can I hide?"

"In the changing room, behind that curtain. The shop isn't open yet, so there won't be any customers. You'll be fine in there."

"Okay."

I'd only been in there for a couple of minutes when I heard a knock at the door.

"Coming!" Kathy shouted.

"I'm Boris Charming." The man had an incredibly deep voice. "Thank you for seeing me."

"That's okay, but I don't have a lot of time to spare because I'm preparing for the big opening on Friday."

"I understand. I'm hoping that I might be able to convince you to change your mind about the lookalike you've booked."

"As I explained on the phone yesterday, I did a lot of research before I made my booking with Double Take. Their lookalikes receive rave reviews. When I was looking at companies to approach, I didn't even see your name listed."

"That's because we don't advertise. The majority of our business comes through word of mouth, which I'm sure you'll agree is the best form of advertising. I believe you said that you've booked a Lucinda Lazenby lookalike for Friday?"

"That's right."

"I have an excellent Lucinda Lazenby lookalike on my books. I could provide her for half the price that Double Take are charging you."

"But I haven't even told you what they are charging me." Kathy was playing the part like a pro. All those years at the amdram hadn't been for nought.

"It doesn't matter. Whatever it is, I'll halve it."

"How do I know that your lookalikes are any good?"

"They're all top notch. You can't tell them from the real thing. Was Lucinda Lazenby your first choice?"

"No, I actually wanted Leroy Dulce, but he was already booked up for several weeks."

"I could do you a Leroy Dulce, and I'll still do him for half the price of the Lazenby lookalike."

"Just like that?"

"Yes. How about it? Can I make the booking for you?"

"At Double Take, I was able to see photos of all their lookalikes online. Do you have a website?"

"No, we've never needed one."

"A brochure, then?"

"No, but like I said, you don't need to worry. All my lookalikes are indistinguishable from the real thing."

"I'm not prepared to take the risk. I'm going to stick with Double Take."

"But you'll be paying over the odds."

"Sorry, but I've made up my mind."

"You're a fool, then." He stormed out of the door, slamming it closed behind him.

Once the coast was clear, I came out from behind the curtain.

"Did you hear all of that, Jill?"

"I did, and it all sounds very dodgy. Thanks for doing this, Kathy. I have to go because I want to follow him."

"Be careful. He looks like a wrong'un."

"Don't worry. I'll be fine. Thanks again."

Chapter 18

Obviously, I hadn't been able to say anything to Kathy, but as soon as the man had walked in, I'd sensed he was a wizard. I followed him out of the shop and tucked in a few yards behind him. After about ten minutes, he stepped inside a building, which was a few doors down from the council offices. I quickly cast the 'invisible' spell and followed him inside. His office, which had no signage as far as I could tell, was on the ground floor. I just managed to squeeze in behind him before he closed the door. The room was only big enough to accommodate a desk, a chair, a single filing cabinet and a table, on which was a kettle and a couple of tea-stained mugs.

He sat at his desk and began to play a stupid game on his phone. I'm no gamer, but I could see he didn't have the first clue what he was doing. After a few minutes, he stood up and walked out of the office. As he didn't lock the door behind him, I figured he wouldn't be gone for long, so I had no time to waste. I started with the filing cabinet, but all three of the drawers were empty. Next, I checked the desk where I found a page-a-day diary. As I flicked through it, it became clear this was where he recorded his bookings. I still had the list of Double Take's cancellations, and it didn't take long for me to confirm that each one had a corresponding entry in the diary. I turned to today's date and saw that there was a booking in half an hour's time for a lookalike called Jenny Diamond who, once again, I'd never heard of. She was no doubt another reality TV star. Just then, I heard footsteps coming towards the office, so I closed the diary and put it back in the desk drawer.

Once inside the office, he stood in the middle of the room and transformed himself into an attractive female with long blonde hair. Now everything began to make sense. This guy didn't employ 'real' lookalikes; he was simply using the 'doppelganger' spell to make himself look like the appropriate 'celebrity'. No wonder he'd been able to offer Kathy whichever lookalike she wanted.

He started for the door, no doubt on his way to his next booking. Once again, I slipped out behind him, then I waited until he was out of the building before I reversed the 'invisible' spell.

I now knew who was behind Double Take's string of cancelled bookings, but how did this guy know which bookings Double Take had on their books? I could only assume that he must have someone on the inside who was tipping him off. But who? The only way to find out, would have been to follow him, but I didn't have the time. Edna was already following Devon, but it occurred to me that she might know someone who could help. I gave her a call and, moments later, she appeared on my right shoulder.

"I don't have anything to report yet, Jill."

"I didn't expect you to. It's just that there's someone else that I need following."

"I know I'm good at what I do, but I can't follow two people at the same time."

"I thought you might have a contact in the same line of business."

"As it happens, I do. My friend, Irene Ironside, is an excellent surveillance fairy. Not as good as me, obviously, but good enough for your needs."

"Could you get in touch with her, Edna?"

"Sure." She took out her phone and made the call.

No sooner had she finished than another fairy appeared on my left shoulder.

"Hi, Irene," Edna said. "Thanks for coming over so promptly."

"No problem, Edna."

The two of them were talking across me as though I wasn't there.

"I have to get going, Irene," Edna said. "I'll catch up with you later."

"Bye, Edna." Irene turned to me. "I assume you're Jill."

"That's right. I'd like you to follow someone for me if you can."

"No problem. Give me the details."

"It's a wizard, but he currently looks like an attractive young woman with long blonde hair."

"I don't understand."

I quickly explained what was happening with the Double Take agency.

"Okay, let me get this straight," she said. "This guy is stealing the other agency's bookings by passing himself off as a lookalike, but he's actually using magic."

"Pretty much, yeah. He must be getting details of the bookings from someone on the inside at Double Take. I need you to find out who."

"Okay. Where will I find this wizard?"

"He's got a booking at this address in a few minutes time." I handed her a slip of paper.

"Did Edna tell you that I charge the same rate as her?"

"She didn't, but that's fine. I assume you'll want paying in custard creams?"

"Good gracious, no. Why would I want those horrible

biscuits?"

Horrible biscuits? I was beginning to have my doubts about Irene. "How do you want to be paid, then?"

"In ginger nuts."

"You can't possibly prefer ginger nuts to custard creams, the king of biscuits."

"I most certainly do. Do we have a deal or not?"

"Err, yeah." Despite my misgivings vis-à-vis her dubious take on the relative merits of biscuits, I was willing to risk it. "We have a deal."

***

After Irene had left, I made my way to the car park. I was just about to turn the ignition key when I happened to glance in the rear-view mirror. Staring back at me was a pair of eyes. I jumped so much that I banged my head on the roof of the car.

I turned to face the man in the back seat. It was a man I recognised; a man who looked very much like myself. For most of my life, I hadn't known that I had a brother. When he came into my life a few years ago, I was both shocked and delighted, but then he'd disappeared as suddenly as he'd appeared.

"Martin?"

"Hello, Jill. I hope I didn't scare you."

"Of course you scared me. I thought you were —" I hesitated.

"*Dead*? Not yet. I'm sorry that I haven't been able to contact you before. How are you?"

"I'm fine. Or at least I was until you scared me to death just now. Are you sure you're alright, Martin? You don't look great."

"The last few years have taken their toll on me, I'm afraid."

"Where have you been? What happened?"

"Do you recall our last phone call before I left?"

"Of course I do. I remember your exact words. You said that he had you fooled. That he wasn't dead, and that you had to stay there to try to keep my child safe. I assumed you were talking about Braxmore?"

"Correct."

"What's happened since then?"

"Now's not the time to go into that."

"Just tell me this, then. Is Florence safe?"

"For now, yes."

"What does that mean?"

"It means that I've done all I can alone, but I'm going to need your help."

"What do you want me to do?"

"There isn't time to explain everything now. I'll call you in a few days' time, so we can get together and discuss it properly."

"Won't you at least come with me and meet Florence?"

"There's nothing I'd like more, but I really do have to get back."

"But Martin—"

It was too late, he'd disappeared again.

It took me several minutes to compose myself enough to drive home. The thought that Braxmore might try to snatch Florence terrified me, but there was no way I could tell Jack because it would destroy him. I would have to keep it to myself, at least for now.

Jack and I had arranged to go out for dinner with Mad and Brad, which was the last thing I felt like doing, but if I told Jack that I didn't want to go, he would know that something was wrong. I would just have to put on a brave face and pretend everything was okay.

***

"They're here!" Jack shouted from the lounge where he'd been keeping watch for Mad and Brad.

I was in the kitchen, playing snakes and ladders with Florence. After talking to Martin, I felt the need to spend as much time as possible with her. So far, she'd won all three games. With anyone else, I would have resorted to magic, but Florence would have realised what I was up to, so I'd never get away with it.

"Can we play one more game, Mummy, please?"

"No, darling, there isn't time. My friends have just arrived, and they want to meet you. Why don't you put the game away while I go and let them in?"

"But, Mummy, you said I could play one game of snakes and ladders with Sarah when she comes."

"Okay, but you have to go and put your pyjamas on now."

While Florence was getting ready for bed, I went through to the hall where Jack was waiting by the open door.

"You've scrubbed up nicely," I said as Mad walked up the drive.

"We thought we'd better make an effort, seeing as we're going out with an old married couple."

"You're married now too, or have you forgotten

already? And less of the *old*, thank you. Come on in."

Mad glanced around. "Where's that beautiful daughter of yours?"

"She's just putting her PJs on. Let's go through to the lounge. She'll come and join us."

We'd been chatting for a few minutes when I saw something scurry in through the door and head towards the bookcase.

Mad must have seen it too because she said, "Have you got a mouse, Jill?"

"I think we must have." I hurried over to the bookcase, scooped up the little creature, and took it through to the kitchen where I put it on the table. "Florence, what do you think you're playing at?"

"I wanted to show your friends how I can do the 'shrink' spell."

"What did I tell you about when you can and can't do magic?"

"I thought your friends would like to see it."

"Brad is a human, and you know you mustn't do magic in front of humans. Now, reverse that spell quickly."

"Okay, Mummy." She did as I said.

"Climb down from the table and come and say hello to my friends." I led the way into the lounge. "Mad, Brad, this is Florence."

"Aren't you beautiful?" Mad said. "Come here and give me a hug." Florence walked over to her and gave her a cuddle. "And this is my husband, Brad."

"It's very nice to meet you, young lady." He shook her hand.

While Mad, Brad and Florence were getting acquainted, I gestured to Jack that he should follow me into the kitchen.

"I didn't know we had a mouse," he said.

"We don't. That was Florence."

"What do you mean, *it was Florence*?"

"She'd made herself tiny using the 'shrink' spell."

He shook his head. "I thought she'd agreed not to use magic when there was anyone else around."

"So did I, but that little madam has a mind of her own. I'm beginning to think we might have made a mistake by listening to Aunt Lucy."

Twenty minutes later, Sarah and Florence were at the kitchen table, just about to start a game of snakes and ladders. Mad and Brad said their goodbyes to Florence, and then the four of us made our way across the village to The Middle where Jack had phoned ahead to book a table for four. Judging by how few customers were in the pub, he needn't have bothered.

We ordered our drinks at the bar, and a few minutes later, Arthur Spraggs, the landlord, came over to our table to take our food orders.

"Terrible business at the tea room, Jill," he said.

"Yes, it was."

"I know no one liked Miss Drinkwater, but she didn't deserve that. Have they caught anyone yet, do you know?"

"Not that I'm aware of."

"Rum business. Still, maybe that couple will get the chance to buy the tea room after all."

"Sorry? What couple?"

"They came in here a few weeks ago to celebrate buying the tea room. They obviously thought it was a done deal."

"What happened?"

"Apparently, Miss Drinkwater vetoed the sale at the very last minute."

"Do you know why?"

"I've no idea. One minute the sale was on, the next, it was off."

"I don't suppose you happen to remember the name of the couple, do you?"

"I do, but only because they had a very strange surname. Peep. P-E-E-P, as in Little Bo."

"Do you know their first names?"

"Joe and Flo. They live in Wash Edge, I believe."

Despite my earlier reservations, I managed to forget about Braxmore and enjoy the evening. Jack and Brad really hit it off, based on their shared bad taste in music.

After seeing Mad and Brad off, Jack and I walked back to the old watermill.

"Is everything okay, Sarah?" I asked. "I hope Florence didn't try to keep you playing snakes and ladders all evening."

"No, she went straight up to bed after we'd finished that one game. She was feeling very pleased with herself because she beat me."

"She's really lucky when it comes to snakes and ladders. She beat me too."

"The funny thing is, I thought I'd won, but then I landed on a snake just before the finish line. I know this sounds crazy, but I could have sworn that snake wasn't there when I threw the dice."

"Err, right. Jack, can you give Sarah her money, please?"

Jack paid her and showed her to the door. When he came back, he said, "Are you thinking what I'm thinking?"

"That Florence used magic to cheat at snakes and ladders? I'd put money on it. I can't believe she would do something like that."

"Hmm." Jack grinned.

"What?"

"Nothing. I was just thinking the apple doesn't fall far from the tree."

Chapter 19

I could hear Florence's screams coming from the next room, but I couldn't go to her aid because my feet were bound by heavy chains that I was unable to break, even after I'd cast the 'power' spell.

"It's alright, Florence!" I yelled. "Mummy's coming." I continued to tug at the chains but to no avail.

Every time Florence called my name, it tore my heart apart.

"Jill, wake up!"

"Jack?" I opened my eyes and realised I was in bed; my feet had become tangled up in the sheets.

"Are you alright, Jill? You must have been having a nightmare. You kept shouting Florence's name."

Florence!

I jumped out of bed and sprinted to her bedroom where I found my little angel, still fast asleep. I backed quietly out of the room and went to re-join Jack.

"What was that all about?"

"Sorry, I dreamt that someone was trying to take Florence."

"Are you okay now?"

"I'm fine. You go downstairs and start breakfast. I'll get my shower and then come and join you."

By the time I got downstairs, Florence was seated at the kitchen table with Jack. The two of them were giggling at something.

"What are you two laughing at?"

"Nothing," Jack said, somewhat unconvincingly.

"Come on. Share the joke."

"Why don't you tell Mummy, Florence?" he said.

"Daddy says you're going to dress up as a pirate."

I glared at Jack. "Did he now?"

"Can I see your costume, Mummy?"

"I don't have it with me. It's at work."

"Can I go to the fancy dress party too?"

"It isn't a party. It's just something that I have to do for work, and children aren't allowed. Sorry."

"Aww." She pouted. "I want to dress up as a pirate."

"The next time we go to Washbridge, why don't you ask Daddy to buy you a pirate costume from the fancy dress shop?"

"Will you, Daddy?" Florence said eagerly.

"Err, yeah, I guess so." It was Jack's turn to shoot me a look.

When Florence had finished her breakfast, she went upstairs to play.

"Will there be photos?" Jack said.

"Photos of what?"

"Your costume of course. I'm looking forward to seeing you, as a cat dressed in a pirate's costume."

"There most certainly will *not* be photos. And I don't appreciate you telling Florence about it."

"Come on. You have to admit it's funny."

"Oh yeah. It's hilarious. It's not like I don't have anything better to do than turn myself into a cat and dress up as a pirate."

"Now there's a sentence I never thought I'd hear."

"I have to go to work." I went upstairs, gave Florence a kiss, and grabbed my bag.

"Ahoy, matey, don't I get a kiss?" Jack shouted after me

as I headed out.

"You don't deserve one."

"Come on. I was only joking."

"Okay." I gave him a quick peck. "But no more pirate jokes."

"Aye, aye, captain."

I'd just stepped out of the house when who should walk through the gate, but my favourite postie.

"Good morning, Oscar."

"Morning, Jill. Is Jack in?"

"He certainly is."

"I thought I'd pop over to check how he's doing with his stamp collection."

"I know he's keen to show you what he's done so far." I opened the door. "Jack!"

He came out of the kitchen. "What have you forgotten, Jill?"

"Nothing. Oscar's here. He's come to see how your stamp collection is coming along."

Jack's face fell. "Great."

***

"Morning, Mrs V."

"Good morning, Jill. Did you check your coins?"

"Sorry?"

"Don't you remember I told you about that rare ten-pence piece? The one that's worth twenty-thousand pounds."

"I'll take a look." I took all the change out of my pockets and purse, and checked the dates, but there was no sign of the rare coin.

"Nope." I sighed. "No twenty-thousand pounds for me."

I'd no sooner walked into my office than Winky shouted, "Close your eyes."

"I don't have time for your nonsense, Winky. I've got a busy morning ahead."

"Just close your eyes."

"Oh, alright, but be quick."

"Ta-da. You can open them now." He was holding up the pirate costume that I'd ripped. It looked as good as new.

"I'm impressed. Are you sure that's the same one?"

"Of course it is. Sid the Stitch is a genius."

I took it from him and examined it. "He's done a brilliant job. If I need anything repairing in future, I'll know where to come."

"So, it's all systems go for the contest this afternoon?"

"I suppose so." I had been hoping that the ripped costume would mean the contest would be a write-off, but now I had no excuses. I handed the costume back to him. "You'd better hang on to this until this afternoon. I've got tons of stuff to do today."

"You'd better not let me down because there's a lot riding on this."

"Don't worry. I'll be back."

"Was that your Arnie impression?"

"Good, eh?"

"Not really. It sounded more like Elmer Fudd."

"Have you been talking to Jack?"

"And how, pray tell, would I do that?"

Just then, Bobby and Bertie landed on the ledge outside the window. They both looked down in the dumps, but I was about to change all that. "Hi, guys. How are things?"

"Not too great, to be honest, Jill," Bertie said.

"Yeah, pretty rubbish." Bobby nodded his head.

"I take it you haven't found your lady friends yet."

"We've looked everywhere, but there's no sign of them. It's back to the single life for us."

"It just so happens that I have Bianca and Briana's numbers in my phone."

"Is that a joke, Jill?" Bobby said. "Because it's not funny."

"I wouldn't do that to you."

"How on earth did you get their phone numbers?" Bertie asked.

"Yesterday, your two lady friends were standing exactly where you two are now."

"They were here?" Bobby said. "How come?"

"It seems you two made a big impression on the ladies, but Bianca lost her phone which had your numbers in it, so they had no way of contacting you. They've been checking every building in Washbridge to try to find you."

"That would explain why we didn't see them in the park," Bobby said. "This is fantastic news."

As soon as I'd given them the numbers, both pigeons got on the phone to their girlfriend.

Another two satisfied customers.

My phone rang.

"Is that Jill?"

"Yes, Jill Maxwell speaking."

"It's Sam from U-City. You asked me to call if there were any developments regarding my missing horn."

"Has something happened?"

"I've actually got it back."

"You have? How?"

"The queen's brother, Devon, managed to recover a number of the horns from Candlefield."

"I knew he'd recovered some, but I didn't realise it would be possible to identify who they belonged to."

"Every horn is unique, so it was easy to return them to their rightful owners."

"That's great. I don't mean to be rude, but is it any good to you now?"

"Oh yes. I've already fixed it in place. I feel one-hundred percent better already."

"Won't it get in the way of the new one growing underneath? I'm sorry if these are stupid questions, but I'm not very well versed in matters unicorn."

"That's okay. I've placed the old horn just in front of the new one. As soon as the new horn reaches a respectable length, I'll no longer need the old one. I'm feeling so much better already."

"I'm really delighted for you, Sam. Thanks for letting me know. Bye."

That got me wondering. Had the two ladies-in-waiting had their horns returned too?

A quick phone call revealed they both had them back. Hopefully, that meant Missy would have hers back too. I gave her a call.

"Missy? It's Jill Maxwell. Are you okay to speak or are you busy with your little one?"

"I'm okay to talk because Lola is asleep."

"I wondered if by any chance your horn had been returned to you?"

"No. Why do you ask?"

"A number of the stolen horns were recovered from Candlefield. I've just spoken to three other unicorns who have all had them returned to them, and I was hoping that yours might have been too."

"I'm afraid not," she sighed. "Do you know who found the horns, Jill?"

"It was the queen's brother, Devon."

"Do you think they might find the others?"

"I don't know. Hopefully."

By rights, I should have been done with the unicorn case, but there was something about it that still bugged me, so I gave Ursula a call.

"Ursula, it's Jill Maxwell."

"Hi, Jill. I wasn't expecting to hear from you again."

"I know you told me to forget about this case, but could I ask you a question relating to it?"

"Of course. What do you want to know?"

"I understand that you were able to identify the owners of the recovered horns?"

"That's right."

"I don't suppose there's any chance that you could send me a list of the unicorns who got their horns back, could you?"

"I really don't think you should be spending any more time on this, Jill."

"Humour me, would you? What harm can it do?"

"Okay. I'll get Ronald to send you a text with the details."

"Thanks, Ursula."

***

I was gagging for a coffee, so I decided to risk a visit to Coffee Animal. I'd given the place a wide berth since the incident with the snake, but my need for caffeine had now overridden my fear.

I was almost at the shop when I bumped into Norman, AKA Mastermind, who I hadn't seen for ages.

"Hello, Norman. Long time, no see."

"Hi, err—"

There was no way of knowing how long it might take him to remember my name, so I prompted him. "Jill."

"Oh yeah, I remember now."

"How is your bottle top shop doing?"

"It's doing well from what I hear. I sold it."

"Really? Did you get fed up with bottle tops?"

"No, I could never get fed up with them."

"Of course not. Silly of me to even suggest it."

"I'm still a keen collector, but I got an offer to buy the shop from the biggest chain of bottle top retailers in the country. It was so much money that I simply couldn't turn it down."

"Does that mean you've retired?"

"Financially, I don't need to work again, but I got bored after a few months of sitting at home all day. That's why I'm about to embark on a completely new business venture."

I should have known better than to ask, but curiosity got the better of me. "What is your new business, Norman?"

"Stamps. I've collected them ever since I was a child. Although, they've always come second to my bottle tops, obviously."

"Obviously."

"I've already turned one hobby into a business, so I thought why not try to do it again?"

"That sounds like a great idea. Coincidentally, my husband, Jack, has just started to collect stamps."

"There does seem to have been something of a revival of interest in stamp collecting recently."

"Will you just be trading online, Norman?"

"No, I'm opening a shop here in Washbridge. Do you know the old cheese shop at the bottom of the high street?"

"Do you mean the Cheese Hole?"

"That's the one. The guy who owned it retired. The shop fitters finished last weekend, and the grand opening is this Saturday."

"You don't let the grass grow, do you?"

"What grass?"

"Never mind. Do you have a name for your shop?"

"I'm going to call it Norman's Stamps."

"Inspired. I'll tell Jack; I'm sure he'll be keen to check it out."

It didn't take long to figure out what the animal of the day was because a frog jumped onto the counter while I was waiting to be served.

"Hiya," he said.

"I thought you were meant to say *ribbit*?"

"Why would I say that? What does it even mean?"

"I don't know. I just thought it was what frogs said."

"You have been badly misinformed."

"I'm not sure you should be on the counter. It's not very hygienic."

"Are you calling me unhygienic?"

"No, I'm just saying—"

"Jill?" Dot gave me a puzzled look. "Are you okay?"

"Yeah. Fine."

"It's just that I thought I heard you talking to that frog."

"No. Why would I talk to a frog? That would be a crazy thing to do."

"Sorry, my mistake. What can I get for you?"

"My usual, please."

"A caramel latte and a blueberry muffin?"

"Yes, please."

She gave me the coffee, muffin, and a small plastic cage inside which was another frog. I was just about to take a seat when someone called my name.

"Jill, over here!" It was Deli. She too had a frog in a cage on the table in front of her.

"Let me out!" my frog shouted, but I ignored him.

"Taking a break, Deli?" I took a seat opposite her.

"Yes, I've had a hectic morning, and Nails is getting on my nerves. Take a tip from me, Jill, never work with your husband."

"Don't worry. There's no chance of that ever happening. Jack and I went out for a meal with Mad and Brad last night in Middle Tweaking."

"Did you now? That's charming. I've been asking them to come out with me and Nails ever since the two of them moved back to Washbridge, but Madeline always insists she's too busy."

Oh bum! It looked like I'd dropped Mad in it.

"Still, they have only recently opened the shop, so they probably have tons to do."

"And yet, they managed to find time to go out with you and Jack. Just wait until your daughter has grown up and she doesn't want to know you. Anyway, you don't want to listen to me moaning. I hear there was a murder in your village."

"Yes. Miss Drinkwater, the woman who ran the tea room."

"A little bird also told me that your grandmother had been taken in for questioning."

"Word certainly travels fast. It's true, she was, but she didn't have anything to do with it."

"Are you sure? Your grandmother has an awful temper."

"Of course I'm sure. In fact, I'm working on the case at her request."

"That could just be a smokescreen."

"Grandma isn't that devious."

What was I saying? Of course she was.

Chapter 20

Although I'd lived in and around Washbridge all my life, I'd never visited Wash Edge. That was about to change because I was on my way there to speak to the Peeps: Joe and Flo. I'd had no difficulty tracking them down because, unsurprisingly, they were the only Peeps in the area.

The property they lived in had once been the local railway station, before that branch line had been closed more than fifty years ago. The building still retained many of its original features and was bursting with character. The gates to the property resembled a miniature level crossing, and the brass knocker on the door was shaped like signals. I gave it a rattle and moments later, the door opened, and a funny little man appeared.

"Mr Peep?"

"Yes, you must be Jill. Do call me Joe. Flo is in the waiting room."

"Waiting room?"

"Just our little joke. It's what used to be the station's waiting room but is now our living room. Come on through."

I followed him into the living/waiting room where the décor was all railway themed.

Flo, who was much taller than her husband, greeted me like a long-lost friend. "It's good of you to visit us, Jill."

"This is a beautiful place you have here. It's very unusual."

"We adore it. It probably won't come as a surprise to learn that Joe and I are both rail enthusiasts. In fact, that's how we met, on the North Yorkshire Moors Railway. Isn't that right, Joe?"

"Yes, darling." He beamed. "That was the happiest day of my life. Can I get you a drink, Jill?"

"Tea would be nice."

"Tea it is."

Flo gave me the guided tour of the living room, pointing out each piece of railway memorabilia, and telling me where she and Joe had purchased it. Mr Hosey would have been in his element there.

Joe returned, carrying a tray on which there were three cups, and a teapot shaped like a steam engine.

"Let's take a seat over here." Flo gestured to the railway carriage seats that lined one wall of the room. "Joe said that you wanted to talk to us about Tweaking Tea Rooms."

"That's right. My husband and I were in the village pub the other night, and we got talking to the landlord. He mentioned that you'd been in there recently, and that you'd told him you were thinking of buying the tea room."

"That's right. In fact, we went into the Middle to celebrate because we thought it was a done deal, but then it fell through at the last minute."

"You aren't thinking of leaving this beautiful property, surely?"

"Definitely not," Joe said. "We'll be here until they carry us out, won't we, Flo?"

"That's right, but we both retired recently, and we're finding retirement rather boring, so we decided to look for a small business to run. We thought a small cafe or coffee shop would be ideal."

"I'm curious how you happened to hear that Tweaking

Tea Rooms was for sale? Where did you see it advertised?"

"We didn't. We placed our own advert in the commercial property section of The Bugle, saying that we were looking for a small cafe or coffee shop within approximately a twenty-mile radius. Not long after the ad appeared, we were approached by Ryan Drinkwater who told us about the tea room in Middle Tweaking. It was a little further out than we would have liked, but it sounded ideal, so we agreed to take a look. We immediately fell in love with the place and made an offer on the spot, which he accepted."

"Was Miss Drinkwater there when you viewed the tea room?"

"No, it was just Ryan. We had no idea that anyone else had an interest in the business, but a few days later, he called us to say he wouldn't be able to proceed with the sale because his sister, who was a part owner, had refused to sanction the deal. We were both very disappointed, weren't we, Joe?"

"Devastated. We're still on the lookout for somewhere suitable but we haven't seen anywhere that comes close."

"I assume you've heard that Miss Drinkwater has been murdered?"

"Yes, we saw it on the news. It's a terrible thing."

"Have you heard from Ryan since his sister died?"

"No, but then I'm sure the poor man has more important things on his mind at the moment."

"Would you still be interested in purchasing the business? After what happened, I mean?"

"I think so, but we'll just have to see what happens."

Was it possible that Ryan Drinkwater had been trying to sell the tea room without his sister's knowledge? That made no sense. Surely, he would have realised that she would veto any sale. It was clear that I needed to speak to him, but that would have to wait for another day because if I didn't get back to the office on time, Winky would have my guts for garters.

I made it there with only a few minutes to spare.

"Are you alright, Jill?" Mrs V said. "You look out of breath."

"I've been running."

"What's so important that you had to run back?"

"I don't want to be late for the — err — " I caught myself just in time.

"For what, dear? You don't have any appointments as far as I'm aware."

"You're right. I just thought the exercise would do me good."

"That's probably a good idea. You have been looking a little out of shape recently."

Out of shape? Me? Cheek!

Winky was tapping his watch and looking very annoyed. "One more minute and you'd have been late."

"I'm here now. That's all that matters."

"Come on, then." He started towards the door. "Let's get going."

"Hold on. You have to go in your basket."

"I hate that thing. It smells."

"It only smells of *you*! If you want to go to the contest,

you have to go in the basket."

"Alright, then, but you'll have to carry these." He handed me a bag containing the costumes.

"Where are you taking the cat?" Mrs V said, as we walked through the outer office.

"Err, he has to go to the vet for his flea treatment."

"Not before time. I've been doing a lot of scratching recently. I suspect I've got fleas from him."

"How dare she!" Winky snapped.

Ignoring him, I continued towards the door. "Right, Mrs V, I'll see you in the morning."

Winky was still grumbling as we made our way down the stairs. "How dare the old bag lady say I've got fleas?"

"Never mind that now. Where is this contest, anyway?"

"I'll give you directions once we're in the car."

I placed the costumes in the car boot, and then put the cat basket on the front seat next to me. I was just about to start the car when Winky said, "Hold on!"

"What is it now?"

"You need to learn the pirate song."

"Sorry?"

"I said you need to learn the pirate song for the contest."

"You never mentioned anything about a pirate song. You told me it was a fancy dress competition."

"Are you sure? I thought I'd mentioned it."

"No, I would definitely have remembered. How am I supposed to learn it now?"

"Don't worry. It's really simple. I've got it on my phone. Listen to it a few times, and then we'll sing along together."

"I'm not sure I want to sing in front of an audience."

"Come on, Jill. Only the other day, you were telling me what a fantastic singer you are."

"It's true. I do have a good voice."

"Right, then. Let's get on with it."

As soon as we were under way, Winky took out his phone and began to play the pirate song. Thankfully, it really was very simple.

Winky sang solo the first three times while I tried to memorise the lyrics.

"You join in this time," he said.

"Okay, I'll try."

"On three. One, two, three."

"I'm a pirate on the high seas. I don't care about the law. I sail near and far and do just as I please. The pirate life for me. Oh, the pirate life for me."

"Very good." Winky nodded his approval. "I think you've got it."

Just then, the glove compartment popped open, and Henry stuck his head out. "What's that awful noise, Jill?"

"I was singing the pirate song."

"Please stop. It's giving me a headache."

"Get back inside there, you." Winky slammed the glove compartment closed.

Poor old Henry. That would be another bruise on his head.

By the time we arrived at the hall where the contest was to be held, I was more or less word perfect on the awful pirate song.

"Where do we go?" I said, as we got out of the car.

"Around the back." Winky jumped out of the basket. "Hurry up, we don't have much time."

There were two huge cats standing guard on the basement door.

"Hi, Bomber." Winky nodded to one of them.

"Hey, Winky. What are you doing here?"

"I'm here for the contest. More to the point, what are *you* doing here?"

"I work for Felix Security these days. They've got us guarding this place. I'm not sure why, though, it's not like anybody's going to break in." He glanced at me. "Who's your two-legged friend?"

"This is Jill."

"She can't come in. It's felines only, Winky. You know that."

"It's alright, Bomber. She's a witch. She'll turn herself into a cat once we're inside."

Bomber hesitated for a moment, but then waved us through. "Okay, but only because it's you, Winky."

Once we were inside, Winky pulled me into a small room.

"Come on, then. Do your magic. Turn yourself into a cat."

"Turn around first."

"Why?"

"Because I have to take my clothes off."

"Hurry up, then." He turned his back.

I magicked myself into a cat and slipped on the costume. "Okay, you can turn around now."

"You look good." He nodded his approval. "All you have to do now is to learn the dance."

"What *dance*?"

"The pirate dance, obviously."

"We have to sing *and* dance?"

"You don't think they'd put up this kind of prize money for us to just stand on stage and look pretty, do you?"

"That's exactly what I thought because that's what you told me."

"Come on, there's nothing to it. It's barely a dance at all. More like a jig."

"A jig *is* a dance."

He took out his phone and played a video of himself and Mimi dancing.

"See! Didn't I tell you it was simple?"

He was right. There was nothing to the dance, just a few steps to the left and then to the right.

"I'm still not sure about this, Winky."

"Just think of the prize money. Come on. I'll play it again and we can sing and dance along." He pressed play, and I did my best to follow what Mimi was doing on-screen, but I kept getting my left and right mixed up.

"Concentrate, Jill, or we'll never win."

"I'm doing my best."

We ran through the routine another five times, by which time, I'd more or less got the hang of it.

"That'll have to do," he said. "Let's go and join the others."

The spectators were seated in the centre and left-hand sections of the auditorium; all the competitors were seated in the right-hand section.

The first couple called onto the stage were Joshua and Jordan.

"These are the favourites," Winky whispered. "This is who we need to beat."

"I don't think much of their costumes," I said, and then glanced around to check out the other competitors. "Our costumes are the best by far."

"I know. We have this in the bag as long as you don't mess up the song and dance routine."

No pressure, then.

In total, there were ten couples competing. According to the draw, Winky and I would be the last ones to go on stage. By the time I'd watched all the others, I was feeling much more confident. Most of the singing had been abysmal, and at least three of the couples had messed up their dance routines.

The MC took to the mic. "Our final couple is Winky and Mimi. Please welcome them on stage."

"Why is he calling me Mimi?"

"I didn't get around to changing the entry form. Come on. And don't let me down."

"Don't worry. I've got this," I reassured him.

Once the music started, we began to sing and dance. I was growing more and more confident because my voice was clearly much better than those who'd gone before. Our dance routine was perfect, and I was starting to count the prize money.

But then, disaster struck!

As we came to the last few bars of the routine, I stepped left when I should have stepped right, causing me to bump into Winky and fall off the stage. Slightly dazed, I looked up to see Winky glaring down at me.

"How very unlucky," the MC said. "And it had been going so well too."

We drove back from the contest in silence. Winky hadn't spoken a word since we'd come off the stage. He hadn't even asked how I was feeling after my fall. Fortunately, I wasn't hurt at all, except for my pride.

When we pulled up outside the office building, I opened the car door for him.

"I'm sorry about the contest, Winky."

"It's my own fault," he snapped. "I should have known better than to ask you, with your two left feet."

"That's a bit unfair. I was doing really well right up to the last minute."

"I'm going inside." He jumped out of the car and disappeared into the building.

That would be the last time I volunteered to help that ungrateful so-and-so.

***

When I arrived home, Jack met me at the door.

"How did it go?"

"Don't even ask."

"That bad, eh?"

"Where's Florence?"

"She was really tired, so she went to bed a few minutes early. She was asleep before I'd finished the first page of her story."

"That's a shame. I was really looking forward to seeing her. I thought she might cheer me up."

"Are you sure you don't want to tell me about the contest?"

"Definitely."

"Did you take a photograph of yourself in your pirate outfit?"

"No, I told you I wouldn't."

"Oh dear."

"*Oh dear*, what?"

"I kind of promised Florence that you would. She said she was really looking forward to seeing it in the morning."

"Why did you go and do that?"

"I just assumed Winky would take photos. She's going to be really disappointed. I don't suppose—"

"What?"

"Do you have the costume with you?"

"It's in the car."

"If you were to put it on, I could take a photo of you, and we could pretend it had been taken at the contest."

"I—err—"

"Florence is going to be really disappointed otherwise."

"Oh, okay then."

I hurried out to the car, grabbed the costume, took it upstairs to our bedroom, turned myself into a cat, and then put it on.

"Wow. You look great." He grinned.

"Just take the photograph, will you?"

I did my best to look cheerful while he snapped the photo. "Got it?"

"Yeah. Florence will love this."

"What's for supper?" I took the costume off and reversed the cat spell.

"Are you really hungry?"

"I'm starving."

"I thought maybe we could stay up here and mess around for a while."

"You thought wrong."

Chapter 21

The next morning when I came down for breakfast, Jack and Daddy's girl were already at the kitchen table, tucking into their bowls of muesli. I was convinced those two only pretended to like that awful stuff just to annoy me.

"Would you like me to pour you some, Jill?" Jack picked up the muesli box.

"No thanks, I'm going to stick to my own cereal."

"But, Mummy, Chococandy Pops are bad for you. They rot your teeth. Daddy said so."

"Did he now?" I shot Jack a look. "Maybe I'll just have toast instead."

This is what my life had come to. I was being told what I could and couldn't eat by my five-year-old daughter, aided and abetted by my muesli-loving husband.

Once I had my toast, I joined them at the table. "I've got something to show you, Florence."

"Is it a caterpillar?"

"Err, no."

"I like caterpillars. They're furry and they walk really funny."

"It's not a caterpillar."

"I saw two caterpillars at school yesterday. Wendy says she saw three, but I don't believe her."

"Right, okay. Anyway, I've got a photograph to show you."

"Is it a photograph of a caterpillar?"

"It's got nothing to do with caterpillars. Do you remember last night when Daddy said that I was going to bring you a photograph to look at? Well, here it is."

"Is that really you as a cat, Mummy?"

"Yes, darling, it is."

"I like your pirate costume."

"Thank you."

"Did you win the contest?"

"I'm afraid not."

"Did you come second?"

"Not quite."

"Where did you come, Mummy?"

"I forget, but it wasn't first or second."

"Can I keep this photograph?"

"Of course you can."

"Can I show it to my friends at school?"

"You can, but you mustn't tell them that I'm the cat."

"Thank you for giving me this, Mummy, it's a lovely surprise."

"A *surprise*? I thought Daddy told you that I was going to bring you a photograph?" I glanced at Jack who was grinning inanely.

"Daddy said you wouldn't be able to take any photos."

"He did, did he?" I glared at him.

"I want to turn myself into a cat," Florence said. "I'm going to learn that spell."

"It's very complicated. It might be too difficult for you."

"But I'm really good at magic. Great-Grandma said so. I'm going to learn it after school."

"Okay, but you mustn't be too disappointed if it doesn't work out."

"Is it alright to go and play with Buddy now that I've finished my breakfast?" She held up her empty bowl.

"Okay, but only until it's time to get ready for school."

As soon as she'd gone outside, I turned on Jack. "You

said you'd promised her that I'd have a photograph to show her this morning."

"Okay, I admit it. I just wanted to see you as a cat, dressed as a pirate."

"You are a very sick man."

"But you love me anyway."

"Hmm. You never told me how it went with Oscar yesterday."

"It was purgatory. He spent half an hour criticising the way I'd arranged my stamps, and told me that I'd need to start again."

I laughed. "Serves you right."

"You've not heard the best of it. He wants me to go to StampCon with him. It's in a couple of weeks."

"I hope you told him you'd go."

"I didn't really have any choice. I thought we'd seen the back of cons after we left Tony and Clare behind in Smallwash."

"It'll be fun."

"You can come with us if you like."

"I'd love to, but I have to cut my toenails that day."

"Oscar also mentioned that there's a new stamp shop opening somewhere in Washbridge."

"I know. It's in what used to be the Cheese Hole, and it opens on Saturday."

"How do you know that?"

"Do you remember Norman, AKA Mastermind?"

"You mean the guy who has the bottle top shop on the high street?"

"Yeah. I bumped into him yesterday and it turns out he's sold his shop."

"Who on earth would want to buy that?"

"Apparently, he was bought out by a major chain of bottle top shops. According to him, they paid him enough to retire on."

"So how come he's opening another shop?"

"Seems he's bored, and he's always had an interest in stamp collecting."

"I've no doubt Oscar will want to drag me in there."

"You'll never guess what the shop is going to be called."

"Norman's Stamps?"

How did he do that?

***

It was time to go to work, so I went outside to say goodbye to my darling daughter.

"Florence, I'm going to work now. Come and give me a kiss."

She came running over, gave me a hug, and planted a big sloppy kiss on my lips.

"Bye, Mummy."

"Don't forget that if you show anyone that photograph, you mustn't tell them that Mummy was the cat."

"I won't. I promise."

"Is Buddy playing nicely?"

"No, he just keeps looking at that tree. He won't play with me."

I glanced up to see what the dog was staring at. And that's when I saw it. That same squirrel was eyeballing me again.

"Shoo! Go away!" I waved my arms around to try and spook it, but it took no notice.

"What are you doing, Mummy?"

"I'm trying to scare off that squirrel. Can't you see it?"

She took a few steps back to get a better look. "I can see it now. I think squirrels are cute. Do you think he'll come down and play with me?"

"Not while Buddy's here, he won't."

"He might play with me after school."

"He might, but don't get your hopes up because squirrels are very shy creatures. Anyway, I have to go now." I took one last look up at the tree where that nutty squirrel was still watching me.

I was half-way down the drive when I suddenly felt something land on both of my shoulders. Edna was perched on one, and Irene was on the other.

"You two really do have to stop doing that. Couldn't you have just landed on the gate?"

"Where would be the fun in that?" Edna chuckled.

"We have to get our laughs where we can," Irene said.

"You really shouldn't visit me out in the open where someone might see you."

They both glanced around. "There's no one here, Jill. It's just us."

"Fair enough. Do you have something to report?"

"I most certainly do," Edna said.

"Me too." Irene nodded. "I think you're going to be very interested to hear what I have to tell you."

"Go on then, ladies. What are you waiting for?"

"I don't think so." Edna shook her head.

"What do you mean? Why not?"

"No report until we get paid."

"I've never had to pay in advance before."

"Times are hard. Needs must."

"I don't have any biscuits with me."

"You'd better go back into the house and get some, then."

"I can't. I ate the last custard cream last night, and I know we don't have any ginger nuts."

"In that case, you'll just have to wait for the reports. Come on, Irene."

"Wait. I need those reports."

"No biscuits. No reports."

"Okay, I'll nip to the store and see if they have any. Will you two wait here?"

"We've got better things to do than hang around here all day," Edna said. "Irene and I will go for a coffee, and we'll meet you at your office in an hours' time. How's that?"

"Okay. I'll see you then."

Why was nothing ever straightforward?

I didn't have the time or inclination to wander around the store, trying to second-guess where the Stock sisters might have put the custard creams and ginger nuts, so I went straight to the counter where Marjorie was busy doing a crossword.

"Good morning, Jill."

"Morning, Marjorie. Are you by yourself this morning?"

"I shouldn't be, but I am. That lazy sister of mine is still in bed."

"She isn't poorly, is she?"

"No. She hasn't been sleeping well recently, so she bought some kind of sleeping draught. It seems to have knocked her out."

"I'd tell her to lay off that if I were you. Two of my PA's

friends ended up in hospital after taking a sleeping draught."

"How awful. I'll tell her."

"I'm in a bit of a hurry this morning, so do you think you could tell me where I'll find the ginger nuts and custard creams."

"They're pretty much where you'd expect them to be. The ginger nuts are in 'G' section and the custard creams are in 'C' section."

"Right, that's much more straightforward than I was expecting. Thanks." I turned around and walked down the first aisle.

Letter A.

Letter V.

Letter E.

Huh?

Confused, I returned to the counter.

"Marjorie, the different sections don't appear to be in alphabetical order."

"People were complaining that they found it difficult to locate things."

"Really? I'm shocked."

"So were we, but the customer is always right, so we went back to the drawing board and came up with a better system."

"When will you be implementing it?"

"We already have."

"Oh? And how exactly does this new system work?"

"We realised that it would be better to have the more popular items closer to the counter, so that's what we've done."

"Hang on. Let me make sure I understand. Are the

goods still stocked alphabetically?"

"Yes, they're placed on the shelves as before, so for example, ginger nuts are still in the 'G' section."

"Okay, I understand that part, but where do I find sections 'C' and 'G'?"

"Hmm, I'm not sure where specific sections are now, but I can assure you that the most popular items will be closest to the counter."

"Brilliant."

"We thought so."

I walked down the first aisle but drew a blank. I did find 'C' section in the second aisle between letters 'J' and 'S'. Fortunately, they had plenty of custard creams, so I grabbed several packets. I didn't find 'G' section until I reached the last aisle where it was located between letters 'B' and 'F'. Once again, I took a handful of packets.

"You managed to find them, Jill?" So far, Marjorie had only filled in two lines of her crossword puzzle.

"Just about."

"This new system is so much better, don't you think?"

If I hadn't been in such a rush, I would have told her exactly what I thought of her new system. Instead, I just paid for the biscuits and got out of there before my brain exploded.

I'd been driving for about five minutes when the glove compartment opened, and Henry peered out. "Is the coast clear, Jill?"

"What do you mean?"

"That psycho cat isn't in here again, is he?"

"No, you're okay. That was Winky — he's in the office."

"What about that crazy old witch?"

"No, it's just me today."

When Henry jumped out, I noticed he had another plaster on his forehead. "What is it with the passengers in your car, Jill? They're all very violent."

"I'm really sorry about what happened, Henry. Grandma can be a nasty piece of work, and Winky just wanted us to focus on learning the pirate song."

"That song was truly awful."

"I know, but we were practising for a contest."

"Did you win?"

"No, we didn't."

"Did you come second?"

"No."

"Where did you come, then?"

"I don't rightly recall, but it wasn't in the top two."

***

When I arrived at the office, there was no sign of Mrs V, but she had left a note on her desk. Apparently, Armi had gone to the hospital because he'd got his toe stuck in the tap. She said she hoped to be in later.

When I walked through to my office, Winky was sitting on the sofa.

"Good morning, Winky."

He stared blankly at me but didn't speak.

"What's wrong with you today?"

He reached down to the pile of cards next to him on the sofa, picked up the first one, and held it up for me to read.

I'm not talking to you.

"Why not? Is it because of the contest?"

He picked up the next card in the pile.

Yes.

"Don't you think you're being a little childish? I did my best."

He continued with the next card.

I was banking on that prize money.

"I've said I'm sorry." I shrugged. "There's nothing else I can do."

Another card.

I want salmon.

"What's the magic word?" He picked up the final card.

Now!

"If you want salmon, you'll have to ask me properly. With your mouth. With actual words. Not with cards."

He just turned his back to me.

"Please yourself." I went over to my desk and was just about to start work when Edna and Irene appeared on the windowsill.

"Do you have the biscuits?" Edna said.

"I do." I picked up my bag, took out the custard creams, which I handed to Edna, and the ginger nuts, which I gave to Irene.

As soon as Edna saw the ginger nuts, she pulled a face. "*Ginger nuts*, Irene? I thought you had better taste than that."

"I don't know what you're talking about," Irene scoffed. "Everyone knows that ginger nuts are the superior biscuit."

"Don't be ridiculous." Edna laughed.

"Ladies, please! I'm really busy. Can you let me have your reports?"

Edna ripped open the packet of custard creams and began to devour one. That was Irene's cue to give her report first.

"I followed the wizard, and last night, he went into a bar in Washbridge city centre, where he met a guy. They were talking for about an hour."

"Could you hear their conversation?"

"Some of it. Enough to know he must be the guy you're looking for—the inside contact."

"How could you tell?"

"I heard them mention *bookings* a number of times, and I also heard the names of several celebrities. And, most importantly, I definitely heard them refer to Double Take."

"That's brilliant. Can you describe the man he was talking to?"

"I can do better than that. I took a photo of him." She took it out of her pocket and handed it to me. "Do you recognise him, Jill?"

"I most certainly do. Thanks, Irene, that's a job well done." I turned to Edna who had just finished eating one custard cream and was about to start on another one. "Hold on, Edna. What do you have to report?"

She put the biscuit back in the packet. "I have to be honest, Jill. Following a unicorn is not my favourite pastime. They might be nice to look at, but boy, are they boring! They don't do anything."

"Did you see Devon talking to anyone suspicious?"

"Possibly."

"What do you mean, *possibly*?"

"It might be something or nothing, but he did meet up with a couple of sweetheart fairies in a coffee shop."

"Did you hear what they were talking about?"

"No, I couldn't get close enough."

"That's a fat lot of good."

"Hear me out. I've come across this pair before, and I happen to know that they've both done time behind bars."

"For what?"

"Theft, blackmail and assault."

"*Assault*? But they're such tiny things."

"Looks can be deceiving. These two are real bad eggs."

"Do you have photos of them?"

"No, but I know their names and address." She handed me a piece of paper.

"Karen and Sharon? Is this a wind-up?"

"No, those are their names."

"There's only one address here."

"That's because they share a flat. There's something else, Jill. This Devon guy paid several visits to a small industrial unit in Candlefield."

"Doing what exactly?"

"I don't know. Everything was boarded up and the place was locked, but I have the address for that too." She handed me another piece of paper.

"That's great. Thanks, ladies, you've both thoroughly earned your biscuits."

"Our pleasure," Edna said. "You know where we are if you need us again."

Chapter 22

The two surveillance fairies had certainly come up trumps. I still found it hard to believe that sweetheart fairies could have been responsible for taking the unicorn horns, but Edna had pointed out that this particular pair had been in trouble with the law before, so they were definitely worth further investigation. I was also intrigued by Devon's visits to an industrial unit. What possible interest could he have there?

Irene too had done well. The person in the photograph that she'd given me was none other than Wayne Crabtree, the elderly Alex Wilder lookalike who had seemed so nice and unassuming when I'd spoken to him at Double Take. Maybe our Mr Crabtree was not the wholesome character he liked to portray.

When I looked up, Winky was facing me.

"Have you decided to talk to me yet?" I said.

He didn't say a word. Instead, he picked up another card and held it out in front of him; this one was blank.

"You've got that the wrong way around."

He flipped it over to reveal a single word.

Sorry.

"I'm really sorry, Jill," he said. "I shouldn't have had a go at you like that."

"You're dead right. You shouldn't have. Whatever got into you? I've never seen you overreact like that before."

"I was banking on the prize money from the contest to pay off a debt."

"What kind of debt?"

"I bought a lot of presents for Mimi. More than I could

afford. Then there were the pirate costumes, which cost an arm and a leg. I borrowed some money from Lenny the Lender, and I'm supposed to pay him back by seven o'clock tonight."

"Can't you just tell him that you'll pay him later?"

"You don't tell Lenny that you can't pay your debts on time. If I do that, he'll send his brother, Kenny the Knuckles, around."

"Are you telling me if you don't pay by tonight, someone is going to come around here and beat you up?"

"Yeah."

"Why don't you go and hide somewhere?"

"Where would I hide? And if I did, it wouldn't do any good because he'd still be waiting for me when I come back."

"How much do you owe him?"

"Two-hundred pounds."

"With all the money you've been raking in, you must have thousands stashed away. What about your lottery win?"

"It's all tied up in long-term bonds, so I can't get hold of the cash quickly enough."

"You're an idiot!"

"I know. And I'll be a dead idiot if I don't come up with that cash today."

"I suppose I could lend you the money?" What was I saying?

"Would you do that?"

"It would only be a loan. I want it back by the end of the month."

"No problem. I'll even pay interest."

"There's no need for that. I'm only doing it because I

feel like I let you down in the contest."

"I love you, Jill." He leapt from the sofa to the desk and then launched himself at me.

"Yuk! Get off!" I had to pull him off me.

"You're my favourite two-legged person."

"Yeah, yeah. I might be now, but for how long?"

"Forever. I'll never forget this."

"We'll see. I need to go and see someone. I'll get your money on my way back."

"You're the best. I've always said so."

I headed down the high street to what used to be the Cheese Hole but was now Norman's Stamps. Or at least, it would be after tomorrow's grand opening. Inside, it was a mecca for stampers.

Yes, I do realise they're normally referred to as philatelists, but I think *stamper* is a much better name. So sue me.

Norman was standing in one corner with his back to me, so I tapped on the window to get his attention. As always, it took him a couple of minutes to place me, but then a light seemed to go on behind his eyes, and he opened the door.

"Hi, Jill." He glanced over my shoulder. "Have you brought your husband with you? Because we don't actually open until tomorrow."

"No, it's just me. I know you aren't officially open yet, but do you think I could talk to you for a few minutes?"

"Sure, come in. I can't offer you a drink, I'm afraid. All the refreshments are being delivered in the morning."

"That's okay. It's actually your grand opening that I want to talk to you about. I need a big favour."

"What's that?"

"How would you feel about hiring a lookalike to take part in tomorrow's promotional activities?"

"A *lookalike*?"

"Yeah, specifically I'd like you to hire an Alex Wilder lookalike."

"*Alex Wilder*?" His eyes lit up. "I'm a massive fan of his."

"You are? I didn't think you would have heard of him."

"Of course I have. He made some classic movies back in the nineties. How much does it cost to hire a lookalike?"

"Not much for this guy, but I'll reimburse you anyway."

"Why do you want me to do it?"

I told Norman about Double Take and the problems they'd been having.

"And you think this guy might have something to do with it?"

"I'm positive that he does."

"Okay, but what happens if this particular lookalike already has a booking for tomorrow? It's very short notice."

"I really doubt that he will, but if he does, give me a call. What time is the grand opening tomorrow?"

"Midday."

"Okay, I'll be here at least half an hour before that. And thanks again, Norman. I'll recommend you to all my stamp collecting friends."

After leaving Norman's Stamps, I stopped off at an ATM and drew out two-hundred pounds, then made my way back to the office with the cash still in my hand.

Mrs V was behind her desk.

"Jill, why are you carrying all that money in your hand? Someone could have mugged you."

"I—err—I had to draw it out for Jack. He's going to book a place at StampCon."

"I didn't know he was interested in stamps."

"Oh yes. He can't get enough of them."

"Don't you normally pay for that kind of thing by card these days?"

"Usually, yes, but stamp collectors are an old-fashioned bunch. They insist on cash. Anyway, how's Armi?"

"He's fine. The only damage is to his pride. He's back home now."

"How did he manage to get his toe stuck, anyway? He wasn't tap dancing, was he?" I laughed.

"Not funny, Jill."

"Sorry."

"It's something he's always done, and I have no idea why. Whenever he sits in the bath, he always pokes his toe into the end of the tap. Only, this time, he poked it in too far and it got stuck."

"What did you do?"

"I had to take him to the hospital to get it removed."

"You took the bath to the hospital?"

"No, silly. I sawed off the end of the tap first, so now I have to call a plumber, to get a new tap installed. I've told Armi the money is coming out of his cuckoo clock fund."

"Did you get the cash?" Winky said as soon as I walked through the door.

"Here you are. I want it back by the end of the month."

"No problem. Is there anything else I can do for you?"

"You can stop being such a bootlicker. It doesn't suit

you."

***

It was time to pay Ryan Drinkwater a visit. If what the Peeps had told me was correct, he'd tried to sell Tweaking Tea Rooms behind his sister's back, which must have taken some nerve. Or maybe he was just stupid? Either way, when his sister found out, she'd slapped him down and stopped the sale. Was that enough for him to have resorted to murder? That's what I hoped to discover.

He lived in an apartment block in the city centre, not far from where Mad and Brad lived. Once inside the building, I found a quiet spot and used magic to change my appearance to that of a police officer.

He was clearly surprised to see me. "Officer?"

"Mr Drinkwater. I'm Constable Trulady. Can I come in and ask you a few questions regarding your sister's murder?"

"But I answered all your questions when I came down to the station. I spent several hours with Detective McDonald."

"I understand that, but Big—err—Detective McDonald has asked me to do a short follow-up interview. It shouldn't take long."

"Very well, but I have to go out in about half an hour."

"Don't worry. That's more than enough time."

"Okay. You'd better come in."

He led the way into the living room.

"Right, Mr Drinkwater, if you wouldn't mind just confirming the last time you saw your sister alive?"

"It was the weekend before last."

"And where was that? At the tea room?"

"No. As I told Detective McDonald, I went to her house."

"I understand that you tried to sell the tea room."

"Who told you that? That's not true."

"A certain Mr and Mrs Peep, who live in Wash End, might beg to differ."

"That was a complete misunderstanding. I was doing them a favour."

"A *favour*? What does that mean, exactly?"

"They're thinking of opening a café and they wanted to see how a good tea room is run, so I gave them a tour of Tweaking Tea Rooms."

"That was a very generous thing to do. It's strange that they thought you were offering to sell the business, don't you think?"

"They're both old. They must be confused."

"Your sister can't have been happy when she discovered you'd been trying to sell the tea room behind her back."

"I'm sorry, but this is ridiculous. I'm going to have to ask you to leave. I won't answer any more questions unless my solicitor is present."

His reaction was not that of an innocent man, and I had no intention of leaving. First, I cast the 'forget' spell, and then the 'sleep' spell. Once he had nodded off, I began to search the apartment, starting with the living room, then the dining room and kitchen. I drew a blank in all three. Same went for the master bedroom. One of the two smaller bedrooms was being used as an office. In the bottom drawer of the desk, I found two separate files, both containing bank statements. The first one was for

Drinkwater's personal bank account which was considerably overdrawn. The second one was a business bank account in the name of RD Ice Works. I assumed that RD stood for Ryan Drinkwater. This account too was massively overdrawn. Beneath the files was a pile of letters. Some of the correspondence was from the bank that held his business account. The gist of it seemed to be that they would not agree to his request for an increase of his overdraft facility. Even more concerning was the pile of bills, personal and business, many of which were long overdue. It was clear that Ryan Drinkwater was in serious financial trouble. That might explain why he'd tried to sell the tea room, but was it motive enough to kill his sister? I needed to find out more about his business, RD Ice Works.

On my way out, I reversed the 'sleep' spell, and while he was still drowsy, I left. I'd just stepped out of the apartment when the lift doors pinged at the far end of the corridor. My heart sank when the doors opened and out stepped Big Mac and a uniformed officer. Fortunately, they were deep in conversation, so they hadn't seen me. I magicked myself back into my own clothes, and then hightailed it the opposite way down the corridor towards the stairs.

That had been too close for comfort.

***

Back in Middle Tweaking, a police car was just pulling away from the old watermill. Had someone spotted me at the apartment block? Had something happened to Jack or Florence? Fearing the worst, I jumped out of the car and ran down the drive.

I burst through the door and shouted, "Jack, where are you? Florence?"

The lounge door opened, and Jack appeared. "Why are you shouting, Jill?"

"Is everyone alright? I saw the police car pulling away."

"We're fine."

"Where's Florence?"

"I sent her to her bedroom and told her she had to stay there until you came home."

"Is she poorly?"

"No, she's been naughty."

"What did she do?"

"Come into the lounge and I'll tell you." Once we were inside, he closed the door. "That's why the police were here."

"What could Florence have done to warrant a visit from the police?"

"They received a phone call from someone to say that they'd seen a lion in our back garden."

"What! Do you mean what I think you mean?"

"Yes. Florence was trying to turn herself into a cat. I'd just stepped out into the garden to see what she was up to when it happened. Luckily, she reversed the spell straight away."

"How come the police heard about it?"

"Just our luck. Barbara Babble, of all people, happened to be walking past at that precise moment. She was the one who called the police."

"What did you tell them?"

"Fortunately, I used to work with one of the officers who came to the house. I took him to one side and explained that Barbara was the village gossip, and that she had a vivid imagination. They took a quick look in the garden, just to cover themselves, then I gave them both a cup of tea."

"What did you say to Florence?"

"I didn't need to say much of anything. She already knew she'd done wrong. I told her she had to go to her bedroom until you came home."

"I'd better go and talk to her."

Florence was playing with her dolls' house. She certainly didn't look very contrite.

"Hello, Mummy. Have you had a nice day at work?"

"Yes, thank you, darling. How was your day?"

"I found two more caterpillars at school."

"That's nice. And did anything happen after you came home from school?"

"Not really."

"Did you practise any magic?"

"A little bit." She held up her hand and illustrated just how little with her thumb and forefinger.

"Which spell did you practise?"

"I turned myself into a cat."

"And how did that go?"

"I got it a bit wrong."

"Daddy told me you turned yourself into a lion."

"I didn't do it on purpose, Mummy. And I turned myself back straight away."

"But someone saw you, didn't they? And they called the police."

"Are you mad at me?"

"I'm not angry, but you have to be very careful when you're learning new spells, particularly dangerous ones like that. You should have done it out of sight of the gate. That way, no one would have seen you."

"Can I come downstairs now?"

"Yes, come on."

***

"I can take Florence to bed if you want to get going," Jack offered.

"No, it's okay. I want to do it, and besides, I don't plan on going until it's dark."

"What is this place you're going to, anyway?"

"It's the company owned by Miss Drinkwater's brother. RD Ice Works."

"What do they do?"

"I've no idea. Manufacture fridges, maybe."

"Do you think he had something to do with his sister's death?"

"I don't know. I do know he was trying to sell the tea room behind her back, though."

Florence came running downstairs. "Am I still going to Wendy's house tomorrow, Mummy?"

"If you want to. Her mummy said you could."

"I do. We're going to hunt for caterpillars in her garden."

"That sounds — err — great."

That night, Florence insisted I read Harry The Caterpillar Finds A Sponge, which was without a shadow of a doubt one of the weirdest stories I'd ever come across. Still, it did the trick because she was fast asleep five minutes after I started reading.

After sneaking downstairs, I gave Jack a quick goodbye kiss, and then drove to RD Ice Works. I parked half a mile away from the industrial unit and made my way from there on foot. It was dark, and there were no cars in the car park. A blinking red light drew my attention to a single CCTV camera, mounted just below the roofline. Staying in the shadows, I walked around the side of the building, and peered through one of the windows. There was very little to see, just a corridor with several doors leading off it.

I magicked myself inside, started at one end of the corridor, and checked each door in turn. They were all locked until I came to the final one. That opened onto the shop floor which was full of machines. As I got closer to one of them, I could feel cool air coming off it, but there was nothing to indicate what the machine did. In one corner of the room there was a shelving unit on which was a pile of brochures, which showed that the company produced and sold ice blocks of all sizes.

On the opposite side of the room, another door led to a corridor identical to the one I'd already checked. Some of the doors on this side of the building were unlocked: Two of them were being used as storerooms. The third room was much smaller and contained the CCTV monitoring system, displaying an image of the car park. On a whim, I checked the footage for the night that Miss Drinkwater was murdered. I started to view the recording from six o'clock that night, at which time there were still several cars in the car park. By the time the footage reached the eight o'clock mark, all of the cars except for one had left. Over the next hour of footage, nothing much happened, but then a figure came out of the building and approached the remaining car. It was Ryan Drinkwater and he was carrying a box.

And not just any old box; it was a freezer box.

Chapter 23

Florence had finished her breakfast and was in the garden on a caterpillar hunt. Jack and I were still at the kitchen table, and for some reason, he had a stupid smirk on his face.

"What's tickling you?"

"Nothing." He shrugged.

"Come on. Something obviously is. Spit it out."

"I was just thinking how lucky you are to be going to the grand opening of the stamp shop." He grinned. "I'm sooo very jealous."

"It's not by choice, I can promise you that. But if my hunch is correct, I should be able to solve the Double Take case, so it'll be well worth it. What are you planning to do with yourself all day, seeing as Florence is going to Wendy's house after dancing?"

"It looks like it's going to be a beautiful day, so I thought I might get out the deckchair and spend a nice relaxing afternoon in the garden."

"I'm surprised you didn't arrange to go golfing."

"I did call a couple of people, but they already had other stuff planned, so I'm going to give it a miss this week. Will you be coming with us to Florence's dance class or do you have to shoot off before then?"

"The grand opening isn't until midday, so I'll have time to go with you. There is something I need to do before then, though."

"What's that?"

"I'm going over to the hotel to tell Grandma I know who murdered Miss Drinkwater."

"You do? How come you didn't tell me?"

"I didn't get the chance last night, but if my suspicions are correct, it was her brother, Ryan. He's in dire straits, financially. From what I can make out, he's very close to bankruptcy. That's why he tried to sell the tea room behind his sister's back."

"I don't understand how he hoped to get away with it."

"Me neither. I can only assume he thought if he could get a good enough offer, he'd be able to persuade his sister to accept it, but she turned him down flat, which left him with nowhere to go."

"And you think that's why he killed her?"

"Yeah. As far as I know, Miss Drinkwater had no other family, so chances are, he'll inherit her half of the business, which means he'll be free to sell it. I first became suspicious when Arthur Spraggs told us that the Peeps thought they'd purchased the tea room, only to have the sale cancelled by Miss Drinkwater. On the strength of that, I paid a visit to her brother's apartment."

"A *visit*? Is that code for breaking-in?"

"I didn't *break in*, exactly."

"You used magic, I assume?"

"It's best you don't know. Anyway, that's how I found out about his financial situation. That gave him the motive, but I still needed to find out how he did it."

"And did you?"

"Of course. Super sleuth, that's me."

"And modest with it."

"When Marian found Miss Drinkwater's body, it was in a pool of water."

"What's so significant about that? Presumably, she'd been holding a glass of water when she was attacked."

"That's what I thought at first, but on the crime scene

photo, there was no sign of any broken glass."

"Hang on. How did you get to see the crime scene photo?"

"I may, quite inadvertently, have stumbled into the incident room at Washbridge police station."

"*Inadvertently?*"

"Absolutely. Anyway, while I was there, I just happened to check the whiteboard. That's when I saw the photo, which showed the pool of water around the body."

"I still don't understand why the water is significant."

"Because that was the murder weapon."

"Now I'm totally confused. Are you saying someone drowned her?"

"No, I'm saying they hit her with it."

"With water? I'm beginning to think you've lost the plot."

"Not with *water*. With *frozen water*."

"Ice?"

"Bingo! When I went to Ryan Drinkwater's factory last night, I discovered that they make blocks of ice for commercial use. While I was there, I checked the CCTV footage from the camera in front of the building. On the night his sister was murdered, I saw him leave the premises at nine o'clock. He was carrying a box. A freezer box."

"You think he hit her with a block of ice?"

"Yeah."

"But surely someone would have seen him carrying the box into the shop."

"I think he left the box in the car and carried the ice block in, probably under his jacket. The next morning, when the waitress arrived for work, the building was so hot that she had to turn down the heating."

"What does that have to do with anything?"

"I think Ryan turned it up before he left so that what was left of the block of ice would melt."

"Have you told the police any of this?"

"No, not yet."

"Why not?"

"Because I want Grandma to know that I was the one who cleared her name." I checked my watch. "I'd better get going or I won't be back in time for Florence's dance class. I'll see you two there."

"Okay, but I still think you should tell the police first."

I was just about to leave the house when Oscar Riley knocked at the door.

"Good morning, Oscar. Aren't you working today?"

"I should have been, but I managed to swap shifts with a colleague so that I'd be able to attend the grand opening of the new stamp shop. In fact, that's why I'm here. I know Jack won't want to miss it either."

"You're absolutely right. In fact, he was just bemoaning the fact that he didn't have anyone to go with. He's in the kitchen. Why don't you go through and surprise him?" I stepped aside to let him pass.

Snigger and double snigger.

***

The receptionist at the hotel recognised me. "Are you here to see your grandmother?"

"Yes, please."

"I'll just give her a call to see if she's available." She grabbed the phone and spoke for no more than a few seconds. "Mrs Millbright says she can spare you a couple of minutes. You know where her office is, don't you?"

"I do, indeed. Thanks very much."

I was feeling rather pleased with myself. It would be nice to receive praise from Grandma for a change.

As soon as I walked into her office, she pointed to two small safes on the floor. "Which one do you like the best?"

"Err, they look very similar. What's wrong with the one you've already got?" I gestured to the one in the corner of the room.

"These aren't safes. They're minibars. I'm thinking of having them installed in all the rooms."

"Is there much call for minibars?"

"Of course. People love to indulge themselves when they're on holiday, and the mark-up on the drinks and snacks is phenomenal. So, which one do you like best?"

"Err, that one. Look, I can't stay long because it's Florence's dance class this morning. I just wanted to tell you that I know who murdered Miss Drinkwater."

"So do I."

"You do?"

"It was that brother of hers."

"If you knew who'd done it, why get me involved at all?"

"I didn't know until the police told me."

"When did they tell you?"

"They came around here about an hour ago. They said they'd made an arrest, and that I was no longer a suspect. I believe her brother is already in custody, pending charges."

"Yes, but I bet they haven't worked out what he used as a murder weapon, have they?"

"You mean the block of ice? Are you sure you like this minibar best?"

"Who cares about stupid minibars?"

"I do. They're going to make me a small fortune."

"But this isn't fair. I was the one who solved the murder."

"Too late, apparently. If I'd realised how dilatory you were going to be, I'd have left it to the police."

"*Dilatory*? I was not *dilatory*! I've given this case my full attention, and I solved it."

"I only have your word for that. For all I know, the police could have told you who did it."

"But, I — err — it — err —"

"Shouldn't you be going? You don't want to be late for my great-granddaughter's dance class."

Somewhat deflated, I made my way over to the village hall where Jack and Florence were waiting for me.

"Was your grandmother impressed?" Jack said.

"Not really."

"What's wrong with that woman? She's never grateful."

"The police had already told her that Ryan Drinkwater had been arrested."

"But I didn't think they knew it was him."

"Neither did I. What a complete waste of time."

Florence grabbed my hand. "Come on, Mummy. It's time to go in."

"Okay, darling."

As soon as we were inside, Florence ran over to join Wendy, and within a few minutes, the lesson had begun.

"I hear you're going to the stamp shop too," I whispered to Jack.

"So much for my relaxing afternoon in the deckchair. Oscar and I may as well travel into Washbridge with you."

"Sorry, but that won't work because I need to get there early. And besides, you'll enjoy it much more if it's just the two of you. You'll be able to discuss stamps on the drive in."

"Hmm."

When the dance lesson had finished, Florence came running over to us. "Is it alright if I go with Wendy now?"

"I just need to check with her Mum first, to make sure everything is still on."

Before I could, the woman who ran the dance class called for everyone's attention.

"Parents, if I could just have a moment of your time. I've already told the girls about this, but I thought I'd better make this announcement in case they forget to tell you. In two weeks' time, it's the mother and daughter dance competition."

That didn't sound good. Not good at all.

"It'll be great, won't it, Mummy?" Florence was bubbling with enthusiasm.

"The thing is, Florence, I'm not very good at dancing, so I'm not sure I'll be able to do it."

"Don't listen to her, Florence," Jack said. "Mummy is just being modest. She's a brilliant dancer. You two are bound to win."

Jack still had that stupid grin on his face as we walked back to the old watermill.

"What now?" I snapped.

"Nothing. I'm just looking forward to seeing you and Florence in the dance competition."

"You're stone out of luck, then, because you're forbidden to come."

"Spoilsport."

Just then, Oscar came running down the road. "Jack, are you ready?"

"It's not time to go yet, is it?"

"No, but I thought you could come over to my place first, and we could discuss some of the things that we want to look at when we get to the shop."

"But, I—err—there's something I have to do at the house first."

"Don't worry, Jack," I said. "I can see to that. You go with Oscar. You clearly have a lot to talk about."

"Thanks very much, Jill."

"Before you shoot off, Jack, can I have a quick word?" I pulled him to one side. "Will you do me a small favour?"

"You've got a nerve, after landing me with Oscar."

"Pretty please."

"No."

"With sugar on top."

"What do you want?"

"I need you to go online and find a photo of the real Alex Wilder, so you know what he looks like. Then, when you get to the shop, I want you to keep your eyes peeled for him."

"I take it that will be you?"

"One of them will."

"One? How many will there be?"

"At some point there will be two of them: Me and the guy from Double Take. I plan on confronting him, and I need you to video the encounter."

"Okay. I guess."

"Try to do it discreetly. Don't get too close because I don't want the other guy to notice."

"Okay, but you owe me."

"I'll make it up to you. I promise."

***

I headed back to the old watermill alone, and I'd just started down the drive when I saw something that stopped me dead in my tracks. There, standing by the door, was that darn squirrel again. This was getting way beyond a joke.

Enough was enough. It was time to have it out with him once and for all, but before I could say anything, he got in first.

"Hi there. I hope this isn't an inconvenient time."

"An inconvenient time for what, exactly?"

"I wondered if I could have a word?"

"I don't think so."

"Why not?"

"Because I have better things to do than talk to squirrels, especially nutty ones."

"Please. If you give me the chance, I can explain everything."

"Okay then, but be quick."

"Could we possibly go inside? If someone was to see me talking to you, they might think something weird was going on."

"Are your feet clean?"

"Of course." He lifted each one in turn.

"Okay, then. Come with me."

We both took a seat at the kitchen table.

"You've been following me around, haven't you?" I said.

"Guilty as charged. I've been waiting for the right opportunity to talk to you, but you're a very busy lady."

"That's true. What exactly is it you want to talk to me about?"

"Donuts."

"Sorry?"

"Squirrel donuts are the best in the world, and we'd like to give you a year's supply of them. That is, if you'll accept."

"I do love donuts, but why would you want to give them to me?"

"A few weeks ago, there was some trouble in the squirrel community. We were being blamed, very unfairly as it turned out, for throwing acorns at humans."

"I know. It was actually shape-shifters, posing as squirrels, who were doing it. I was the one who reported it to the rogue retrievers. Sorry, I don't imagine you know what shifters or rogue retrievers are, do you? Being a squirrel, I mean?"

"Of course I do. We squirrels are very familiar with all matters paranormal, and we also know that it was you who reported the shifters. In fact, that's the reason I'm here today. The squirrel community is very grateful for what you did. Our good reputation was being tarnished by those imposters, and there was a danger that we might have forfeited our cute status. But, thanks to you, that won't happen now."

"It's nice of you to say so."

"The squirrel seniors got together to discuss what we should do to show our gratitude, and they came up with the idea of giving you a year's supply of our world-famous donuts."

"A whole year's supply? That's very generous. Do you have some with you?"

"No, but if you'll accept our gift, we'll see they're delivered to your door as soon as possible."

"I accept. Definitely. Thank you."

Chapter 24

I arrived at Norman's Stamps an hour before the grand opening was due to take place. The man himself was inside, preparing a table full of refreshments. The door was locked, so I tapped on the window to get his attention.

"Good morning, Jill. Help yourself to a snack and a drink."

"Thanks, I don't mind if I do." I grabbed a cupcake and a can of Coke. "Are you expecting a big crowd today, Norman?"

"I'm not sure, to be honest. I haven't done any advertising, but I hope word will have got around."

"Is it okay if I go into that back room over there?"

"Sure, if you want to, but it's a bit of a mess."

"That's okay. I'll leave the door ajar so I can see out."

"Do you want me to tell the lookalike that you're in there when he arrives?"

"No, I'd rather you didn't mention that I was here at all."

"Okay. What do you want me to do?"

"Just act normally." And yes, I did realise that was quite an ask. "I'll do the rest."

By eleven-forty-five, a sizable crowd had gathered at the front of the shop. Among them was Oscar who was practically salivating at the thought of all the stamps inside. Standing beside him was Jack who looked almost comatose. Judging by the number of punters who had turned up, without a penny spent on advertising, it seemed that Norman was onto another winner.

At five minutes before midday, someone knocked on the door. I assumed it was one of the stampers keen to get inside.

It was actually Wayne Crabtree AKA Alex Wilder.

Norman spotted him, and whispered to me, "What do you want me to do, Jill? Shall I let him in?"

"Yes, please."

"What do I say to him?"

"Tell him you want him to cut the ribbon and declare the shop open."

"I don't have any ribbon."

"Hold on." I took a step back, so that I was out of sight, and then used magic to produce a length of ribbon and some scissors. "Here you are, Norman."

"Where did you get those?"

"I always keep them in my handbag, just in case of emergency."

"Err, right. Thanks."

Once Wayne was inside, the two of them exchanged a few pleasantries.

"What exactly would you like me to do today?" Wayne said.

"I'm going to put this across the doorway." Norman held up the ribbon. "I'd like you to cut it and say a few words."

"Is there anything in particular you'd like me to say?"

"Just thank everyone for coming. Oh, and you can tell them that there's ten percent off everything today."

"Okay."

Norman attached the ribbon and then opened the door.

"Hi everyone," he said. "Welcome to Norman's Stamps. I'm going to hand you over to Alex Wilder who will perform the opening ceremony."

Wayne, AKA Alex stepped forward, scissors in hand.

"Good morning, everyone. Are any of you old enough to remember my movies?" A couple of hands went up, but the majority of the crowd stared blankly at him. "It's good to see I have a few fans here today. I'll be happy to sign autographs for those who want them." That fell on deaf ears because most of the stampers just wanted him to get on with it. "It is my honour to declare Norman's Stamps officially open." He cut the ribbon and stepped aside, and the crowd surged forward.

A few people stopped at the refreshments table, but the majority of them headed straight for the display of stamps. Wayne was standing just in front of the door behind which I was hiding. He had his pen poised, ready to sign autographs, but there were no takers.

I cast the 'doppelganger' spell to make myself look like Alex Wilder, then I made my move. As I stepped out of the back room, Norman did a double take, but fortunately, he didn't say anything.

"Hey!" I tapped Wayne on the shoulder. "What are you doing here?"

He spun around and stared at me, clearly gobsmacked. "What do you mean, what am *I* doing here? What are *you* doing here? Who are you?"

"I was supposed to open this gaff."

"I've already done that."

"I can see that."

"Who booked you to do this gig?" he said.

"Some guy called Boris Charming."

"That's impossible. He can't have."

"Well, he did. Do you know him?"

"No, yes, sort of."

"Do you, or don't you?"

"Hold on." He took out his phone and made a call. "Boris? It's me. Did you book a lookalike for Norman's Stamps today? No? Well, there's one here. An Alex Wilder lookalike. Yes, I know that's who I do. That's why I'm calling you. This guy reckons someone called Boris booked him to do the gig. No, I don't understand it either."

That was my cue to leave. "Sorry, but I don't have time to hang around here all day, especially if I'm not getting paid. I'm off."

"Hold on a minute!" Wayne shouted after me, but I was already headed for the door. Once outside, I glanced back through the window where Jack was obviously trying to catch my eye. He was shaking his head and mouthing something, but I couldn't make out what he was saying. He was probably hoping that I would rescue him, but he was plain out of luck.

I hurried down the street until I found a quiet alleyway where I reversed the 'doppelganger' spell, then I grabbed my phone and called Raymond Double.

"Rock, it's Jill."

"Oh. Hi, Jill. I was just thinking about you. Do you have any news for me yet?"

"I do. I now know who's behind the problems you've been having."

"Who?"

"You're not going to believe this, but it's Wayne Crabtree."

He laughed. "I assume that's a joke?"

"No, I'm deadly serious."

"There's no way Wayne could be behind this. That guy is the salt of the earth."

"He certainly goes out of his way to give that impression, but there's no doubt about it. He's been passing on details of your bookings to another agency, who then jump in and offer to provide the same lookalike for a better price."

"I still think you're mistaken."

"There's no mistake, Rock. I have the evidence to prove it."

"What kind of evidence?"

"A video of him talking to another Alex Wilder lookalike, in which he admits exactly what he's been doing."

"There's another Alex Wilder lookalike? I'm amazed. I can barely find enough work for one of them."

"The video leaves no doubt that Wayne is the one who's been sabotaging your business."

"Can you send it over for me to see?"

"It's not actually on my phone. My colleague recorded it, and I won't have access to it until this evening, but I can send it over to you then."

"Okay, but I have to warn you that I'm still very sceptical about all of this."

Having alerted Raymond Double to Wayne Crabtree's skulduggery, I now needed to put paid to Boris Charming's evil doings, so I made a phone call to Daze.

"It's Jill. Are you busy?"

"Not at the moment. I'm in Cuppy C with Blaze."

"Is it alright if I come over and join you?"

"Sure. Come on over."

When I got to Cuppy C, Amber and Pearl were both behind the counter.

"We were just about to call you, Jill," Amber said.

"Oh? What about?"

"Take a look at these." Pearl handed me an envelope.

Inside it were a number of photographs. All of Florence. One of them was of her in our back garden. Another was of her walking through the village with Jack. There was one with me in Tweaking Meadows. And the last one was with Wendy and her mum.

"Who gave you these?"

"A man came into the shop about five minutes ago."

"Who was he?"

"I don't know. Neither of us does."

"What did he look like?"

"No idea. He was wearing a dark cloak with the hood pulled down over his face. As soon as he walked through the door, I said to Pearl, this guy looks like a nutter. He came over to the counter, slapped the envelope down, and said give this to your cousin."

"What else did he say?"

"Nothing. As soon as he'd put it down, he left."

I checked the envelope again, half-expecting to find a note of some kind, but there was nothing.

"Did you see which way the man went?"

"No, sorry. Did you want your usual?"

"Err, yes please, but I need to speak to Daze and Blaze."

"Is everything alright, Jill?" Daze said. "You look a little pale."

"I'm okay. I think. You two didn't happen to see the man who was in here a few minutes ago, did you? He was wearing a cloak with the hood pulled down over his face."

They both shook their heads.

"Sorry, no. We were busy chatting. Why? Is something wrong?"

"Err, no, it's okay. I wanted to tell you about a case I've been working on in Washbridge. I was hired by the owner of a lookalike agency called Double Take. They've been having lots of problems with people making bookings, then cancelling them. It turns out that someone on the inside was feeding details of the bookings to a wizard called Boris Charming. He's been using the 'doppelganger' spell to make himself look like the various celebrities, and he's been undercutting Double Take's prices. I've told the owner about the traitor in his midst, but I thought you guys would want to know about his partner, the wizard."

"Did the human realise he was working with a wizard?" Daze said.

"No. At least, I don't think so. I'm pretty sure he assumed he was just dealing with a competing lookalike agency. I've contacted a couple of the people who cancelled, but they refuse point blank to talk to me about it. I have no proof, but I suspect Charming may have offered the reduced price on the strict understanding that they don't reveal the details to anyone."

"Or threatened them to keep quiet?"

"That's possible, I guess."

"Do you happen to have an address for this Charming guy?"

"Yes, I've been to his office."

I scribbled down the address and passed it to Daze. "Look, guys, I'm sorry, but I have to get going." I stood up and started for the door.

"What about your coffee?" Amber shouted after me.

"Sorry, I'll have to leave it."

My heart was pounding like a drum. Who had taken those photos of Florence and why? Was she in some kind of danger? Could this be related to what Martin had told me about Braxmore?

I wanted to check that Florence was alright, so I magicked myself straight to the old watermill and dashed inside.

There was no sign of her or Jack.

"Jack! Florence! Where are you?"

Jack appeared out of the lounge. "Where's the fire?"

"Where's Florence? Where is she?"

"At Wendy's house. It's not time to pick her up yet."

"Are you sure she's there?"

"Positive. What on earth's the matter?"

"Nothing. Sorry." I wanted to tell Jack everything, but how could I? "What time are we supposed to pick her up?"

He checked his watch. "In about twenty minutes."

"I'll come with you."

"Okay."

"Can you send me that video you recorded?"

"I don't have it."

"What do you mean, *you don't have it*? Why don't you have it?"

"I tried to tell you when you were leaving the shop. I must have forgotten to put my phone on charge last night, so when I took it out to make the video, the battery was flat."

"That's just great!" I screamed at him. "I ask you to do one simple thing and you mess it up!" I burst into tears and slumped to the floor.

"Jill, whatever's wrong?" He crouched down next to me. "I've never seen you like this. I'm really sorry about the video."

It took me a while, but I eventually managed to compose myself. "It's not about the video. I don't care about that."

"Then what's wrong?"

"Nothing."

"I know something is and I'm not moving until you tell me what's going on."

"I'm scared, Jack. Someone is after Florence."

"What do you mean? Who's after her?"

"I don't know." I took out the photos and handed them to him.

"Who took these?"

"I've no idea, but I think it may have something to do with a wizard called Braxmore."

"Who's he?"

"I don't really know. No one does. He's been lurking in the background ever since I discovered I was a witch. Do you remember Drake?"

"*Drake*? The name rings a bell, but I—"

"I went on a date with him a couple of times around the same time as you and I started seeing one another. You did meet him once."

"Oh, yeah. I think I know who you mean now, but what does he have to do with anything?"

"Drake wasn't his real name. He'd been sent by Braxmore to kill me, and he almost succeeded."

"Where is he now?"

"He's dead. I killed him. Do you remember when my brother, Martin, suddenly disappeared some years ago?"

"Of course I do."

"The last thing he said to me was that he had to leave to make sure my child would be safe."

"But that was before Florence was born."

"I know."

"And you never thought to mention any of this?"

"I wasn't sure what he meant, and I didn't want to worry you."

"I'm Florence's father. I'm supposed to worry if someone means my little girl harm. You had no right to keep it from me, Jill."

"I know, and I'm really sorry. I just didn't know what to do for the best."

"What are we going to do now? Should we go to the police?"

"That won't do any good. Braxmore lives in the paranormal world. How are we going to explain that to them? Martin came to see me a few days ago, to tell me that he needed my help to stop Braxmore."

"What does he want you to do?"

"I don't know yet."

"When will you know?"

"Soon, I hope."

"Is it safe for Florence to go to school? What about dance class or Wendy's house?"

"We have to carry on as normal. We can't let her know about any of this; it will terrify her."

"That's not going to be easy."

"I know, but we have to do it, anyway."

"I'm scared, Jill."

"I am too, but we have to be strong. For Florence's sake."

"You're right."

"We'll both have to be ultra-vigilant. If you see anything unusual, let me know."

"Can you stop this Braxmore guy?"

"I have to."

Chapter 25

It was Sunday morning. Florence had finished her breakfast and was in the garden, playing with Buddy. Jack and I were still at the kitchen table, both bleary-eyed.

"Do you think I should go out and watch her?" Jack said.

"No, she'll be fine."

"But one of those photographs was taken in our garden."

"She's with Buddy. He'll bark if anyone tries to get in. If we start following her around, she's going to pick up on it and realise that something's wrong."

"I guess you're right. Did you get any sleep last night?"

"Not much. What about you?"

"No." He yawned. "I couldn't stop thinking about those photographs. Have you ever met this Braxmore guy?"

"No, or at least, I don't think so."

My phone rang; it was Martin.

"Where are you, Martin?"

"In Candlefield. How are things with you?"

"Not great. Someone left an envelope full of photographs with the twins at Cuppy C yesterday. They're all of Florence and they were taken around the village where we live. Someone has been stalking us."

"Who dropped them off at the tea room?"

"I don't know. The twins said it was a strange man, wearing a long cloak, with the hood pulled down over his face. Do you think it could have been Braxmore?"

"Definitely not. It would probably have been one of his minions. Don't worry about it, Jill."

"Easier said than done."

"I know, but its only purpose is to scare you. Braxmore can't get to Florence. Not at the moment, anyway."

"That's not very comforting."

"Let's meet later today and I'll explain everything."

"I can come over now."

"Sorry, there's something I have to do first. How about we get together straight after lunch? Say one o'clock?"

"That works for me. Where?"

"Cuppy C?"

"Okay. I'll see you there."

"I take it that was Martin?" Jack said.

"Yes, I'm seeing him this afternoon."

"What did he say about the photographs?"

"He reckons there's nothing to worry about, and that they're just intended to scare us."

"They succeeded."

"He's adamant that Braxmore can't get to Florence at the moment."

"None of this is very reassuring, Jill."

"I know. Hopefully, I'll learn more this afternoon. Is it okay if I nip out now for a while? I need to pay a visit to a couple of sweetheart fairies, and then I want to pop into the office."

"Sure. Wendy is coming over to play with Florence in about fifteen minutes, so that will keep her busy this morning."

"I'd totally forgotten she was coming over."

"Will you be back for lunch?"

"Yeah, but I'll have to go straight out afterwards, to see Martin."

"No problem."

"You're the best." I gave Jack a peck on the lips. "I'll just go and say goodbye to Florence."

I found her staring up at the tree.

"What are you looking at, darling?"

"I'm trying to see that squirrel, but I think he's gone."

"It looks like it."

"Aww, not fair. I liked the squirrel."

"Me too. Maybe he'll come back one day. Mummy has to go to work for a little while now."

"How long is it until Wendy comes over?"

"About ten minutes. What are you two going to be doing?"

"Looking for caterpillars."

"Again? You're really into caterpillars at the moment."

"That's because they're super brilliant. They have lots of legs and they walk really funny. Do you like caterpillars, Mummy?"

"Not particularly, but I do like them when they've turned into butterflies."

"How do they do that?"

"I—err—I don't know."

"Do they use magic?"

"No, but it's like magic, isn't it?"

"I think caterpillars must be sups."

"Hmm, I don't think so."

"Mummy, did you ask the queen unicorn if I can go and see her?"

"Err, not yet."

"You said you would. You promised."

"And I will."

"Wendy too."

"We'll see."

Edna had given me the address for the two sweetheart fairies who'd been seen talking to Devon. They shared an apartment in Angel Buildings, which was in the Fairy Parade district of Candlefield. Before magicking myself over there, I turned myself into a sweetheart fairy because their buildings were tiny, and I didn't want to crush them underfoot. When I arrived outside the third-floor apartment, I could hear loud, heavy-metal music coming from inside. If this was typical of their behaviour, I didn't envy their neighbours.

I knocked on the door, but there was no reply, which was hardly surprising, given the volume of the music coming from inside. I tried again, hammering on it much louder this time. A couple of minutes later, a sweetheart fairy opened the door. She wasn't typical of the sweetheart fairies I'd encountered before. They'd been delicate, charming little things. This one was covered in tattoos; she was leaning against the door, chewing gum, and had apparently applied her makeup with a trowel. All in all, she looked a real ruffian.

"Yeah?" She somehow managed to speak and blow a gum bubble at the same time. "What do you want?"

"Are you Sharon?"

"No, I'm Karen. I asked what you want."

"I'd like to speak to both you and Sharon, please."

"What about? Who are you, anyway?"

"My name is Jill Maxwell, and I'd like to talk to you about Devon."

"Isn't that a county in the human world?" She laughed.

"I mean Devon, the unicorn. Queen Ursula's brother."

"Never heard of him."

"That's not true, is it?"

"We're busy. We're doing our nails."

She tried to close the door, but I'd already wedged my foot in the gap. "I really think you should talk to me."

"Do you have any idea who you're dealing with?" Without any warning, she threw a punch, but I managed to duck out of the way. After casting the 'power' spell, I grabbed both of her arms and dragged her, kicking and shouting, into the living room where a second sweetheart fairy was lying on the sofa, smoking a cigarette.

"Turn that music off," I shouted.

The second sweetheart fairy, who I assumed to be Sharon, jumped off the sofa. "Who are you? What are you doing here? Let go of Karen."

"I'll let go of her when you turn off that awful music."

"It is not awful! This is Oliver More and the Empty Bowls."

"I don't care who it is. It's making my ears bleed. Turn it off."

She walked over to the record player and lifted the needle off the vinyl record. "Okay, now let Karen go."

"My pleasure." I released her. "Why don't you both sit on the sofa, so we can chat?"

They hesitated but then did as I said.

"What do you want?" Sharon snapped.

"I'm the one asking the questions, and if I don't get answers, I'll turn you both over to the authorities."

"What are we supposed to have done?"

"Are you deaf? I said I'm the one asking the questions. Why don't you start by telling me what business you have with Devon?"

They exchanged a glance, then Karen said, "We don't have any business with him. You've got the wrong people."

"You're lying. I've had Devon followed, and he was seen talking to both of you on a couple of occasions. Devon is definitely going down. The only question is whether you two want to go down with him."

"Go down for what? We haven't done anything."

"Don't come the innocent with me. I know you've been stealing unicorn horns."

"We did no such thing," Sharon said.

"Okay, if that's the way you want to play it, I guess I'll just give the police a call."

"No, hang on. There's no need for that."

"Are you saying that if we tell you everything we know, we'll get full immunity?" Karen said.

"I can't guarantee that, but if you come clean, I promise that I'll put in a good word for you."

They had a brief, whispered conversation, and eventually agreed to co-operate.

"Okay. What do you want to know?" Sharon said.

"What do you do with the horns?"

"We don't do anything with them. We just give them to Devon."

"What does he do with them?"

"No idea." Karen shrugged.

"You said that you'd tell me everything."

"We don't know what he wants them for. He pays us and that's all we care about. We don't ask any questions."

"How did this little arrangement come about?"

"He approached us not long after we'd come out of

prison. We couldn't get any other work."

"When was this?"

"About seven years ago."

"*Seven years*? But the thefts only started recently."

"I'm talking about the first time we worked for him."

"Let me get this straight. Are you saying that you two were stealing unicorn horns for Devon seven years ago as well?"

"Yeah, we were making a killing until he suddenly called a halt to it."

"Why did he do that?"

"No idea. Like I said, we don't ask questions."

"How do you decide which unicorns to target?"

"We don't. Devon tells us who to take them from."

"How do you two tiny things manage to carry those horns?"

"We're stronger than we look. We can carry one between us easily, can't we, Karen?"

"Yeah, no problem."

"And how do you remove them? Do you use magic?"

"Nah, a hacksaw."

***

I had planned to drop into the office, but after hearing what Karen and Sharon had to say, I decided instead to check out the industrial unit that Edna had seen Devon visit. There was no signage on the building to indicate what was inside. In fact, from the exterior, it looked as though it could have been abandoned.

I magicked myself inside, but I didn't bother with the 'invisible' spell because it was obvious that the place was deserted. In the centre of the unit was a small assembly line. At one end of the conveyor belt were boxes full of small, empty glass bottles. At the other end was a machine with a glass tank mounted on top; it was full of powder of some kind. When the production line was running, the bottles presumably travelled along the conveyor belt, were filled with powder, and then labelled. I picked up one of the sheets of labels. On each one was printed the name of the product: U-Sleep. Underneath that were the words: *the world's most effective sleeping solution.* That name rang a bell: It was the one that Mrs V had used. The same one that had put one of her friends in hospital.

The adjoining room, which was much smaller, appeared to be the despatch office where several boxes, full of bottles, were waiting to be collected. I opened one of the boxes, took out a bottle, and poured some of the powder onto the back of my hand. It had a very pleasing smell, and one that I recognised.

I called Ursula and arranged to pay her a visit the following day.

***

There was no sign of Martin when I arrived at Cuppy C, where Pearl was by herself behind the counter.

"Pearl, have you seen Martin?"

"Who's Martin?"

"My brother of course."

"I haven't seen him in years."

"I arranged to meet him here. Maybe he's running a little late."

"Where's he been hiding all this time?"

"It's complicated."

"*Complicated?*" She rolled her eyes. "That's what people say when they don't want you to know something. Why the big secret?"

"I can't go into it right now. I'll tell you another time, I promise."

"Fair enough. Did you find out who was behind those photographs?"

"No. That's one of the things I want to talk to Martin about. Could I get a caramel latte, please?"

"I'll pay for that." The voice came from behind me. I spun around to find Martin standing there.

"Long time, no see, Martin," Pearl said.

"Hi. How are you and your sister?"

"We're both fine, thanks. What can I get for you?"

"I'll have an Americano, please. Black. I see you've closed the cake shop."

"We did that some time ago. It's much better now that we only have the tea room to deal with. Why don't you two go and grab a table? I'll bring the drinks over for you."

"I haven't paid you yet," Martin said.

"That's alright. These are on the house. Call it your welcome back present."

"Thanks."

We grabbed a table by the window.

"Are you sure that I don't need to worry about those photographs, Martin?"

"Positive. Like I told you this morning, Braxmore just wants to scare you."

"So, what's the plan? How do we keep Florence safe?"

"There's only one way to ensure Florence's long-term

safety. And yours, for that matter. That's to kill Braxmore."

"Is that all? For a horrible moment there, I thought it might be something difficult."

"You can do it, Jill. Remember that Braxmore tried to destroy you once before, but failed."

"When he sent Drake to kill me, you mean?"

"Yeah. Having missed that opportunity, he realised he had no option but to bide his time."

"Until when?"

"Until he could match your power."

"Hang on. Are you telling me that I'm more powerful than he is?"

"It's close, but I would say so, yes. But that won't always be the case. He's spent the last few years expanding his powers. It's only a matter of time until he'll be able to match you in a head-to-head confrontation."

"What do you mean when you say he has been *expanding* his powers? How does he do that?"

"By absorbing the power of others."

"Is that as grisly as it sounds?"

"Worse."

"And when he believes that he's powerful enough?"

"That's when he'll come after you, and —" He hesitated.

"Florence?"

"Yes. She's inherited your powers. If he can absorb both of you, he'll be unstoppable."

"What can we do about it?"

"You have to go on the offensive. You have to destroy him before he destroys you."

"How?"

"Braxmore is no fool. He knows he's vulnerable, so he's

put in place a number of defences to stop you getting to him. To breach those defences, you're going to need the four compass stones."

"And where can I find them?"

"Each stone has its own guardian who knows the stone's location."

"Okay, so I'll need to speak to all four guardians."

"Correct, but you'll need to find them first."

"Are you telling me you don't even know where I can find the guardians?"

"That's exactly what I'm telling you. You're going to have to track down each one of them in turn, and get them to tell you where the individual stones are."

"That could take ages. How long do I have before Braxmore comes after us?"

"Long enough, hopefully."

"You aren't filling me with confidence here, Martin."

"Sorry, I'm just trying to be honest with you."

"Okay. Where do I start?"

"With the North Stone. Its guardian is a woman who goes by the name of Madam Rodenia."

"And you have no idea where she might be?"

"The only thing I know is that she'll be somewhere in the northern quadrant of Candlefield. Each of the guardians has to remain in their own quadrant."

"How come I've never heard about these stones before?"

"The compass stones are older than time. The only people who know of their existence are the guardians themselves, Braxmore, me and now you." He checked his watch. "I'm sorry, Jill, but I have to get back."

"Okay. I appreciate everything you've done."

"I'm just sorry I can't do more. You'll keep me posted on how you get on, won't you?"

"Of course."

We hugged and then he disappeared out of the door. A few minutes later, Pearl came over.

"Do you know what I don't understand?" she said.

There were so many things to choose from.

"What's that?"

"How does someone like you have a brother who's so good looking?"

"Cheek."

***

That evening, after Florence had gone to bed, I told Jack about the four compass stones.

"And you have to collect all four of these stones in order to get to Braxmore?"

"That's right."

"And you have no idea where they are?"

"Correct."

"But there are people who can direct you to them?"

"Yes. The guardians."

"But you don't know where they are either."

"Also correct."

"So, essentially, you have absolutely nothing to go on."

"That's not quite right. I do at least know the name of the first guardian. Now all I have to do is find her."

"What do we tell Florence? Anything?"

"No. Definitely not."

Chapter 26

The next morning when I walked into the office, Mrs V was sharpening a pencil with an electric sharpener. She had a pile of pencils, at least twenty of them.

"Is that new, Mrs V?"

"Yes, isn't it amazing? It used to take me ages to sharpen my pencils, but with this little beauty, I can do them in seconds. Look." She picked up another pencil and stuck it in the sharpener. Moments later, she pulled it back out. "See how sharp it is, Jill?"

"That's — err — brilliant."

"Isn't it just? There was a delivery for you earlier. Donuts, apparently."

"Oh?" I hadn't expected them to be delivered to the office. "Did the squirrels bring them?"

It was only when I saw her puzzled expression that I realised what I'd said.

"How could *squirrels* deliver donuts?"

"Did I say *squirrels*? Silly me. I meant Cyrils."

"*Cyrils*?"

"Err, yeah. It's a little bakery I discovered called Cyril and Cyril."

"I see. These came in plain brown boxes. What are you going to do with all of those donuts?"

"Eat them of course. By the way, Mrs V, how is that friend of yours who was in intensive care?"

"She pulled through and should be home in a few days' time."

"That is good news."

My desk was hidden behind a huge pile of boxes. I

ripped one of them open to find the most delicious looking donuts. I took a step back and counted the boxes; there were twenty-four in total.

Oh bum!

When the squirrel had told me that they were going to give me a year's supply of donuts, I'd assumed they would deliver a batch each week. Or each month. I hadn't expected them all to be delivered at once.

"Do you think you've got enough donuts there?" Winky grinned.

"Too many."

"Where are they from?"

"The squirrel committee gave them to me for services rendered."

"Lucky you. It's a well-known fact that squirrels make exceptionally good donuts."

"That may be true, but what am I going to do with this lot? I'll never eat them all."

"I could take a few off your hands."

"You're welcome to, but that will still leave me with dozens."

"I know someone who could shift them for you."

"What do you mean?"

"Billy the Baker would sell them for you, but he'd want fifty percent of the takings."

"That sounds fair."

"And of course, I'd want twenty-five percent."

"Why should I give you a cut?"

"Because I'm the middleman, and without me you'll be stuck with this lot."

"Okay, but I'm deducting the money you owe me first."

"Fair enough. It's a deal."

I wasn't looking forward to this phone call, but it was time to come clean with Raymond Double.

"Jill? I thought you were going to send that video over on Saturday night."

"That was the plan. Unfortunately, my colleague had a problem with his phone, and he wasn't able to record the video."

"Does that mean you don't have any evidence to back up your accusation against Wayne?"

"Unfortunately not, but I was right there, Rock, and I overheard the conversation. Wayne is definitely the one who's been sabotaging your business. Every time you took a booking, he passed the details on to his colleague at the other agency who then undercut your price."

"That's a very strong accusation, Jill."

"It's the truth."

"But we're talking about a man I've known for years. A very honest man who I would trust with my life. He'd never do something like this."

"It's very admirable of you to show him such loyalty, but he doesn't deserve it."

"I'm sorry, Jill, but without evidence, I'm simply not prepared to accuse him of this."

"Where does that leave us?"

"I'm sorry to have to say this, but I think you've failed to find the real culprit, and now you're using Wayne as a scapegoat. I suggest you find out who's really behind this, and we can talk again then."

"Hold on, Rock."

It was too late because he had already ended the call.

As usual, it was Ronald who met me at the gates to the palace.

"Hello again, Jill. You spend more time here than I do."

"It's certainly beginning to feel that way."

"Her Majesty and her brother are waiting for you in the throne room."

"Devon's here?"

"Yes, is that a problem?"

"It could be, but I have to go through with it now that I'm here."

After he'd shown me through to the throne room, Ronald took his leave. The queen was on her throne. Devon was standing beside her, glaring at me.

"I was surprised to get your call, Jill," Ursula said. "And to learn that you're still working on the case. I thought we'd agreed there was no need for you to do anything else."

"We did, but don't worry because I won't be charging you for the additional time that I've spent on it. It's just that I felt there were some matters still unresolved." I glanced over at Devon. "And, as it turned out, I was right."

"I see," Ursula said. "What exactly have you discovered?"

"I really do think it would be better if you and I could speak in private, Ursula."

She looked to Devon for his approval, but he shook his head. "I'd rather my brother stayed. Anything you have to say to me you can say in front of him."

"Okay. Despite what you've been told, the unicorn

horns were not being stolen in order to sell them in collectibles shops."

"What makes you say that?"

"Because they're being ground into a powder, which is being sold in the human world as a sleeping draught."

Before Ursula could react, Devon snapped, "This is nonsense. Why are we even listening to this woman?"

"Just a minute, Devon," Ursula said. "Jill's been good enough to come here today. We should at least hear her out. Jill, would you care to elaborate?"

"I'd be happy to, but maybe Devon should be the one to tell you. After all, he's the one behind this little escapade."

"That's outrageous." Devon looked like he wanted to kill me. "This woman is an idiot."

"Jill?" Ursula turned to me. "That's a very serious accusation. What are you basing it on?"

"My understanding is that some years ago you financed your brother in a business venture that went wrong."

"Why are you bringing that up now?" Devon said. "I just had a spot of bad luck, that's all."

"I don't understand what bearing his previous failed business has on what's happening now," Ursula said.

"I believe you were manufacturing love potions and selling them in Candlefield, weren't you, Devon?"

"What of it?"

"What did you use to make the potions?"

"That's none of your business."

"That's okay. I already know the answer. You were stealing unicorn horns and grinding them down, just like you're doing now."

"Ursula!" Devon turned to his sister. "Are you going to let her slander me like this?"

"It's only slander if it isn't true," I said. "But you and I know that's exactly what happened, don't we? The powder was totally ineffective as an aphrodisiac."

"I've heard enough of this," Devon said.

"Although your love potion business collapsed, there was a silver lining, wasn't there? You discovered that the powder had an unexpected effect on some of the people who took it: It sent them to sleep, which is not exactly the desired effect for an aphrodisiac. Still, being the entrepreneur you clearly are, you saw another opportunity, didn't you?"

"I have no idea what you're talking about."

"I couldn't understand why it took so long to launch this new venture, but then I realised that's how long it took you to work out why the powder had only affected certain people. Once you'd done that, you were back in business."

"Is what she's saying true, Devon?" Ursula turned to her brother.

"Of course it isn't. She's only doing this because she's embarrassed about failing to discover what really happened to the horns."

"Jill, do you have any evidence to back up these claims?"

"Where would you like me to start? How about I begin with Sharon and Karen, the two sweetheart fairies who Devon got to steal the horns, both seven years ago and again now? Because of their size, they were able to get in and out of houses unnoticed. They only need to find a window cracked open wide enough for the horn to fit through."

"More nonsense." Devon scoffed. "Do you really expect

my sister to take the word of two ex-con sweetheart fairies over that of her brother?"

"How do you know they're ex-cons?"

"I—err—I must have read about them somewhere."

"Does your sister know about the industrial unit where you make the sleeping draught?"

"More lies."

"I went there earlier and saw for myself the powder waiting to be bottled and sold to unsuspecting customers. It's not just the damage you're doing to your own people. The sleeping draught is dangerous; it's much too strong. I know of at least one human who was hospitalised after taking it."

"Is this true, Devon?" Ursula said.

"Of course not. Are you really going to take her word over mine?"

"I'm just asking you if it's true."

"I'm not going to stay here and listen to these outrageous lies." With that, he stormed out of the room.

"I'm sorry about that, Jill. Please carry on. I want to know everything."

"As I said, I couldn't figure out why there had been the long gap between the two incidents. At least, not until I checked on the horns that had supposedly been found in collectibles shops, and returned to their owners. I discovered that the only unicorns who didn't get their horns back were mothers with newly-born babies."

"I'm sorry. I don't follow."

"When I visited Missy, one of the unicorns whose horns had been stolen, she mentioned that since the theft, she'd struggled to get her baby to go to sleep. The little one would normally nuzzle up to the horn, which I assumed was like a comfort blanket. On further investigation, I discovered that a new mother's horn changes composition and gives off an aroma which sends the baby to sleep."

"Is that why some of those who bought the aphrodisiac fell asleep?"

"Yes, the powder they took must have come from the horn of a new mother."

"I don't understand, Jill. If it's only those particular horns that have that effect, why steal them from other unicorns too? I know for a fact that several were taken from males."

"Devon knew if he targeted only mothers with newly-born babies, someone might realise what was going on. That's why he got the sweetheart fairies to steal from a cross section of unicorns. The other horns were simply put to one side because they were of no use to him."

"I'm still trying to get my head around all of this, Jill. You mentioned an industrial unit. What did you see there?"

"I have photos." I took out my phone, brought up the images I'd taken during my visit, and showed them to the queen.

"Unbelievable. I'm appalled. I'll put a stop to this. You have my word."

"I hope so. I fear a human might die otherwise. What about your brother? What will you do about him?"

"I don't know. Devon is my only sibling. Our father died when we were young. We promised our mother that we'd look after one another."

"This is the second time he's done this, Ursula. You have to take decisive action."

"You're right, and I will. I'm so very grateful to you for

seeing this through. You must bill me for the extra time you've spent on this."

"Rather than do that, do you think I could ask you a favour?"

"Of course. What is it?"

"My little girl, Florence, is crazy about unicorns. She knows I've been working for you and she asked if she could pay you a visit. I'll understand if it's not something you're comfortable with."

"Of course she can. I look forward to seeing her."

"Thanks. Can I be even more cheeky and ask if she can bring her best friend with her?"

"No problem. I look forward to meeting them both."

***

It was my turn to read Florence her bedtime story. She'd asked for the caterpillar book, which seemed to have displaced Elly and Smelly as her favourite. When she'd finally fallen asleep, I crept back downstairs to join Jack who was watching TV.

"Do you fancy a glass of wine?" he said.

"Why don't we have the beer that Mr Bacus gave us? I need something strong after the week I've had."

"You mean the business with the photos?"

"Yeah, but not just that. There was Miss Drinkwater's murder too. I should have got the credit for solving that, but now Grandma thinks the police told me who did it. I also managed to work out who's been sabotaging Double Take, but the owner of the agency simply won't believe me because I can't provide him with any evidence."

"That's my fault. If I hadn't forgotten to charge my

phone, you'd have the video."

"He should have believed me even without that. At the very least, he should have confronted Wayne, but he simply dismissed the idea out of hand."

"What about the unicorn case? Has that gone pear-shaped too?"

"No, but I'm not convinced that Queen Ursula will take any action against her brother. She seems to have a blind spot where he's concerned. She did say that Florence and Wendy can pay her a visit, though."

"Have you told Florence?"

"Not yet. I'll wait until I've set up a date, otherwise she'll keep pestering."

"Good idea. Now, drink your beer and forget about work."

"I'll try." I took a sip. "Wow, this stuff is strong."

Jack took a long drink. "You're not kidding. It definitely has a kick." He pointed at the TV, which was showing the local news. "Did you hear about this?"

"What is it?"

"The ultimate feelgood story. Do you see that boy scout? Apparently, he was selling cookies to raise money for his scout troop when he found the rare coin that everyone's been looking for in his takings. The scout group stands to benefit to the tune of twenty grand."

I looked closer at the boy's face. It was the boy scout I'd bought the cookies from outside my offices. Did that mean—? No, it couldn't. He'd probably been selling those cookies for several days; lots of people must have given him money.

"Do you know the most fascinating part about this story?" Jack continued. "It seems he'd only been selling the cookies for a couple of hours when he went down with a tummy bug and had to go home. What were the chances of being given that coin during that short window of time?"

Oh bum!

ALSO BY ADELE ABBOTT

The Witch P.I. Mysteries
(A Candlefield/Washbridge Series)

Witch Is When... (Season #1)
Witch Is When It All Began
Witch Is When Life Got Complicated
Witch Is When Everything Went Crazy
Witch Is When Things Fell Apart
Witch Is When The Bubble Burst
Witch Is When The Penny Dropped
Witch Is When The Floodgates Opened
Witch Is When The Hammer Fell
Witch Is When My Heart Broke
Witch Is When I Said Goodbye
Witch Is When Stuff Got Serious
Witch Is When All Was Revealed

Witch Is Why... (Season #2)
Witch Is Why Time Stood Still
Witch is Why The Laughter Stopped
Witch is Why Another Door Opened
Witch is Why Two Became One
Witch is Why The Moon Disappeared
Witch is Why The Wolf Howled
Witch is Why The Music Stopped
Witch is Why A Pin Dropped
Witch is Why The Owl Returned
Witch is Why The Search Began
Witch is Why Promises Were Broken
Witch is Why It Was Over

Web site: AdeleAbbott.com
Facebook: facebook.com/AdeleAbbottAuthor

Made in the USA
Columbia, SC
05 February 2021